MARK MANNOCK

Die As You Kill

The LACHLAN BYRN Thrillers (1)

For my mother
Ann Rew Mannock

When there is no light... seek solace in the darkness.

Contents

Chapter 1

"Please... no... I don't deserve this."

Byrn pressed the barrel of his SIG Sauer P226 pistol hard into the man's temple. His victim shook uncontrollably, sweat streaming down his face, and God only knew where else.

"We've been through this. I thought I'd explained quite clearly the circumstances that have led us to this point," Byrn said.

"I've got money. I... I'll pay any amount you want," the man stammered.

"Thanks, but I've been paid. To take your money as well would be double dipping, and that wouldn't be right."

"And killing me is right?"

Byrn smelled it first, then looked down. The man had soiled himself. It happened a lot. At least that meant he was taking the situation seriously. He should.

"Right, wrong, black, white. It's a fine line, really," Byrn responded.

"I didn't do anything. I was acquitted. The news was all over the media. You must have seen it."

Byrn sighed before withdrawing the gun from the man's temple. In a flash, he flipped it over and smashed it forcefully across his victim's face. A second later, the weapon was back in place. The man slumped in his chair, only held upright by the ropes that bound him. His prey regained consciousness quickly, groaning before spitting several teeth out onto the hard floor.

"I'd prefer it if you didn't interrupt my processes by provoking unnecessary violence. It disturbs my workflow," said Byrn.

"But *you* hit me."

"Because you asked me to," Byrn responded.

"I…"

"Yes, your actions dictate my reactions. You lie. I cause you pain. I thought I'd made the rules clear."

Byrn paused for a moment and gazed at the struggling specimen before him. If he was a better man, Byrn would say he didn't like killing and only did what was required of him. But the truth was, he loved it. Every second of the process. For Lachlan Byrn, killing was an exact science, like an engineer designing a bridge.

It was gratifying work.

"Now we've got to keep this moving along," continued Byrn. "Those teeth you spat out are going to make it that bit harder for the next person who has to deal with you."

The man looked up. His eyes widened, not in fear, but in hope. Maybe Byrn wasn't the last person he'd ever see after all.

"The next person?"

"Yes, the undertaker. He'll have to pretty you up."

The man slumped again, his head resting on his chest.

Hope fallen.

"Now, one last time. We both know that you kidnapped the child. What was she, mid-teens? And we both know that when the father couldn't pay, you killed her. Your acquittal was caused by an unfortunate young law officer not following the correct processes, not because you are innocent. That's something I've learned in life. Processes are important."

"Who's paying you to do this?" asked the man, his voice now barely audible.

"A concerned citizen is all you need to know," Byrn replied. "Apparently, a lot of people are upset with you."

The assassin reached down and grabbed a second rope that lay on the floor behind the chair.

"Let's move on, shall we? I've explained very carefully the reasons why today is the final day of your life. I believe everyone, even the stray, should understand why they're about to die."

Byrn checked his watch.

"Our time together is almost over. The last matter at hand is establishing the process of death."

The man glanced up, his jaw trembling under the white pallor of his face.

"My understanding is that you strangled the girl."

As he spoke Byrn dropped his pistol into his pocket and passed the rope into his right hand allowing his victim to see it for the first time.

"No... no... I beg you."

Byrn looped the rope and swung it in front of his prey.

"Fair's fair. An eye for an eye and all that."

"Please..."

Without another word, Byrn grasped the rope with both hands, wrapped it around the man's neck, crossed it, and yanked hard. The man struggled ineffectually as Byrn maintained the pressure. His victim tried to kick out, then pushed against the ropes trying to wriggle free. All pointless gestures.

The assassin craned his head around, watching the flailing man lose color. Slowly his skin and lips assumed a blue hue as his oxygen supply deteriorated into nothingness.

"There, there. Isn't it better just to be calm and travel on peacefully? Simply take a deep breath… oh, my bad… that's not possible, is it? Well, rest…."

Byrn stopped talking. The man lay slumped and motionless.

Lachlan Byrn loved his work.

Chapter 2

The salty spray stung Byrn's eyes. He didn't mind. Pain was just nature's way of letting you know you were alive... until you weren't. It had been a hard journey since leaving Barcelona. Although the prevailing winds pushed him along nicely, they'd been strong. When the first big gust peaked the gauge at forty knots, Byrn had reefed his mainsail tight.

He'd been on the water for twenty-four hours and the swell continued to mount, so sleep was out of the question. The assassin reached into his pocket, grabbed out a vial, flipped it open and threw a couple of tablets into his mouth. Modafinil, the Night Eagle, as his former Chinese captors called it. Byrn could stay awake for five days thanks to his little medicinal helper. In his line of work, where he had no one but himself to watch his back, the Night Eagle's wings were a necessity of life.

The kill in Barcelona had been straightforward. The man was a fool to think he could run and hide. Byrn's underground contacts encountered no difficulty in locating him, just as the assassin encountered no difficulty in doing the job.

Kill a kid, lose your life. Black, white. Besides, he'd been paid well.

Byrn's thirty-five-foot sloop rode the swells, crashing

through the foaming wave tops like an athlete. The constant barrage of water, either from the waves or the torrents of rain, soaked the craft's cockpit and Byrn along with it. The boat served as an easy means of extraction. He'd used it many times before. No one suspected a small sailing vessel moored in a quiet area of a harbor to provide a killer's escape. In this case, it didn't really matter anyway because the authorities wouldn't put much effort into finding him even if they located his victim.

The vessel was registered in the Caribbean although Byrn regularly changed its appearance through repainting, adding bow sprits and rear platforms and, of course, altering the craft's name and number. Simple but effective. Lachlan Byrn didn't like leaving a trail for anyone to follow.

The ability to vanish without a trace was more important to him now than ever. He'd assumed the authorities would be looking for him after the incident in Rome. You don't just kill the US Secretary of Defense and slip away into the night. On the other hand, only one, perhaps two, people knew Byrn had survived the affair. They also knew he'd spared their lives, so it could go either way. Still, better to assume the worst. The irony was that the hit on the secretary had been a free job, a labor of love. Well, hate really. Byrn and the man shared a history. Now the SecDef had been consigned to history.

The wounds Byrn incurred in his escape were debilitating, at least for a while. He'd spent several months lying low, moored off the island of Paros in Greece. The kill in Barcelona was his first time back on the job. Like workplace rehabilitation, he was easing himself back in. Light work initially, then perhaps something more challenging.

His next job would step things up a notch.

A large wave crashed over the cockpit, sending the vessel sideways down a swell. Byrn heaved the helm to port in correction before checking his compass for confirmation. As a former member of the UK Special Boat Service, the assassin was trained to deal with most of Neptune's challenges.

Byrn gazed into the rain. In a few hours, he'd reach Monte Carlo. A few hours after that, there'd be someone there who'd wish he hadn't.

Chapter 3

The sun was setting slowly into the distant hills as Byrn threw a line over the bollard at Port de Plaisance de Cap d'Ail. The marina was a lot cheaper than the legendary Port Hercule just along the coast. The super yacht owners that filled Monaco's most famous marina spent over fifty thousand euros a month for the pleasure. Byrn had been well paid throughout his career, so money wasn't an issue. However, the lower profile of Port de Plaisance de Cap d'Ail offered greater anonymity.

The assassin wouldn't be here long. All the required planning and preparations were made earlier. Lachlan Byrn wasn't an improviser, at least not unless a changing situation forced his hand. Tonight was all about the execution, in both senses of the term.

After a restless attempt to catch a couple of hours' sleep, Byrn climbed out of his bunk, showered, dressed, popped some more pills, and then checked his equipment. When he was done, he checked it again. Once in the military, always in the military.

By the time he set foot on the dock, the storm had subsided. Byrn scrutinized his new environment. Even though this wasn't millionaire's row, there were some fine craft surrounding his humble vessel. It didn't matter that much if his boat stood out a little. He'd be gone by dawn.

With his backpack slung over his shoulder, Byrn commenced the stroll towards the casino. Although he didn't intend to enter the establishment, he looked forward to catching up with an old acquaintance as he left. Byrn was quite pleased with what he'd planned. There would be a certain poetry to the process that he would find satisfying.

After paying too much for a quick meal at a café on the Boulevard Louis II, Byrn hiked up the hill to the casino carpark. It was fully dark now, and numerous shadowed areas provided suitable points of concealment. His first task was to identify his target's car. In any normal parking area, a jet-black Porsche 918 Spyder would stand out. At the Casino de Monte-Carlo, every vehicle stood out.

The assassin found the car, did what he had to do, and then settled in.

It was good to be back.

SCOTT TUNNERSON

Scott Tunnerson was extremely pleased with himself. The evening couldn't have gone any better if he'd planned it. The businessman won at blackjack, and he'd had a long winning streak at the roulette wheel. Tunnerson hadn't been that surprised at his good fortune. Every morning he woke up considering himself one of life's winners. He'd been successful in business, he'd made a heap of money, and because he had the courage to make hard decisions, the single major problem he'd encountered in recent years was about to be eliminated.

Of course, in retrospect, he should never have taken on

a partner. But Iqbal Ramez's funds had been just what he needed to get his latest venture off the ground. Money attracts money, and the investors had come running. Tunnerson hadn't anticipated Ramez's sudden attack of conscience when things got a little sticky with the environmental regulators. His first move had been to throw enough shade on Ramez so that any investigation into the company's activities would find his partner to be the sole instigator. Either way, if Ramez would just shut up, Tunnerson could control the situation. He bought the right people, and they came with the right answers.

But Ramez wouldn't shut up, so Scott Tunnerson had needed to make further arrangements. It was a road he hadn't traveled before, but the businessman was certain of a successful outcome. He'd hired the best.

"Good evening."

Tunnerson swung around to see the beautiful woman from across the roulette table now standing before him. Her dark hair was pinned up, but long strands extended down to frame her exquisite face.

"Yes."

"I couldn't help noticing your success at the wheel. It seems a shame to celebrate such a win on your own, does it not?"

Tunnerson eyed her up and down. Was she on the make? Some high-class hooker? He was way too smart for that.

"I'm afraid you'll have to find someone else," the businessman began. "You see, I'm not that…"

At that moment, one of the maître d's who'd been looking after the roulette players appeared.

"Lady Adeer, your limousine is waiting as requested."

Tunnerson stopped talking, looked at the maître d', and

then took a step sideways to look out the large casino window. Sure enough, a gleaming black limousine stood waiting in the circular driveway, its driver standing beside an open door.

Scott Tunnerson prided himself on being able to read any situation.

"Forgive me," he began. "Perhaps you'd care to join me for a drink? If you're happy to dismiss your chauffeur, I'd be delighted to drop you at your hotel afterward."

The woman paused, thinking. Tunnerson liked that. A genuine reaction.

"Why, of course, that would be lovely. Thank you."

She reached forward and offered the businessman her hand. "I am Chantelle Adeer."

Tunnerson pressed his fingers into hers.

"And I'm Scott Tunnerson. Shall we? He gestured his free hand in the direction of the lounge.

Tunnerson felt like saying 'I'm Scott Tunnerson, complete freakin' winner'.

As they strolled into the lounge area, the businessman nodded toward two large men in dark suits standing near the front door, his security team. He gave them the prearranged slice across the throat, meaning you have the rest of the night off. The boss just got lucky.

LACHLAN BYRN

It had drawn close to midnight when Byrn saw them appear through the casino's massive doors. They descended the steps, the grand floodlit facade looming behind them like a fairytale castle. The assassin retreated fully into the shadows.

As their shoes clacked across the roadway, the couple walked right past him without so much as a glance.

Perfect.

Scott Tunnerson clicked his key, the Porsche's lights flashed. Attempting his best impersonation of a gentleman, the entrepreneur stepped around the passenger door and opened it. At that moment, the woman placed a hand over her stomach and bent forward. Byrn couldn't hear everything, but he caught her saying *'S'il vous plaît excusez-moi'*. Please excuse me.

She hurried back towards the casino doors. As she passed the spot where Byrn stood concealed in darkness, she glanced toward him and nodded.

Perfect.

The actress, the maître d', and the limousine. All money well spent.

Lachlan Byrn stepped quickly out of the darkness, withdrawing his SIG as he crossed the driveway. Within half a dozen steps, he stood opposite Scott Tunnerson.

"You?" said Tunnerson.

"Yes, Scott, me."

Chapter 4

"Get into the car and close the door."

"I'm not taking orders from…"

Byrn pointed the weapon directly at Tunnerson's face.

"Get into the car, Scott."

Tunnerson's shoulders sagged in defeat. He opened the driver's door and climbed in. By the time his hands touched the wheel, Byrn was sitting beside him.

"Start the engine, pull out quietly and head toward Av. d'Ostende."

"But Chantelle…"

"Chantelle won't be back," said Byrn.

Reluctantly, Tunnerson started the car and reversed out of the space.

"Why are you doing this?"

"Don't speak, Scott. We'll talk when we get there. Just concentrate on your driving."

"Where's there?"

"Drive through the tunnel and keep going. I'll tell you when to turn."

The Porsche's roaring motor dominated the next few minutes.

"Here, right onto Route de la Turbie."

Tunnerson swung right, and they began to climb, leaving the lights of Monte Carlo behind. As the entrepreneur pressed down hard on the gas pedal. The vehicle lurched forward.

"No Scott. You can't drive your way out of this. If I feel unsafe, I'll simply shoot you and take the wheel. Focus, man."

The road twisted and turned, rising rapidly, demanding concentration. Even at night, the heights were dizzying.

After a few more minutes.

"All right, pull over here. There's a small space."

"There's not enough room."

"It's fine, Scott. Pull over."

Tunnerson swung the wheel to the right and braked sharply. The car skidded to a halt. It was almost as though they'd parked in mid-air. The vehicle sat stationary amidst a one-hundred-and-fifty-degree hairpin bend. The Porsche's headlights shone into the nothingness, the ground falling away steeply just in front of the wheels.

"Turn the engine off."

Tunnerson pressed the off button before turning to face Byrn. The assassin's face remained half hidden in the shadows. Recovering some fortitude, Tunnerson attempted to assert himself.

"Have you finished the job as instructed? And why the hell have you insisted on bringing me up here?"

Byrn sat silently. Experience had taught him that silence bred nervousness. A minute later, Tunnerson started tapping on the wheel.

"No, Scott," Byrn began. "Your assignment is not yet complete, but the file will be closed by the end of this evening, I promise. By the way, I recommend you leave your CEO boardroom aggression for circumstances more appropriate than this."

"What do you mean?" asked Tunnerson.

"You lied to me, Scott. I'm a very dangerous man. Lying to me is a very dangerous thing to do."

"I didn't…"

"Hush, Scott. That time has passed."

"What do you want?"

Again, Byrn paused. He would be the one controlling the conversation.

"I want to reach a satisfactory conclusion. I'm fairly certain we can achieve that."

Even in the half light, Byrn noted Tunnerson's skin begin to pale.

"I believe the brief you gave me, Scott, was that your partner had absconded with a great deal of your company's money and assets. You indicated that he left you and many of the fine people who work for you exposed. Vulnerable. I'm sure you mentioned the possibility of families losing their homes. You told me that if your partner was dead, and I recall we spoke of a car accident, you could claw those assets back for the good of everyone."

"Yes, that's true."

"No, Scott. We both know it's not," Byrn responded.

Silence.

"Your mistake was being too explicit. You laid out a trail for me to follow that was too directive. Everything you told me to check supported your story. Unfortunately, my additional research indicated otherwise."

"Someone must have lied to you, I swear…"

"Don't swear Scott. In fact, for now, just shut your fucking mouth." Byrn continued, "It turns out you were cutting corners, and your partner was about to throw you to the regulatory wolves. My research was confirmed after a lengthy conversation with Mr. Ramez, who incidentally had a substantial trail of paperwork to back up his perspective."

"You weren't meant to speak to him. You were hired to kill him."

"Shhh. Yes Scott, that was your instruction, and your deposit was received. Thankfully, it has covered my expenses."

"Then why…"

Byrn's patience was fast running out. While holding his SIG in his right hand, he leaned forward, balled his left fist and launched a forceful blow into the side of Tunnerson's face. The entrepreneur's head slammed back onto the headrest as blood seeped from his nose and eye.

"I shall now continue uninterrupted. I made it crystal clear to you, from the beginning of our relationship, that I would undertake my own investigations. I'm certain I emphasized the point that if I discovered I'd been lied to, or my services had been exploited under a false premise, then there would be repercussions."

Tunnerson's head slumped to his chest.

"Yes, Scott, you're now facing those repercussions."

"I can pay you more."

Byrn released a violent backhand. His victim lapsed into silence. After a minute, the trembling started. No surprise. A normal bodily reaction at the point of acceptance.

"So, Scott. I'm going to demote you."

Tunnerson turned his head toward him, but Byrn raised a palm.

"Let me finish. You are no longer a CEO or whatever you like to call yourself. You are a messenger. You will help send a message to all my future clients that I don't deal in deception. I'll give you a minute to think that through."

Byrn allowed Tunnerson a couple of moments to come to terms with his circumstances before continuing.

"Now, let's discuss the process. I've actually brought you to a significant location in local history tonight. This very corner, in all its danger, is known as 'Devil's Curse'. In 1982, the actress Grace Kelly, by then Princess Grace of Monaco, suffered a terrible mishap right here. Her vehicle plummeted one hundred and twenty feet down that slope. Sadly, she succumbed to her injuries the following day."

Tunnerson's eyes started to widen. Fear.

"There's a good news side to the story, Scott. Kelly's daughter, Stephanie, survived the accident, receiving relatively minor injuries. So perhaps there's hope."

Tunnerson raised his head, craning to get a look at the drop in front of them.

"So, here is how it will play out. You're going to reverse the car back up the road about fifty feet. I'll get out and be standing on the rock wall between the two sides of the hairpin. My gun is going to be aimed at your head. So, if you try anything but what I instruct, I'll just shoot you."

Another sagging of the shoulders.

"On my cue, you will accelerate down the road, break through the small brick barrier, and fly into the night. From then on, it's a gamble, and we know you like to gamble, Scott. The question is, which princess are you? Do you survive or die?"

Tunnerson turned back to Byrn and began to open his mouth before realizing the futility of his efforts.

"All right, let's get to it. Start the engine and reverse the car up the hill, Scott."

Almost in a trance, Tunnerson followed the assassin's instructions.

Byrn opened the passenger door, putting one foot on the road before turning back to his prey.

"If you've learned nothing else tonight, Scott, it's to never play out of your own league."

Byrn stepped onto the wall and motioned with his gun for Tunnerson to begin the process. He knew it would be difficult for the man; that made it all the more satisfying for Byrn.

Eventually the Porsche's revs increased. Byrn wondered whether it was despair or anger that motivated his victim now. It could go either way. Finally, the car lurched forward. Byrn kept his pistol trained on Tunnerson's head. They both knew it was an easy shot for a professional.

A moment later, in a cloud of dust and raging metal, the vehicle tore through the brick barrier and off into the abyss. Byrn darted ahead to see the results.

About a hundred feet down he saw the car hit the ground nose first before somersaulting over itself and coming to rest against a tree. There were no flames.

Byrn waited. After a minute, he concluded the petrol tank of the Porsche had remained unruptured. The crash was, therefore, possibly survivable. The assassin reached into his pocket and pulled out his cell. He dialed a number before pausing one more time to view the wreckage. Satisfied, he pressed the call button. Instantaneously, the vehicle below exploded, the flames reaching high above the tree beside it. The package of C4 had done its job.

Byrn leaned forward, a wry grin appearing on his lips. "Sorry motherfucker, I don't gamble."

Chapter 5

The distant waters of the Mediterranean glistened in the mid-morning sun. Lachlan Byrn sipped his coffee. The Greeks understood coffee. Small servings, thick and intense. The growing tourism industry had introduced a myriad of variations, but to Byrn, nothing tasted better than the traditional Elleniko Kafe, made from Arabica coffee beans. Byrn couldn't see his boat from the taverna perched high on the hillside, but knew she'd be swaying gently on the soft swell.

Byrn enjoyed the Greek Islands. The waters, the sparse, sunburnt countryside and the welcoming yet slightly narcissistic manner of the younger locals all appealed to him. He'd allow himself a small amount of time here before moving on. Lachlan Byrn had his favorite haunts in many parts of the world, but the assassin never frequented any too often. Unpredictability was a required professional trait.

Byrn didn't mind the downtime between jobs, but inactivity brought unwanted reflection. There wasn't a whole lot of Byrn's life that he needed or wished to revisit in his thoughts. Better to hold on to whatever sanity he could.

Byrn took a slow sip of his coffee.

'Sanity.' That was a term that defied description, at least

to Byrn's way of thinking. It seemed to him that 'sanity' was a state of mind humans forced themselves into, to cope with the enigmas that life presented. Byrn's life was indeed a complex enigma. An unsolvable puzzle of pain, frustration and disappointment that had forced him to redefine a level of rationality that allowed him to exist. And, truth be told, that's all he really did. Exist. The need or desire for positive emotion abandoned him long ago. A simmering rage filled the hole where hope may have once dwelt.

The assassin refused to dwell on excuses. The abuse and ensuing death of his sister. His father, the abuser, who died at Byrn's hand. The mother… well, what mother, really? She was just a woman in a house he lived in for a while. Then there was the system that wouldn't allow a teenage vigilante to run free, and the years of institutionalization that followed. That, of course, inspired a separate trail of crushing disappointment.

Amongst it all, a small glimmer of light had appeared to a then young nineteen-year-old. His acceptance into the military. The recognition of Byrn's unparalleled skills as a marksman, and their willingness to overlook his tendency toward violence. After all, he was a warrior. His eventual approval to join the British Special Boat Service followed. Byrn had chosen that path because his contemporaries told him the SBS made the SAS look like a bunch of scouts. Probably untrue, but Byrn rose to the challenge.

Then came the first mission. Unsanctioned, as it turned out. Byrn had been captured by the enemy and disavowed by his leaders.

The enemy.

The Chinese.

Another sip of coffee.

Time to run interference on his brain. Byrn attempted to terminate his own train of thought by absorbing his surroundings. The whitewashed wall of the taverna, the old men chatting at a table in the corner, the cheeky flirting of the young waitress. He stared back down the hill, his thoughts wandering...

The Chinese.

Abandonment from his own. Years of interrogation and torture from his captors. Pain beyond description.

Yes, sanity had to be reimagined. Now, what was left of Lachlan Byrn was a man who lived for the deaths of others. Killing was his only satisfaction, his 'happy place', or more exactly, his 'less disappointed place'.

So be it.

Sanity redefined.

The cell phone in Byrn's pocket buzzed. That was rare. Not more than half a dozen people in the world had his number. The assassin yanked it out and stared at the screen.

Damn.

He knew the caller.

The Chinese.

Chapter 6

Lachlan Byrn stared down the cobblestone alleyway. It was an atmosphere of boisterous anticipation. For now, the foot traffic was sparse, only a few folk heading out for the evening ahead. As the night drew on, things would get busier, and Byrn appreciated that. It was always like that in Athens.

The sun was drawing the day to a close, yet there was still enough light to observe the comings and goings, the people. That's exactly what Byrn was doing, observing people.

The assassin had arrived a full hour before his agreed meeting time. He loitered, out of sight, in a doorway fifty feet along the laneway from the taverna. Byrn had picked the spot. He and his Chinese minder had twelve locations in Europe marked for their meetings. Each had an allocated number, so real locations were never referred to by voice or text. Number eleven. Byrn chose this one because it was outdoors, virtually on a vacant lot. Access in and out was suitable. The ability to scrutinize from a distance, adequate.

It wasn't that Byrn didn't trust Zhen Su; Lachlan Byrn didn't trust anyone.

At two minutes before seven, Zhen appeared, strolling

down the alleyway, as though he didn't have a care in the world. Byrn's gut felt like a lead weight. He'd considered himself liberated from this relationship. He and Zhen hadn't spoken in over a year. The agreement had been that the assassin's last job for Chinese intelligence would be his swan song. He'd worked his way free over the preceding years, or at least he thought he had.

The journey from captive to trusted informant and eventually hired assassin had been long. It had taken more from Byrn than he'd cared to give. Yet his keepers took it, anyway.

Byrn studied Zhen as the waiter guided the agent to a table in a corner of the yard, away from prying ears. The man ordered a drink. It would be sparkling water. It always was. Just another Asian businessman in a dark suit.

Byrn knew better. Zhen Su was anything but a harmless businessman. The Chinese operative was a shrewd negotiator, a meticulous planner and manipulator, and when required, a merciless killer. Byrn waited five minutes. Satisfied no one else was checking out the taverna, he approached.

The maître d' guided him to Zhen's table. The agent didn't even raise his eyes.

"Lachlan, it has been too long, my friend."

Byrn sat down.

"That's entirely a matter of perspective, Zhen. I would suggest it hasn't been long enough."

"Come now," Zhen's English was flawless. "We've been through a lot together."

"I've been through a lot, Zhen. You just watched."

A wry grin appeared on the agent's face.

"As you say, a matter of perspective," he agreed.

The waiter approached. Byrn waved him away.

23

"Why am I here?" Byrn asked.

"Because I invited you, Lachlan. I didn't put a gun to your head."

Byrn paused, lingering on a memory.

"The last time I declined an invitation from you, three of your goons tracked me down and put me in hospital for the best part of a week."

"Yes, I recall that. You know you were very difficult to find. It took them two months to locate you. You may also remember that two of my men's bodies were later recovered from the river Seine. The third only just made it back to Beijing. My understanding is he has permanently lost the use of his right arm."

"I needed a messenger," Byrn responded. "I'd hoped you understood the message."

"Message understood and ignored." Zhen smiled. "And here we are."

Byrn nodded.

"I also understand you've sent another message recently. Postmarked Monte Carlo."

Byrn was almost taken aback, but nothing Zhen uncovered surprised him anymore.

"So," said Byrn.

"So," replied Zhen. "I have an offer for you, a job."

"An offer infers an opportunity to refuse."

"All right then, I have a job for you. This shall be your final commitment to my government."

"You said that last time," Byrn replied.

"The world has changed, Lachlan, and it continues to change. My president is not convinced that the changes at hand will be beneficial to our nation. The politburo agrees."

"I won't be part of any action commissioned by a group of politicians. The possibility of leaks, weaknesses in security and reprisals is too great." Byrn sensed his own edginess as he spoke.

"Relax, my friend. Only two people on the planet know of this mission. You will be the third."

"You lied to me about the last assignment being my final task. Why on God's earth should I believe you this time?"

Zhen gazed across the table at Byrn.

"Two reasons, Lachlan. The first is this."

Zhen reached into his jacket pocket and produced the printout of a bank deposit. The sum deposited was significant.

"That is the first payment. A payment of equal amount will be deposited into your account on completion."

"I find your generosity chilling," Byrn responded. "Why do I suspect you are about to ask the world of me?"

"Because we are."

"If the job is doable, the payment is fair. But what assurance do I have that this is my final operation for your government?"

Again, Zhen stopped to consider his words.

"A minute ago, you accused me of a lack of participation in your activities for us. I told my chairman that despite the money, and the threat of ramifications, you would probably decline. He suggested I put some, what you would call, 'skin' in the game."

For a moment, Byrn considered that Zhen may actually be nervous. There was a slight tremor in his movement as he reached once more into his coat pocket, perhaps even a tiny bead of sweat on his forehead. Byrn dismissed the observations as ridiculous.

"Here is your guarantee, Lachlan."

Zhen produced a white envelope and set it down on the table.

Byrn reached over and picked it up before carefully opening it. Inside was a picture of a woman and two young children, girls.

"My wife and my daughters. On the back is our home address in Beijing."

Byrn titled his head quizzically.

Zhen continued. "If I or any member of my government call on your services again, I will gift you the lives of my family. I envisage that you would have no trouble seeking them out."

Byrn was momentarily confused.

"Don't speak Lachlan, unless of course, it is to say yes. You should know that if you fail in your mission, my president, in his infinite wisdom, has indicated that my life will also be forfeited."

"And I thought western politics was tough," Byrn responded.

Byrn considered his position. Despite the gesture, he still didn't trust Zhen Su an inch. On the other hand, this could be his one chance to escape the tentacles of the Chinese intelligence system for once and for all. The assassin scrutinized Zhen's features, looking for any sign of vulnerability or deception. Of course, it was pointless. The Chinese agent was too professional to send any physical tell he didn't want sent.

Several minutes passed in an awkward silence. Zhen chose not to interrupt Byrn's thought processes, and Byrn had a lot to process.

"You haven't told me the target, Zhen."

"You will be informed after you have committed. We cannot risk a leakage of information to anyone not directly involved."

Another minute passed.

"I'll tell you what," Byrn began. "I will go this far. If the job is doable, I'll commit to it. How's that?"

The Chinese agent considered Byrn's proposal before nodding slowly.

"I suspect there is virtually no job you would be incapable of succeeding at Lachlan. Your terms are accepted."

"So…"

"So, your task is to assassinate a major figure in the world's political landscape."

"What tinpot country has pissed you off this time, Zhen? Will I have even heard of it?"

"I believe so Lachlan. The nation concerned is the Russian Federation. Your assignment is to eliminate Vadim Aleyev, its president."

Chapter 7

Lachlan Byrn sat back in his chair. He hadn't seen that one coming.

"The Russian president?"

"That is correct."

"You must know that the assassination of a man with such a high level of security is almost impossible."

"Yes, Lachlan, we are aware of that. The reason you've been tasked with the assignment is in your own words."

Byrn nodded. He walked right into that one.

"*Almost* impossible."

"Yes. Most operatives would have simply stated it was an impossible commission. That is why we've come to you."

Byrn chuckled out loud. "So, your confidence in telling me this is my last mission for your people lies in the fact I'll probably be killed trying to complete it."

Byrn remained silent.

"That's entirely possible, but I suspect not. You, like the proverbial cat, seem to have a number of lives up your sleeve."

Byrn remained silent.

"Of course, you should have died in Colombia. But we rescued you," said Zhen.

"Interesting definition of the word 'rescue'."

"Perhaps, but everything turned out for the best, didn't it?"

Byrn was past feeling any emotion towards his then captors. He may not totally control the dreams that still haunted him, but in the waking hours, his emotional composure was resolute. He chose not to respond.

"There were other instances," continued Zhen, "but of course the most remarkable was the most recent."

Byrn had no idea what the agent was referring to, so he maintained his silence.

Zhen smiled once more.

"Oh, come on Lachlan, don't be coy. It takes a special skill set to eliminate the US secretary of defense and come out alive while convincing the authorities you died in the act."

"How the hell…"

"Does it matter?" Zhen interrupted. "The man was a prick, anyway. You really shouldn't be so surprised at the reach of our intelligence resources."

No, Byrn figured, he shouldn't be surprised at all.

Zhen reached for his drink, took a long swig before waving the server down to order another.

"You sure you don't want anything, Lachlan?"

Byrn nodded toward the bottle of still water on the table.

"Water is fine, thanks."

Once his drink had been delivered, Zhen resumed speaking.

"Now down to business."

"First up, Zhen, explain to me why you want to assassinate Aleyev. Last time I checked the papers, China and Russia were allies. What happened?"

"Our two great nations are allies, but our president feels that if that relationship is to be maintained, Russia is in need of a new leader."

"Why?"

"Vadim Aleyev is living in the past. You are well aware, I'm sure, that Aleyev came up through the ranks as a KGB operative and then headed up the FSB. He was devastated when the Soviet Union splintered. Sadly, instead of moving forward with the times, he's dedicating his final years in office to a futile attempt to reawaken the soviet spirit. First the Crimean Peninsula, then Ukraine, now he has eyes on Estonia, and perhaps even Latvia, Poland and Finland."

"Can't you people dissuade him? Your country wields a great deal of economic power."

"Our president had tried, unsuccessfully. Aleyev won't budge. He has surrounded himself with sycophants who tell him what he wants to hear. Even those close to him are too scared to speak the truth. The Russian president is not a man who tolerates disagreement, either from within, or in our case, from another country."

"There does seem to be an epidemic of powerful people falling out of windows in Moscow," observed Byrn.

"Exactly," Zhen responded. "Our president believes that Russia's expansionist agenda is triggering a strong western coalition with zero tolerance for nations rearranging their borders. If this continues unabated, it may have a negative effect on our own nation's plans."

"You mean across the Taiwan Strait?"

"I cannot say."

"All right. If I take this on…"

"You've already said you will, Lachlan. *Almost* impossible."

Byrn gazed into Zhen Su's eyes. He noted a steely resolve that was disquieting. The assassin had been trapped by his own words.

"The security around Vadim Aleyev and the Kremlin is exhaustive. You would need an insider, in fact several insiders, to have any chance of infiltrating the layers of defense surrounding the man. He even has people tasting his food, for God's sake."

"I totally agree. The Kremlin's security is impregnable. But that won't be your issue, Lachlan."

Zhen Su was not a stupid man. Byrn figured he'd have some kind of ace up his sleeve.

"I've already demonstrated the depth of our intelligence capabilities," Zhen continued. "From this moment on, those assets will be working for you. And I'm certain the first gift from Beijing will reassure you of your chances of success. Our people inform us that you won't need to go anywhere near Moscow. The Kremlin will, in fact, come to you."

One of the first things Lachlan Byrn had learned in his professional life was that targets are more vulnerable when traveling. Even the president of the United States, with his mammoth entourage, resources and pre-planning, was more susceptible to risk when away from Washington. That said, the US Secret Service played one hell of an 'away game', making the president an extremely difficult target anywhere. Byrn wondered if Aleyev's team was as good.

"All right, let's play along for a minute. The Kremlin is incredibly tight lipped about the president's travel arrangements. In most cases, the public doesn't know he's been somewhere until he's already returned. Therefore, I assume you have intel coming from deep inside the Presidential Security Service," said Byrn.

Zhen nodded silently.

Byrn continued. "Okay, so where is Aleyev going? When is he going? And of course, why?"

"The timeline we're dealing with is tight, but not impossible. Vadim Aleyev and his entourage depart Moscow in six weeks. Their destination is Estonia."

Byrn raised his eyebrows. "Estonia is a NATO country."

"It is. It also used to be part of the Soviet Union."

"You have my attention."

"Aleyev is traveling to a high-level summit. And I mean, genuinely high-level. Up for discussion will be the Russian Federation's future plans and international relationships," said Zhen.

"Who is he meeting with?"

Zhen allowed himself a tiny, self-satisfying smirk.

"The president of the United States."

Byrn shook his head.

"I withdraw the *'almost'*. The combined security forces protecting those two men will be an impenetrable fortress. It can't be done." Byrn sat back and folded his arms across his chest.

"I agree," Zhen responded.

Byrn remained silent. He'd give Zhen Su three minutes to clarify the situation, or he was walking.

"Let me explain," Zhen began. "The US president declined to meet anywhere that wasn't a NATO country. His security team requires power and influence wherever their boss goes. Aleyev refused to travel beyond Russia's neighboring nations. Estonia was the compromise. Those close to Aleyev believe he's quite keen to use a visit to Estonia to reinvigorate some of his leaders about his Russian expansion policy. You know the thing... once upon a time, all this was ours, and it can be once more."

Byrn shook his head again.

"Delusional."

"Yes, Lachlan, delusional. But we're way past that being a surprise. The point of relevance for you is that Aleyev has requested some time in Estonia aside from the summit. He wishes to tour some of the former Soviet sites."

"And that will be my opportunity."

"Yes."

"Do you have details? Itinerary?"

"Not yet, but we will."

"You must be confident of your sources?"

"Extremely."

"How do you propose I execute the operation?"

It was Zhen's turn to sit back in his chair.

"Never would I dream of telling the great Lachlan Byrn how to do his job. There are several men on the planet that may give you a run for your money as a marksman, Lachlan. But I'm yet to meet a man that could design and execute an assassination with your skill, precision, and imagination. Anyway, to be perfectly honest, we don't want to know how you're going to proceed. The fewer people that have that knowledge, the greater the chance of success."

Byrn nodded.

"After the event. Extraction?"

"We expect that if you survive, you'll need to get out of the country quickly. We'll make those arrangements, be assured. The Night Eagle will fly again."

Byrn had never liked the handle that his masters had given him. 'Night Eagle'. He supposed it reflected their strategy of getting him at least partially addicted to modafinil, the drug that had seen him through so many operations.

"One last question Zhen. Why six weeks? If the Americans think they have a chance of negotiating their way through this, why wait that long for the summit?"

Zhen rubbed his chin.

"Positioning. Aleyev has refused to meet before that date. It gives him a chance to reposition himself militarily and politically. Essentially, it's the old strategy of grab as much land as you can before you agree to give any back. Of course, during that process, the likelihood is that thousands of innocent people will die."

Zhen paused to allow his words to sink in.

"So, we proceed?"

Byrn considered the man across the table. Despite Zhen's outward manner, there was little love lost between them. Workable tolerance at best.

"I don't like it, Zhen, not one bit. There are holes in your plan big enough to drive an army through. So, I say fuck you, in fact, fuck you big-time."

Zhen Su remained silent before Byrn added.

"But I'll do it."

Chapter 8

Byrn stared at the ceiling. The flaking paint matched the décor of threadbare carpet, stained sink, and bare lightbulbs. An overnight respite for a hungover sailor. Also, a temporary abode for the anonymous traveler.

Byrn had taken three cabs, a train, and a bus to avoid being followed. No mean feat in Athens. Eventually, he found his way here to Piraeus, the chief seaport of Athens. It was a town of transients, Byrn was just one additional unnoticed soul. He was certain his movements hadn't been tracked. No single person had tailed him, and he'd changed modes of transport too quickly for any group operation to keep tabs on him. In the morning, he'd be on the first ferry to Paros before boarding his boat and leaving the area.

Lachlan Byrn hadn't survived this long by not taking precautions. Maintaining a zero level of trust in Zhen Su and his organization was one of those precautions.

The assassin traced the outlines of the room with his eyes, following each cornice into a corner before moving onto the next wall. He did it over and over. Repetition helped him think.

The last thing on the planet he'd wanted to do was work for his old Chinese masters again. Maybe he'd been a fool to say yes. On the other hand, he'd have been a fool to say no. This was his final chance at an out. If Zhen went back on his word, Byrn would kill him. The jury was out on the man's family. Of course, the money was good, very good. If he survived, the assassin would never have to work again. The trouble was that Lachlan Byrn loved his work. He would always work. So, while useful, the money wasn't the deciding factor. Breaking free from Zhen and his cohorts was the decider.

Zhen had known it would be, and that pissed Byrn off.

The assassin would consider the parameters and tactics of the assignment later. For now, it was a case of accepting his fate and finding a clear space to work without looking over his shoulder. It worried him slightly that Zhen knew about the job with the US SecDef in Rome, but it didn't really matter in the scheme of things.

Of course, nothing really mattered to Byrn, but that was an issue to unpack some other time.

Byrn kept tracing the outline of the ceiling.

He questioned if he was being honest with himself. There must be some level of sensitivity lurking deep inside him. There had to be, otherwise he couldn't maintain the rage that drove him. It was always there; he'd just learned to temper it when working.

The rage.

The anger.

The years of pain at the hands of his captors.

The memories.

Byrn began to feel drowsy. He snapped himself awake before drifting off again.

The memories.

The damp ceiling was lined with endless cracks. Byrn tried to follow each crack, imagining each one as a road to freedom. They weren't, they were just cracks. He didn't look anywhere else, just straight up to the roof, the road map.

He lay shackled to a wooden board, its edges digging sharply into his back. The shackles' heavy metal cut into his wrists and ankles. A cross beam supported his arms. He'd overheard the guards describe the irons around his extremities as 'Hell's Shackles' and the plank as the 'death bed'.

Death would be good right now. He'd welcome it.

A muted scream filled the room as the guard ground his cigarette firmly into Byrn's palm. The special services operative didn't plan to scream. He never planned to scream. Despite his haunting cry, the burning flesh of his hand wasn't the worst bit. His dread lay in the anticipation of what came next.

He'd been here for months, many months. He'd figured out his jailers' routines. He knew they wanted him to understand their processes. With understanding came anticipation. The knowledge of imminent pain was often worse than the pain itself.

Byrn started to shake... trepidation. He gazed at the map. Perhaps one of the roads led to the sea. He used to like the sea....

He smelled it before he felt it. The bucket of burning, filthy water. Suddenly, a flash of pain became a cloak of agony. Could something be sudden if you expected it? The agony became suffocating, unbearable. Byrn knew he'd pass out. Fine. The trouble was, he also knew he wouldn't die; he'd be back. Back here.

Screw the motherfucker who put him here.

Byrn awoke, startled. Damn that he couldn't control his sleeping mind. They weren't nightmares. Nightmares were made-up stories that scared kids. These were recollections that kept revisiting. That was much worse.

They were real.

The assassin returned to tracing the corners of the ceiling before slowly drifting off again.

His shoulders ached, as though nails had been driven through every muscle... but there were no nails. Three feet above his head, Byrn's wrists pulsed in agony, bound tightly to the bars of the metal cage. He thought he'd been in that position for at least twelve hours, although he couldn't really be sure of any single passage of time.

The dank smell of the swamp below him devoured his senses, cutting through his pain. As ever, the anticipation hung over him like an acid-filled cloud.

The water started to lap at the soles of his feet. He'd sensed its intrusion only seconds earlier. He knew what would happen the moment he heard the brittle screech of the chain grinding above him. It was an odd sensation. It felt more like the water rising than the crate being lowered.

It lapped around his ankles now.

Byrn knew he would count out two minutes before his knees disappeared into the cold murkiness.

A minute after that, the process abruptly stopped.

The first time that happened, he'd allowed himself a glimmer of hope. Not now, not anymore. Hope was a term he no longer entertained.

Around twenty minutes later, the water rose again. His groin, his chest, and then his neck. Suddenly, the machine jerked the crate to a halt, just as the stale water began to slap at his chin. Finally, a fraction of an inch at a time, the crate was lowered further. Water trickled slowly into his mouth. An unwanted poison.

He strained his neck upward, craning for any air he could find.

When he sensed a gap between the tiny waves that rippled against his face, he drew a deep breath. Invariably it was followed by gagging as a flood of rancid liquid replaced the air. Still, he had to try.

The chain stopped cranking. Now the water enveloped his mouth, teasing mercilessly at his nose. Any movement of his head caused more waves. The waves intruded into his nostrils like an invading army.

Every part of Byrn's body stretched tight. He fought against any reaction his aching muscles demanded.

He wondered if he would survive this for another twenty-four hours. Perhaps it would be better just to submit.... and die.

But he wasn't dead, and there'd be no more attempts at sleep tonight.

Byrn sprung out of bed. He did his usual hundred push-ups to wake himself up, followed by his regular exercise regime. Finally, after showering, packing, and checking the news media, he stole away into the dark early morning.

The assassin was standing at the dock waiting for the ferry as the first rays of sunlight glistened across the water.

Chapter 9

The black Kawasaki ZX-10R under Byrn's legs roared into the night. The journey provided the assassin with an opportunity to review his plans thus far.

R.O.P.E. Research, observe, plan, and execute. They were Lachlan Byrn's tenets for a successful operation. Military people lived by acronyms, and Byrn was no different. He'd completed the research phase and was about to move into the observation stage.

After leaving Greece, Byrn had moved his boat to a safe, secluded harbor off the Turkish coast. He'd used the travel time wisely, researching all that he could online about Vadim Aleyev. Google really did make an assassin's job easier. A trail of false IP addresses and the appropriate crypto software protection rendered Byrn's inquiries untraceable. He accepted that, unlike his usual practice, he couldn't spend much time observing his target. The circles of security around the Russian president were too opaque to allow that. However, there was a chance he may have some opportunity just before the hit in Estonia.

That's where he headed now.

He knew the ride would be long and arduous, but the Kawasaki would straighten every bend in the road. The journey would take him around thirty hours if he didn't stop overnight. Thanks to his pills, that wouldn't be an issue.

Byrn remained focused as his route took him northwest through Bulgaria, Serbia, Hungry, and the edge of Austria before swinging northeast through Czechia, Poland, Lithuania, and Latvia. That was a lot of countries to cover in thirty hours, but the only sights Byrn expected to see were the black tarmac and the white lines of the road. When working internally in Europe, the assassin avoided planes and public transport wherever possible. Transit stations had cameras and security guards. The open highway on a bike allowed him anonymity. The European roads were host to thousands of bikers dressed in dark colors wearing full face helmets.

Perfect.

The motorcycle jiggled under his hands as it flew over a pothole. Byrn finessed it calmly, restoring optimal balance. At around ninety miles an hour, his focus remained intense.

The assassin hadn't worked in Estonia before, so the area was unfamiliar to him. What he needed to do as quickly as possible, and without drawing unwanted attention to himself, was to study and observe the likely locations Aleyev would visit. Byrn had been told by Zhen Su that both the Russian and US itineraries would be in his hands when he arrived in Tallinn, the country's capital.

Byrn didn't care about the US contingent as long as they were out of his way. In the absence of prior information about the Russians' movements, he couldn't fully plan and prepare. No plan, no hit. That meant no money and no freedom for him.

Byrn didn't give a damn about the politics.

Lachlan Byrn regarded all politicians as scum. In his eyes,

they were in the game for money, power, prestige, or all of the above. Time and time again, those who were supposed to lead feigned putting their people first. It was bullshit. The world's leaders, media, and public knew it was bullshit, but did nothing. The few that called them out ended up being drawn into their own dubious swamps.

Well, that wasn't entirely true. From time to time, Byrn did something about it. Just ask the recently demised US secretary. Byrn had no issue being judge, jury, and executioner. Some would say he had an overly developed sense of black and white, but Byrn was happy to accept living on the extreme edges of morality. Life had taught him to embrace his own eccentricities. What others considered abnormal, Byrn considered well balanced. Just like the motorcycle beneath him.

The assassin did not understand guilt. In his adult life, he'd never felt remorse. He was aware of files and dossiers about him in a variety of government archives. Depending on their analysis of his behavior, he'd been branded an assassin, a vigilante, and a serial killer.

Byrn didn't give a shit, although there were times he wondered if the latter category was the most suitable. He may kill for a living, but he passionately loved every minute of it.

A quick glance at the fuel gauge told him a stop would be required soon. He was certain he was in Slovakia, but the borders had passed by at a lightning speed. At the next opportunity, he'd pull over and fill up. A ten-minute break should be enough to revive him.

Fifteen minutes later, the glaring lights of a petrol station appeared. Unsurprisingly, a café was attached to it. A strong coffee would hit the mark. Byrn followed the turn off and decelerated, stopping precisely in front of a pump.

It didn't take him long to fill the tank. Then he moved the bike to a parking spot, ensuring the space was dark enough that his false registration plates were unreadable. It was the small things that mattered.

As he strode along the darkened path, Byrn heard a groan. It seemed like a tiny, distant sound and through his helmet could have easily been missed. A second later, it morphed into a small shriek. Byrn stopped and turned around. He scanned the whole area but noted nothing unusual. He was still some distance away from the main part of the café building and vehicles of all sizes pulling in and out, including large trucks, dominated the soundscape.

The assassin almost dismissed it as his imagination when another scream penetrated the air. It sounded female. He looked around again. No one else appeared alarmed, but no one else was within his immediate vicinity.

The next shriek started loudly, but quickly became muffled. Byrn was now certain it came from the rear of the building.

A smart operator would ignore it.

Byrn took another pace along the path before stopping. He said 'shit' to no one in particular and turned around. He marched purposefully back, retracing his steps. After striding past his bike, he swung around the corner and headed to the rear of the building. No driveway and minimal lighting.

As he rounded the corner, the hair on the back of the assassin's neck prickled.

A girl, probably about seventeen years old, lay on the gravel, her skirt hoisted up. A man, broad shouldered and dressed in black, was lying on top of her. Byrn noted a helmet, not unlike his own next to the man. He also noticed the large hunting knife in his hand, pressing against the girl's throat. Byrn took a step forward and was about to speak when a second man, equally menacing and dressed in leathers, stepped out of the shadows to his left.

Byrn continued his path forward.

"Gentlemen, I would suggest you both get on your metal stallions and leave while you still can."

"Fuck off mate. Piss off out of here, while *you* still can," responded the man from the shadows.

Byrn shrugged. He didn't need this right now.

Byrn took another step forward, but the man stepped out, blocking his way.

"Leave now or pray," he said.

"Nice line," said Byrn, "but sadly ineffective. Now get on your way. If you choose otherwise, this situation won't play out as you see it."

"I've got real good eyes," said the second man, laughing.

As he spoke, he pulled a small pistol out of his pocket. Byrn sighed again.

Four seconds later, the pistol lay on the ground three feet from the figure, clutching desperately at his bloodied eyes, lying next to it.

"How are your eyes now?" asked the assassin.

"Fuck you."

"You're a fucking dead man," yelled the other guy. In one movement, he leaped off the girl and came straight at Byrn, blade pointed in front of him.

Byrn stepped to the side, grabbed the man under his armpits, and launched him into the darkness. The first man, still on the ground, scrambled for his gun a few feet away. Byrn took one pace forward and stamped his boot on the guy's wrist. He grunted in pain. Byrn stepped back, raising his other foot, and slammed it into the man's face.

Byrn heard a sound behind him, feet scuffling on gravel. He pivoted and sidestepped to the right. This time, he grabbed his attacker's knife hand and spun him around. The man attempted to propel himself forward but lacked grip on the gravel. Byrn squeezed his wrist, and the blade dropped. The man looked up just as Byrn brought a knee up under his chin, sending his head snapping backward.

Seeing both men down, Byrn turned to the girl. Without a word, she picked herself up and sprinted off into the darkness.

The assassin stood silently, now at odds with himself. Every fiber of his being wanted to remove these two idiots from the planet. There was no one to stop him… except himself. Too much was on the line to complicate things. As fast as Byrn was traveling through the country, who knew how quickly the police would react to a double murder?

After a few seconds of staring at the groaning men, Byrn retrieved the gun and knife and placed them in his pocket. He shook his head.

"Well, I guess it's your lucky night," he said, before walking off around the building.

The assassin felt incomplete. The situation felt incomplete. Worst of all, now he wouldn't get his coffee. He climbed onto his bike, started the engine, and pulled out into the darkness.

Thirty minutes later, Byrn had almost forgotten about the incident. While dissatisfying, it was also inconsequential both to him and his task at hand. He was now completely focused on the road ahead.

The first thing he noticed was the approaching lights in his rear vision mirrors. They were traveling at a far greater speed than the surrounding traffic. Byrn had eased off on his own speed, trying to avoid attention. The second thing Byrn noticed was that the lights didn't move completely parallel to each other. Two lights, but not a single car. Two separate vehicles. Motorcycles.

The fools.

It never ceased to amaze Byrn how men's egos seemed to control their rational thought processes. In the assassin's mind, it was ego that led those two buffoons to assume they could do what they wanted with the girl. Now their pride had been bruised, so they needed to avenge the damage.

Byrn was quite pleased.

A couple of minutes later, they caught up. The riders pulled up on either side of him. Predictable. The guy on his right made the first move, lunging his bike towards Byrn's own. Byrn braked hard, emptying the space ahead of him. The guy had swerved too fast, and almost collided with his counterpart, now just ahead on Byrn's left. The rider on the left accelerated as Byrn's attacker fought to rebalance his machine. Byrn opened his own throttle, motoring up beside the struggling bike. Taking one hand off his bars, the assassin removed the previously confiscated knife from his jacket pocket, then turned his head toward the other rider. He hoped the other guy could see the smile in his eyes through his visor. A second later, Byrn inched forward, reached down, and thrust the knife into the spokes of his attacker's front wheel before veering away.

That was all it took.

The motorcycle tripped over its own front wheel, sending

its rider somersaulting in the air before crashing down onto the hard road. The bike cartwheeled before crashing down on the rider's chest.

To Byrn, the incident appeared un-survivable.

The assassin looked ahead. The second rider must have seen what happened in his mirror, because he now accelerated away into the darkness. It always amazed Byrn that people bled courage when they became isolated from their peers. Courage, however, wouldn't be all this scumbag would bleed tonight.

Byrn opened the throttle and his machine raced forward.

Five minutes later, the second rider was within spitting distance. It looked to be a Yamaha YZF. Nice bike. What a shame. He must have noted Byrn's presence because he cut in sharply in front of a large truck as the two lanes became one. Not a smart move for a biker. Byrn wondered for a moment if he'd have to act at all, or if the man would just kill himself through his own stupidity.

Byrn waited for a chance to pass the truck on the narrowed highway. A couple of moments later, he performed the move safely. No need to expose oneself to pointless danger. He was pleased to note that his prey had now come up behind another truck. The road was now too windy, even for a reckless fool to overtake. Now traveling in convoy, both motorcycles and the truck maintained a fair speed due to the road's downhill slope.

Byrn edged forward until he sat a foot from the other motorcycle's rear wheel. The rider in front glanced around, confirming his fears.

Byrn held position.

Every moment or two, Byrn would speed up, nudging at his

prey's rear wheel. The man kept looking around. The assassin knew his nerves would be fraying. Every few seconds, the front bike would sneak to the left, seeking an opportunity to overtake.

Byrn mirrored his every move, biding his time.

The piercing roar of both motorcycle engines combined with the whine of the truck's motor would do little to calm the rider in front.

Byrn waited, seeking out his moment, each nudge reminding the other biker of his presence.

Then opportunity knocked.

Headlights reflected on trees across the road. Byrn briefly moved left. A massive truck loomed on the other side of the highway, several hundred yards away, thundering toward them.

Byrn swung back behind the Yamaha and rammed its rear tire firmly. He paused briefly before pushing harder. The rider in front looked around. The third time, Byrn opened his throttle to full and charged at the bike in front. As earlier, he was prepared for the impact, but the other rider was not.

The bike wobbled. Byrn assumed the guy in front was terrified of being pushed under the truck's wheels. That would make sense. The rider looked around again as Byrn sped forward one final time. The biker saw it coming and panicked. With nowhere to go, he leaned to the left, propelling his machine desperately past the enormous truck.

Even over the roar of the engines, the metallic din screeched through Byrn's helmet. He looked up just in time to see the remains of the Yamaha and the man riding it disappear under the oncoming truck's wheels.

Byrn rode on, satisfied.

Accidents happen.

Chapter 10

Despite his medicinal helpers, Byrn was tiring as he rode the final stages of the Via Baltica Motorway into Tallinn. As he reached Laagri, the last of the farmlands gave way to the capital's urban sprawl. Because Estonia was unfamiliar ground to him, Byrn had decided to ride through the city center to familiarize himself with the town. Although keen to get his hands on the Russian itinerary, which would allow him to drill down to specific locations, a working knowledge of the area would be beneficial.

Byrn motored through Toompea, Tallinn's Upper Town and All-linn, the Lower Town. He found the city striking in its beauty, particularly the older sections. Like many modern cities, Tallinn had a mix of old and new. When he detoured down some of the narrower cobblestone streets in the Upper Town, his motorcycle shuddered underneath him.

Point noted, if he needed to move quickly, this wasn't the route to take.

Byrn's research had told him the population of the country was relatively small, yet it was a regional leader in information technology. Skype had its roots here. It astounded Byrn how rapidly the city and the country had modernized after being released from the Soviet grip.

The assassin tracked his way down to the waterfront, where Tallinn Bay led out to the Gulf of Finland. A short distance to the west lay the Baltic Sea. Byrn had already noted that Helsinki, just across the gulf, might provide a suitable point of extraction, if required.

The sightseeing completed, Byrn headed east toward the remote farmhouse he had rented in advance. Everything had been booked and paid for with high quality false identification and credit cards. The assassin would be long gone before anyone suspected they were forgeries.

As he headed out of town, Byrn became aware of the soreness in his body from being frozen in the same position on the bike for over thirty hours. Experience had taught the assassin that he could endure more pain than most. In fact, he'd been trained for it. Consciously by his SBS training, and incidentally by the techniques of the Chinese Ministry of State Security. The MSS had few boundaries when it came to the extraction of information from its prisoners.

The farmland slowly reclaimed the landscape. By the time he hit Voerdla, the green rolling pastures were the dominant feature. Passing Lake Rummu, Byrn looked out for the turn off to Kiiu. After making the turn, he sped north along the decreasingly diminishing roads until turning right down a dusty potholed track at the edge of Valka County.

At the end of the track, backing on to the forest, stood a small, weatherboard farmhouse. Byrn rolled slowly up the driveway.

The location was perfect. Away from any major tourist traffic, close enough to Tallinn, and easy access to most of the locations he may require. The fact it was less than a mile to the coast provided another escape route if required.

At least he'd given Zhen Su options for extracting him from the country.

Byrn hopped off the bike, removed his helmet, and stretched his back before climbing the wooden steps to the veranda. Just as directed, a key safe was fixed to one of the veranda roof supports. Byrn inserted the code he'd been sent, retrieved the key, and opened the front door.

There was no musty smell as he entered. That indicated that the owners had aired the place out prior to his arrival. That wasn't necessarily a good thing. He hoped they weren't nosy hosts. A single face-to-face contact would force him to move on. Apart from that, the house was clean and functional. Compared to many places the assassin had held up, it was luxurious, although it didn't really matter to him. He had a job to do.

After throwing his backpack on the bed in the second bedroom, Byrn returned to the veranda and scanned his immediate surrounds. The distance to other houses, paddocks on three sides, and woods behind the house were as shown on Google Earth.

Excellent.

Byrn returned to his motorcycle, filthy with the dust and grime of the road. He'd wash it later. In the meantime, he climbed on, started the engine, and rode it around the side of the house to the garage behind. As arranged, the building was unlocked. With the bike secure from prying eyes, Byrn walked back to the house, pulled out one of his three cell phones, and sat at the dining table. He placed his thumb on the display while the device identified him. He expected Zhen to have sent the Russian itinerary by now so he could begin work.

He was wrong.

Within seconds, a message in capital letters flashed up on the screen.

YOU HAVE BEED COMPROMISED. GET OUT OF THE COUNTRY IMMEDIATELY.

Z.

At that precise moment, the windowpane above the dining table shattered. Shards of glass sprayed across the room as the grenade landed on the floor. A second later, two more windows suffered the same fate.

The assassin knew he was in trouble.

Chapter 11

Byrn hit the floor.

All three grenades had already begun spewing tear gas across the room. He wrenched the scarf off his neck and wrapped it around his face, covering his nose and mouth. His eyes remained exposed and had started watering. That couldn't be helped for now.

Staying low, he crawled across the floor toward the bedroom door. As he passed the first bedroom, the thud of automatic gunfire smashing the windows and peppering the walls echoed through the lounge room. A few seconds later, the same thing happened in the living area.

Byrn figured his attackers knew the layout of the house. It wouldn't have been difficult to locate online. That was one of the reasons he'd chosen to sleep and stow his gear in the second bedroom. When he reached its door, he noted that his backpack remained on the bed undamaged. Byrn rose to his knees and launched forward, grabbing the pack, bringing it to the ground. Seconds after he secured it, the bed and neighboring walls disintegrated under a slew of gunfire.

Byrn was coughing violently now, and tears were now streaming down his face. The assassin knew he had only seconds to extricate himself from the situation.

With no time to consider who was behind the onslaught, Byrn had to commit to an action and follow through... immediately.

With bullets, glass and plaster strewing in all directions, the assassin crawled speedily to the back door. He decided to break left towards the forest. Byrn figured that the hail of incoming gunfire would stop within the next ten to fifteen seconds so his attackers could assess their initial assault. At that point, all eyes would be on the exit points. Byrn thought he'd have more chance of exiting unnoticed while they were still firing, as long as he wasn't cut down in the onslaught.

Of course, more chance still meant almost no chance.

Either way, if it was Byrn's time to die, so be it.

He opened the door a few inches and pushed his backpack ahead of him along the ground. No one shot it. Fortunately for Byrn, the garden, although not overgrown, did provide some cover. His chances of escape would have been better at night, but there was still a good forty-five minutes of daylight left.

Once committed, the assassin would have to go for it. Staying low, Byrn propelled himself out the door and along the ground, military style.

Ten seconds later, surprising even himself, he'd made it to the first bush. Without pause, he continued forward. The forest stood thirty yards ahead. There was a chance, albeit small.

Every instinct in Byrn's being pushed him to glance back and assess the situation. Fortunately, his training had taught him otherwise. A second lost was a second's more exposure to fire.

Forty seconds later, the gunfire stopped. Clearly, he'd been attacked by a team of hostiles, presumably working under a single commander who'd called the ceasefire. The assassin knew the focus would be on the doors and windows of the building. There would also be someone scanning under the house and another scoping out the roof. All points of exit would be considered and monitored. When Byrn didn't emerge from the building, he assumed they would either conduct a synchronized entry to check on his status inside, or fire on the structure once again.

They chose the latter. The roar of the gunfire exploded in intensity.

Seconds later, the assassin sensed the shadow of the forest closing in around him. He'd made it. Lucky.

Lachlan Byrn detested relying on luck.

In a split second, the assassin's mindset switched from fugitive to hunter.

Now that he could sit up unseen, he pulled his backpack toward him and opened the flap. First to come out was his diver's knife. It had been a preferred weapon of Byrn's since his days in the SBS. He placed it in the sheath attached to his ankle. The assassin already had his SIG Sauer P226 secured under his coat. He'd restrained from using it so far because in the current situation he'd been absurdly outpowered.

The final object Byrn withdrew from the pack was a long, soft case. The oversized backpack had been designed to take the case, which fitted snuggly inside. Byrn laid it flat on the ground and undid the zipper. The matt black Barrett M82 sniper's rifle lay in pieces before him.

Byrn yanked out the lower receiver, lowered the bipod legs and removed the mid-lock pin. He then reached back into the case and retrieved the upper receiver. Byrn took off the rubber battery bumper and slid the barrel forward into its firing position. Holding the weapon against his torso, he pulled the spring-loaded lock into place before inserting the rear and mid lock pins.

Byrn glanced out from his forest refuge at the ongoing salvo on the house. The group's commander would probably be calling another ceasefire and assessment momentarily. Byrn aimed to be in position before the next stage of their operation.

The assassin then inserted the telescopic sight before performing his final task. He reached into the case and grabbed out the magazine assembly before pushing it into place. With a familiar click, the process was complete.

Byrn then launched himself back to the edge of the forest. He lay down next to a log, the rifle before him resting on the bipod legs. He had a reasonable view of the kill zone, but no one position, except from overhead, could provide a full picture.

The house lay around forty yards away. The Barrett had a range of just under two thousand yards.

The imbalance of power was about to change.

Five men, perhaps a sixth, around the far side of the building.

Each man was poised in the kneeling position. Rear knee on the ground, the other leg supporting the elbow of the forward arm. Their elbows were placed on the muscle of their quadriceps, not on their kneecaps where the bone-to-bone contact could cause the rifle to wobble. These operators were professionals, not weekend warriors. It wasn't Byrn's preferred firing position. Unless you were surrounded by waist high cover, the position left you exposed. In addition, the accuracy was questionable. Of course, to the shooters before him, neither mattered. The operation was designed to be a massacre. No one was shooting back at them, and they literally only had to hit the proverbial barn door.

Byrn had a decision to make. He could wait until darkness set in, allowing him to move unhindered, or he could initiate action now. Both points of view had merit, but he chose to go in early. Any minute, these people would stop firing again. If they approached the house with no returning gunfire and entered the building to find him gone, the kill team would probably begin searching the surrounding areas, including the woods where he lay. That would return Byrn to a position of defense, which, to his thinking, was unacceptable.

The assassin now clicked into the process he was trained for. This would be a pleasure.

One by one he brought each man to bear in his sights, making sure he had all their positions marked in his mind. Man one, twenty yards ahead and to Byrn's left. Man two, fifteen yards southwest of the first. Third shooter, ten yards further around what was clearly a semicircle attack formation. On Byrn's right, man number four was positioned on the northern side of the building, some twenty-five yards distant, and another shooter, ten yards on from him.

As he checked the layout, Byrn felt fortunate he'd managed to unknowingly track through a small gap in their formation to get to the forest. The close positioning led the assassin to believe there was probably another agent out of view.

Byrn checked the wind. Negligible, not that it mattered at these distances. He pulled his eye away from the sight and began the process to slow his breathing. Inhale, exhale, fire only while exhaling.

He'd decided to begin with the closest target. He'd then take the two on either side of him, followed by those on the flanks. If the operative hidden from view realized the gunfire he was hearing wasn't from his own team, so much the better.

Closest man in sight. Exhale. One, two...

Suddenly, all the shooting stopped.

Byrn took his finger off the Barrett's trigger and waited.

For three minutes, you could hear the birds in the trees. Then, on cue, each man stood up, now in a stalking position, guns still raised. On what was obviously a command, they all moved slowly forward; their eyes trained on the building.

Perfect.

The assassin allowed himself a brief grin before getting to work.

Exhale. Fire.

The first target recoiled sideways and hit the dirt. Byrn didn't follow his progress. He was certain of the outcome.

Shift aim to the right. Man two. His target was searching for the source of fire, betraying some element of confusion.

Exhale. Squeeze the trigger. Target down.

Byrn swung quickly around, taking the third and fourth shooters down in quick succession.

By the time he re-focused his sight on the location of the fifth man to the northeast, he wasn't there.

As expected.

Aware no professional would stay upright under fire, Byrn had marked the position. He then fired two rounds directly into the base of the bush a yard from where the man had been.

Again, the assassin was confident of the outcome.

The final target would be the most difficult. The man on the other side of the house would be making a decision. To retreat or confront. It would be sensible to pull back, but Byrn's gut told him that wouldn't be the case here. These were extremely capable and focused operators.

Now that a brief respite presented itself, Byrn recognized a nagging doubt in the back of his mind. In his haste, he'd missed something. Why hadn't they covered...

The hail of bullets tore into the log next to him. Byrn felt a sting as a round grazed him. The hit team had an operative deep in the woods, covering their target's only possible escape route.

Self-recrimination would come later. Byrn threw himself over the log as another spray ground into the dirt where he'd just been laying. Now the assassin had a real problem. He lay trapped in a pincer movement. A marksman's worst nightmare. He may be able to hold off the guy approaching through the woods using the log as cover, but at any moment, the absent operative would venture around the building and see him totally exposed.

Which death would he choose?

Neither.

Although the Barrett now sat out of range, Byrn still had the SIG and the knife. He drew out the SIG and fired blindly in the direction he thought the shots had originated. Byrn didn't expect to hit the sniper, but he wanted to draw his fire to pinpoint a position.

The barrage came within a second. Byrn risked a look around the log. Fifty yards deep into the forest, he saw the shooter. Byrn shot a couple more rounds before scrambling to the far end of the log. He waited until his opponent fired again before launching himself toward the nearest tree, ten yards away.

He'd almost made it when he felt the SIG bounce out of his hand. The shooter had missed him but got lucky and hit the gun.

Byrn made it to the tree but kept going. The bush was thicker from this point on, so he'd be harder to spot. Counting on his attacker figuring he'd move carefully from tree to tree, Byrn sprinted in a semi-circle. His aim was to come up behind the shooter before the man had realized Byrn had gone.

He made the ground in less than twenty seconds, but by the time he took cover behind a large oak, the other guy had wised up. He scanned his rifle in an arc, roughly following Byrn's route.

Victory favors the bold.

Byrn swung slightly south to keep out of his hunter's immediate view before sprinting through the forest toward the marksman. Choosing speed over silence, Byrn had almost made him when the shooter suddenly heaved his rifle in the direction of the rustling.

Too late.

The assassin dived forward, below the rifle's barrel, grappling the man mid torso. Without further thought, he slashed his knife across his would-be killer's stomach as the guy went down. His victim grunted in agony. Byrn held the knife high before plunging it hard into the man's throat. His victim fell silent.

Byrn looked up, back towards the house. The final operative was just rounding the corner of the building. Judging by his immediate change in body language, he must have seen something of the altercation. Without hesitation, he lurched down on one knee and started firing in Byrn's direction. The rounds sprayed the surrounding dirt. It would only be seconds until they found their mark.

Byrn wrapped his arms around the bleeding corpse in front of him and propped it up on its side.

Cover.

He then grabbed the man's fallen gun and took aim.

With the shooter at the house now exposed, Byrn now had some level of concealment. He raised the rifle just over the corpse and fired.

Nothing happened. The weapon had jammed.

With zero time to fix the problem, Byrn realized there was only one possible path to success. He had to try.

As bullets peppered the ground nearby, he rushed ahead in a zig-zag pattern, using trees as cover where he could.

Thirty yards.

Twenty yards.

Fifteen.

Five.

His attacker had a clear bead on him now. Byrn knew he wasn't going to make it.

As he lunged forward, sliding across the ground, Byrn felt the stock of the Barrett under his fingers. His opponent was up and moving, sensing he was about to take out a minimally armed target. Byrn thrust the Barrett's stock into his arm pit and took aim. He squeezed the trigger. A red dot appeared on the operative's cheek as he tumbled backward. Byrn fired again. The round went straight up between the prone man's legs, his body jerked in response.

Lachlan Byrn winced before breathing a sigh of relief.

The assassin waited ten more minutes, ensuring nobody else approached. By that point, darkness had begun to set in. Byrn needed to move quickly.

He circled the property, checking that each man he'd taken down was dead. Scene secured.

Byrn then scurried to the forest, packed the rifle, stored it in his backpack, and strode to the garage. He wrenched open the door.

Relief. The motorcycle remained intact, protected by distance.

Byrn grabbed an old section of hose hanging on a hook on the garage wall. He reached down, snatched his diver's knife, and cut a suitable length off the hose. He then unscrewed the cap on the bike's petrol tank, located a rusty old bucket in a corner of the shed, and returned to the bike. After placing one end of the hose into the petrol tank, he covered the other end with his mouth and sucked in two large breaths. He heard the gurgling just in time and aimed the hose at the bucket. The petrol drained out of the tank, gradually increasing its flow. Ensuring he had enough for the task at hand, as well as leaving enough fuel remaining in his tank, Byrn flicked the bucket end of the hose into the air to stop the process.

Bucket in hand, Byrn stepped outside. The early stages of darkness had settled in. That suited the assassin just fine.

After placing the bucket of fuel on the veranda, he circled the grounds once more. This time, his task took much longer as he grabbed each of his victims by the feet and dragged them into the house.

He showed them zero respect yet was careful enough to minimize the blood trail.

As he deposited each corpse inside the house, Byrn relieved them of their MOLLE vests and armory, which he piled just outside the rear door. He fetched a shovel from the garage and headed back to the forest. Nearly an hour later, Byrn had dug a hole big enough to accommodate the weapons and the vests. Twenty minutes after that, he covered the hole over with earth and ground clutter.

The assassin was almost ready to break his lease in an extreme manner. Stepping back into the house, bucket in hand, he splashed the petrol around the lounge room, including over the dead men's bodies. After scanning the area to ensure no incriminating evidence remained, Byrn reached into his pocket, yanked out a lighter, and started the blaze.

If nothing else, Lachlan Byrn was thorough.

As he rode the Kawasaki down the driveway, flames towering into the darkness behind him, Byrn asked himself two questions.

Now that he'd lost his operating base, where would he relocate?

And.

Why were all the burning corpses of the men sent to kill him of Asian descent?

Chapter 12

"What the fuck was that?"

Lachlan Byrn sat at the dining table of his new hide. Always over-prepared, he'd had two other similarly remote dwellings booked and paid for before he even entered the country. They were all in different names and funded with different credit cards.

"There was a problem at our end."

Byrn thought Zhen Su's voice sounded edgy, his normally restrained demeanor faltering.

"I'm assuming that because we're speaking, the kill team has been neutralized?"

"You could say that," said Byrn. Normally he wouldn't communicate with a client by voice, but these circumstances were not normal. "What I want to know is who found out about the mission and sent those guys after me?"

"The problem is at this end," replied Zhen.

"No fucking kidding. If I don't get answers now, I'll withdraw. And then I promise you that you'll have another problem 'at your end,' because I'll be coming after you."

No response.

Then finally.

"You're considering carrying on with the mission?"

"I'm contemplating it, but not if I'm facing a repeat of the last few hours."

"They were an MSS team. Someone at a high level over here got wind of the operation and decided to put it down. I understand a surveillance drone picked you up at the border."

"If only you and your president knew about it, how could a third party find out?"

"I will ascertain that. In the meantime, if the team is out of the picture, I assure you that I can contain the political situation at this end... as long as the operation doesn't in any way lead back here."

"As yet, I'm unconvinced."

"As yet," mimicked Zhen.

Byrn knew it was foolish to entertain the idea of continuing the assignment. It had been an almost impossible task to begin with. Now it was layered with a new level of complexity. The only reason he hadn't walked already was the promise of a complete break of his ties with the Chinese intelligence system. Maybe even that was an impossible task.

But somewhere in his gut, he knew he'd see it through. He had no choice but to try.

"I'm not saying yes, and I'm not saying no. In a few moments I'll send you the coordinates of a suitable extraction point. If I continue, you'll receive a text from me when the job is done.

"So, you'll do it."

"So, I'll consider it. I'll need our target's itinerary and all the updated background you have on him within the hour. At that point, there will be zero communication between us until post the event. If there is an event."

"How do we know if you're proceeding?"

"That's the point. You won't, until it's either done or you

can't find me. And after all that's gone down, I strongly recommend you don't come looking."

"Point taken. Your terms are agreed, not that I have much choice."

"You have no choice," said Byrn. "Just remember that."

He hung up the call.

Shit. He had some thinking to do.

Chapter 13

Laying with his head on the pillow of the bed in the second bedroom, Byrn resumed the familiar task of chasing the cornices around the tops of the walls.

Focus.

He should walk away, but he'd virtually decided he wasn't going to. It wasn't the money, and if Byrn was honest with himself, it wasn't just the thought of freeing his Chinese ties.

It was the challenge.

The job seemed impossible from all angles. Now he had to watch his back as well, although it had been several hours since he'd been attacked at his previous location. Maybe Zhen was as good as his word in that respect.

Nothing attracts a perfectionist like the impossible.

The security around any world leader was an incredible challenge. Even when away from the Kremlin, Vadim Aleyev had hundreds of people protecting him. The advance teams would be thorough. Establishing proximity to the president of the Russian Federation would be incredibly challenging. Byrn could attempt a long-distance rooftop hit, but as he'd just found out, surveillance drones were becoming increasingly effective.

For the past few hours, the assassin had studied the itinerary of the Russian group provided by Zhen. Byrn had paid scant interest to the components that involved the meetings with the US president, Jefferson Blake. Aleyev would be most vulnerable during his time in the country when he wasn't meeting with the American leader. Byrn had circled two locations that Aleyev and his people were due to visit. They were both former military bases. If Zhen was right about the president's mood and the itinerary supported it, these places could be used for Aleyev's nostalgic stroll through Soviet history.

It amazed Byrn that Vadim Aleyev considered these broken relics of the past as a means to inspire his generals to leap into a recreated Soviet future. That said, Aleyev had been underestimated before. His hold on power had been through a mixture of visionary thinking and using terror as an effective weapon against his opponents. Many people currently tenanted in the cells of Russian penal colonies in Siberia would lay testament to that, and they were perhaps the lucky ones.

Lachlan Byrn had no intention of joining their ranks.

He began studying Vadim Aleyev's personal file one more time. The Russian entourage would arrive in Estonia in just under four weeks.

There must be some way in.

Chapter 14

PRESIDENT VADIM ALEYEV

It was in the darkness of the early hours of the morning that Vadim Aleyev felt the most restless. The president's daylight hours were packed with meetings, decisions, directions, and other duties befitting the leader of a great nation.

Aleyev believed he'd been put on the planet to restore the Russian empire's former glory. He held his predecessors in absolute contempt. They had literally sold off the farm piece by piece. They called it modernization and naively attempted to move the country towards a democratic system.

The fools.

The resulting federation was a pale shadow of the great Soviet Union. That would change. Now, heading in a new direction, showing the world how strong they could be, Vadim Aleyev held no doubts about the success that awaited his people. If only they would stay the course.

He glanced at the clock on his bedside table: 3 a.m. The president reached over until his fingers clasped his glass of water. Experience taught him that he'd now be unable to sleep until dawn. He knew the tiredness made him irritable during the day, but he didn't really care.

As he sat up, Aleyev turned to the vacant space in the bed beside him. Things had been different when his Tatiana had been alive. She may not have been the great love of his life, but their partnership had seen success beyond their dreams. Without her, he would certainly not have made it this far, and neither would the nation. There was no one else he truly trusted on the planet except for Tatiana, and now she was gone. Now there was no one to soothe him, no one to calm his moods nor temper his ambitions for his country.

As the night wore on, Aleyev reflected, as he often did, on his achievements and his frustrations.

The expansion had begun well, or so he'd been informed. His generals had told him Ukraine would be theirs within days. That was over a year ago. In the end, he knew the Russian bear was a patient and dominant beast. Just ask the Germans how their invasion of Mother Russia imploded many decades earlier. The bear would again prevail, although it was taking a little longer than expected. Aleyev was already making plans for the next stage. Estonia and Latvia would once again fall under the Russian umbrella when the time was right. NATO would be polarized in fear. Then, who knows what?

The president sighed and threw the sheets and blankets aside. If he was awake, he may as well work. He put on his fraying slippers, a present from Tatiana, and shuffled over to his comfortable winged chair. A gracious relic from dynasties' past. He eased himself down before reaching to the small wooden table to his right. Reports stacked several inches high. He took the first and began reading.

It was always the same. The Russian forces have achieved great success in the north. We are dominating the enemy. Pushing south is slower than expected. Opposition is strong.

"Of course it's strong, you idiots," the president said out loud to no one in particular.

The opposition was strong due to the generals' insistence on a gradual and controlled invasion to avoid alarming the West. That had been a colossal mistake. Their lack of impetus had allowed Ukraine to gather a western coalition behind them. Now the Russian troops faced western weapons and unlimited technology. And the Russian people at home faced the indignity of embargos and moratoriums.

The unexpected strength of the enemy cost many young Russians their lives. Aleyev knew he wasn't being told the whole truth. Why were the idiots around him too scared to speak their minds?

Fear. The president had already begun replacing the weakest. Yet even as he dispatched them, those he'd thought to be strong cowered. Where were their backbones?

In the big picture, it didn't matter to Aleyev. He had a vision.

By the time they attended the worthless summit in Estonia, Russia would be unstoppable. He'd arranged forces to move on a number of borders in preparation for the event. The West would have knowledge of this. That pleased him. It would keep them distracted as other plans were finalized.

If there was one single thing in this world that Vadim Aleyev was certain of, it was that Russia would never again be subdued in her quest for glory.

As the sun rose over the Kremlin walls, Aleyev found himself dozing. He cast aside his papers, ambled over to the sideboard, and poured himself a quick shot of Ararat brandy.

Two minutes later he'd reclaimed his bed, and slowly drifted off to catch a final hour of sleep.

A smile crept across his weary face.

Soon.

Chapter 15

LACHLAN BYRN

Byrn had been through the itinerary and Aleyev's file with a fine-tooth comb. Apart from the inspections of the old Soviet sites, there was nothing to help him. In the morning, he would visit both locations. The first would be the Keila Joa air base and missile site in the west. He'd then move onto the Hara submarine base on the eastern coast. At this point, after searching both spots online, Byrn figured either could be a potential locale for his purposes.

The assassin still had no definitive strategy, and that annoyed the hell out of him. With just under four weeks until Vadim Aleyev set foot on Estonian soil, Byrn would have to firm up his plans soon. Once the advance security teams moved into position, it would be too late.

Byrn had destroyed the phone and SIM card he used to talk to Zhen Su. He had two cell phones remaining. If that wasn't enough, he'd grab a couple of burners. He'd transferred the files Zhen had sent him onto a new phone and then removed that SIM card. Ever cautious.

Byrn had no intention of relying on the Night Eagle, the modafinil, to keep him awake and alert. That time would come closer to the main event. He hadn't taken a pill since arriving in the country, so his weariness slowly took a hold. Maybe some sleep would shed some clarity on the situation. It often did.

Although remaining fully dressed, Byrn allowed himself to doze. He figured that if there was going to be any more action, it would have happened by now. To be sure, he'd set up perimeter sensors at the front gate and at several sections on the property's boundaries. The retrieved SIG lay under his pillow, the knife, cleaned of his victim's blood, remained sheathed to his ankle and the Barrett was within easy reach in the backpack on the floor beside the bed.

If he had to move, he could move fast.

In the end, he didn't have to move at all.

The first rays of the fresh Estonian morning lit up the bedroom. Byrn listened to his environment before opening his eyes. Old habits die hard. When nothing alarmed his senses, he scrutinized the room before easing himself out of bed. He was surprised how well he'd slept. Obviously riding non-stop across Europe, eliminating a pair of local morons, and taking out an entire MSS kill team was good for your sleep. Although the assassin doubted he could utilize that technique on a daily basis, as tempting as it sounded.

Byrn was reassured by the fact he'd made it through the night undisturbed. His clean up at the previous location had been thorough, but it had been rushed. He was aware that at some point in the next twenty-four hours or so, authorities would conclude that the seven charred bodies found in the farmhouse were not Estonian nationals. Byrn hoped they wouldn't find the buried weapons, but it didn't really matter that much either way.

As long as nothing pointed to him or an assassination plot concerning the summit, all would be well. If the papers reported otherwise, Byrn's Plan B was to phone in a couple of death threats to some local dignitary to throw them off the track.

He'd prefer not to have to resort to that.

The assassin took a brief shower, changed, and psyched himself into tourist mode. A vital professional trait in his line of work was the ability to act. Byrn was of the 'method' school. Live the part until you didn't have to. The skill played out not just in the way he spoke, but also in his body language and movement.

Many people hadn't lived to regret their misjudgment of Lachlan Byrn as being a threat to their welfare.

Keila-Joa was a disappointment. The facility served as an airfield in WWII and as a missile base during the Soviet era. As Byrn wandered around the site, he wondered if it had been worth the ride out. Although only fifteen miles west of Tallinn, there wasn't really much to see. The old control tower remained standing amongst a smattering of trees and unkempt grassland. To Byrn's mind, if Vadim Aleyev brought his generals out here for inspiration, it would be an exercise doomed to failure.

Certainly, there was not much here that would suit Byrn's purposes, although the history of the site was something else. As a launch site for S-75M Volkhov, and later the nuclear capable S-300PS missiles, Keila-Joa would have once been one of the most threatening places on earth to western democracies.

Little remained of that ominous power now. Byrn quickly concluded that Aleyev and his Russian entourage would probably not spend much time here, if they came at all.

Byrn decided to have lunch at the neighboring village that shared its name with the base. It was a pretty area, and the assassin needed some sustenance. After all, he was in this for the long game.

Seventy minutes later, with fresh food and strong coffee warming his belly, Byrn was back on the Kawasaki, heading east to the Hara submarine base. He was hoping for a better result.

The Tallinna Ringtee had taken Byrn around the outer edges of Tallinn through Kurna and Maardu. The only time the assassin had felt a little uneasy was passing through Kiiu. The town was a little too close to his now burned-out farmhouse for comfort.

Just over an hour after he began the journey, Byrn transited through the Lahemaa Rahvuspark. As the towering aspen and pines of the national park gave way to a sprawling view of the coast, Byrn sensed that this would be the location he sought. The moment the abandoned Hara Soviet submarine base came into view, he was almost certain. The assassin parked the bike and gazed out over the water.

The long, crumbling stone pier reached well out into the Gulf of Finland. Two equally crumbling buildings lay at different points along its length. An additional structure, just as imposing, sat at a cross angle to the pier. A third building perched on its edge, but there was a small gap of water separating the two, making it inaccessible by foot.

Byrn took a moment to let his imagination wander back in time. Running parallel to the pier, another structure loomed out of the water. Pillars supporting some sort of gangway ran most of its length. In his mind, Byrn could see the large Soviet subs tied up between the two structures as they were being serviced, taking deliveries of torpedoes, and, if his research was correct, undergoing the process of demagnetization to avoid the attention of western mines.

Byrn figured if he could see it, so could Vadim Aleyev. It wouldn't be a huge stretch to take his generals on the same journey.

Yes. This would be the place.

Byrn got off the motorcycle, stowed his helmet and walked towards the entrance. He already knew the base was being run as a tourist attraction, just as he was aware the facility would be shut down for a week before the Russian visit. Byrn needed to have his ducks in a totally straight line, well before that date.

The assassin paid his money and tagged along with a tour that was about to begin. There was no knowledge like local knowledge, so now it was time to play tourist.

Less than an hour later, Byrn understood a lot more about the Hara base than he had read online. While the tour guide's information was intriguing, Byrn was more enthusiastic about the structural features of the first dilapidated building where torpedoes were stored and loaded onto the subs.

When the tour finished, Byrn strolled back along the pier. To any observer, he appeared like an interested sightseer. But he was gauging sight lines and distances. He paid specific attention to the internals of the building. Now covered in graffiti, it was still a most imposing structure. Byrn assumed that the hooks on the walls had been used to hold torpedoes racks in a previous time. Although the building was two stories, there was a subfloor with a variety of entrances and small storage areas underneath the main floor. These areas were of particular interest to the assassin.

When he was done, and after taking over three dozen photographs, Byrn returned to his bike. He had no doubt that Vadim Aleyev would spend time in that building. There was a better than good chance that would be one of the locations he'd use to motivate his comrades.

Now all Lachlan Byrn had to do was figure out how he could get himself alone with the Russian president inside that space.

No big ask.

Chapter 16

It was always going to be difficult.

Lachlan Byrn prided himself on his ability to design and execute a good kill. It took research and imagination to manipulate events that culminated in a positive outcome for the assassin.

He was certain his victims didn't see it that way though.

One of Byrn's great joys was to look into the eyes of an individual facing death. Byrn regarded a good death as an educational opportunity. It was important both to him and his victim that the nearly departed appreciated the reasoning behind their impending demise. Those Byrn killed were guilty of something and considered themselves smart enough to have gotten away with it. Sometimes it was murder, sometimes it turned out to be much more. Either way, Byrn saw it as his duty to educate the person as to the reason for their death. The assassin also thrived on seeing his victim's ego deflate as they realized they hadn't been as smart as they thought.

Every job had its perks.

Byrn considered ego to be the Homo sapiens' greatest weakness. The assassin accepted everybody had an ego; himself included. The way he saw things, it was really just the depth of submission to your own ego that proportionally increased your vulnerability to attack. Fortunately for any professional assassin, politicians were particularly susceptible to their own inflated opinions of themselves.

Byrn kept drilling through the files Zhen sent him. He knew he was missing something but, as yet couldn't identify what.

He decided to put aside the Russian's itinerary. Byrn had squeezed every bit of information he could out of that document. He now focused on Vadim Aleyev's personal history. If the Russian president was using this visit to travel down memory lane, perhaps the secret lay there. Byrn scanned the lengthy file.

History.

Ego.

What in Aleyev's past would trigger his ego now?

Byrn stood up and paced the perimeter of the room. This farmhouse wasn't much different from the previous one. Simple, comfortable, secluded. The assassin had a clear view of the surrounding pastures. There was no wood close by here. That's why it was his second choice. The border sensors remained silent, allowing Byrn to focus on his thoughts. He made a strong coffee, paced some more while it brewed and then sat back down, studying the file on his phone.

History.

Ego.

Byrn began at the start, tracing Aleyev's life. Searching with a different perspective, irrelevant facts could suddenly assume importance.

First hit. Aleyev's father was a conscript in the Soviet Navy, serving in the submarine fleet. Connection. Tenuous, yes, but perhaps part of a bigger picture. Byrn noted the information down on a pad.

Byrn was aware of Aleyev's career in the KGB, but he hadn't really paid huge attention to the details. Now he did. The Russian president began his KGB duties working in the Second Chief Directorate in counterintelligence. After several other postings, including Leningrad and Dresden in Germany, Aleyev was sent to Tallinn in Estonia for five years.

Another hit.

Byrn knew that his target had been posted to Estonia during the Soviet's occupation of the country, but he hadn't explored his activities during that period closely.

That was about to change.

At some point during his time in Estonia, Vadim Aleyev had been appointed to the rank of lieutenant colonel. Byrn figured he must have been doing something right by his bosses. He made another note.

The document Zhen provided suggested that after his previous work in counterintelligence, Aleyev had become somewhat of a specialist in recruitment. During his Tallinn period, it appeared Aleyev recruited spies not only within local government, many members of which were not great fans of their Soviet occupiers, but also within the extensive Estonian resistance movement. Estonia had a strong history of resistance, including the legendary 'Forest Brothers', citizens who exiled themselves to the country's vast forests as a base for revolutionary activity. The tentacles of the more modern resistance spread far and wide, in government, business, and amongst farmers and the youth. Judging from the report in front of him, Byrn figured that Vadim Aleyev's tentacles spread equally far.

But how?

Byrn read on.

Finally, buried deep in the document, Byrn found a reference to Aleyev's preferred method of recruitment. He worked closely with a small group of young Estonian women who had succumbed to his influence to form relationships with vulnerable men within the resistance.

The honey trap.

Many countries had used the practice to gain intelligence about their enemies. Clearly, Russia was no exception and Aleyev was a master of the technique.

The men were turned, and the information Aleyev sought flowed through to him. According to the report, numerous resistance members were caught, imprisoned in Russian camps, and never heard from again...

Byrn placed the phone on the table and gazed out the dining room window. He wondered, could this be the way in? The vulnerability? The seed now planted, he returned to the document, digging deep for any information regarding Aleyev's recruitment activities.

He needed more detail.

Three pages on, he had it.

Well after his promotion, and after almost five years of successful operations in Estonia, Lieutenant Colonel Vadim Aleyev of the KGB was suddenly and unexpectedly transferred back to Moscow. The accompanying documentation portrayed the transfer as a step up. But right at the bottom of a page, Byrn found a footnote.

'There were unsubstantiated rumors around government inner circles in Tallinn that Aleyev's banishment back to Moscow was because he'd become too close to one of his 'honey trap' operatives, causing some skepticism regarding elements of the intelligence

gathered.'

Unknowingly, Byrn held his breath. If he could just find a….

Kristiina Volk.

There it was. The name of the woman that drove Aleyev away.

Byrn wondered if there was any chance she'd still be alive. She'd probably be close to Aleyev's age or a little younger. It was quite possible. A scenario slowly presented itself in Byrn's mind. He pondered the possibilities, as unlikely as they were. For this to come together, the assassin had to identify one of two key elements.

Love.

Or guilt.

Or both.

It was time to get to work.

Chapter 17

The black Kawasaki's motor roared as Byrn hit the outskirts of Tallinn.

After rejecting his instinct for seclusion by reinserting the SIM card to his phone, Byrn had spent nearly two hours trying to track down Kristiina Volk. The problem was, he'd tracked down five of them. Both Kristiina and Volk turned out to be quite common names in Estonia. Byrn had eliminated two due to an obvious age discrepancy exposed by online images, but three remained in question. That is, of course, if the Kristiina Volk he sought was still living.

As he wound his way through the afternoon traffic, the assassin admitted to himself that his chances of success were remote. Yet one of the reasons Lachlan Byrn earned a great deal of money was because he wasn't just another gun-wielding killer. He was employed to do complex jobs. The more elusive or difficult his target, the more sophisticated the kill had to be. Byrn was no stranger to engineering an intricate kill plan that required a lot of different moving parts to come together. Taking out the Russian president was the biggest challenge of his career. It was no surprise that the task would involve a high level of complexity.

Byrn swung the bike to the right as he smiled to himself.

If the scheme lurking in his thoughts materialized, it would also reek of poetic justice.

Not to mention personal satisfaction.

The first address on Byrn's list was a business in Maakri Street, near the city center. The company sold office supplies. From Byrn's position on the opposite side of the road, he could see that the store's location at the heart of a cluster of modern glass-walled skyscrapers enabled custom to blossom. Byrn parked the Kawasaki in a car park a couple of hundred yards away. He loitered on the footpath for a few minutes, watching the foot traffic in and out of the store. The assassin had absolutely no intention of exposing his face unless he had to. Unnecessary witnesses mean unnecessary complications.

The constant flow of people in and out allowed Byrn to slip into the shop unnoticed. He browsed around the store's shelves, picking up the odd bit of stationery now and again. It was fortunate that all the store attendants wore name tags. It took Byrn less than seven minutes to eliminate most of the staff from his search.

A row of glass partitioned offices stood behind the counter. Byrn grabbed a stapler along with a box of paperclips and stepped up to the counter. He held the cash required for the transaction in his hand. It wasn't until he'd almost reached the checkout that he could read the signs on each office door. The third cubicle from the right was open, but the assassin could clearly make out the writing.

Kristiina Volk- Peadirektori Abi

Byrn didn't speak the language, but he'd already ascertained from the store's website that Kristiina Volk was assistant general manager of the business. He glanced through the glass. A woman, dark hair, tidily dressed sat behind a large desk. She appeared to be studying some sort of paperwork in front of her. Byrn didn't have a good enough view to gauge her age while she had her head cast downward. A few seconds later, she looked up and rubbed her eyes.

Forty to forty-five years old by Byrn's calculation. Too young.

Just to be thorough, Byrn proceeded with the purchase. As he paid over the cash, he said to the assistant, "Kristiina seems to be busy today."

The young man glanced over his shoulder before nodding. "Jah, the boss is always working hard."

That settled it. The woman was definitely Kristina Volk, just not the one he was looking for. It had been a small risk to speak English, but the assassin's research had indicated that English was the most commonly spoken foreign language in Estonia, particularly for those involved in commerce.

Byrn left the shop and headed down the street to his motorcycle. One down.

The assassin spent the rest of the afternoon sitting in a hire car, procured with false ID and credit cards, parked outside a small suburban home in Viimsi. Eventually, the lady of the house came back with two young children and a trunk full of shopping. The sign on the letter box said 'Volk' but the woman seemed about thirty years of age. Another Kristiina struck off the list.

Slightly dispirited, the assassin returned the car, retrieved his bike from a separate location around the corner from the rental company, and headed back to his rural base. As he roared along the Peterburi Tee, Byrn allowed his disappointment to vaporize. He hadn't lost all hope, but the odds were certainly stacking up against him.

Perhaps tomorrow.

Chapter 18

The apartment block in Pelgulinn, Northern Tallinn, was just a couple of miles north of the main city. The structure had clearly been there for many years, but its weatherboard exterior was well kept. The place didn't appear upmarket, neither did it look neglected. A high wood fence separated the building from the road, allowing some privacy. On either side of the path leading to the shared front door, were three lockable letter boxes inserted into the fence.

Lachlan Byrn sat on the Kawasaki around the corner from the apartments. He had a clear view of the letter boxes and had already scoped out number four. It was the furthest away, along the right-hand fence. The assassin had masqueraded as a new resident of the suburb to enquire online as to the times the mail was delivered in this area. Byrn had been waiting when the postman had distributed an array of envelopes and flyers into each letterbox. Now all he could do was wait some more.

Eventually, the owner of apartment number four would come out to check her mail. That was the moment Byrn would decide if this Kristiina Volk could be the woman he pursued.

As the morning progressed, he changed position three times

to avoid attracting the attention of locals. At 11.27 a.m., the front door of the building opened. Out of the shadows, an older lady appeared. She glanced around before carefully descending the two porch steps. The cane in her right hand supported her as she slowly edged forward. Byrn gauged her age to be mid-sixties. Aleyev's age of seventy placed this woman in the correct age bracket.

As she stepped into the light, Byrn noticed how frail she appeared. Both hands seemed to have a slight tremor and her skin was pale and chalky, although not overly wrinkled. Her appearance made Byrn wonder if there was a health issue at play. When she reached the letter boxes, the woman took a moment to straighten up and take in her environment. She had a strong jawline and her now gray hair still had some blond streaks. Byrn decided that at some point, this lady would have been a striking beauty.

She leaned forward and stooped down. Key in hand, she opened her letterbox.

Number four. Bingo.

Nothing was yet set in stone, but Byrn figured the scenario was worth pursuing.

The assassin spent the next two hours wandering around the neighborhood, pretending to gaze into shop windows and sitting on a seat in the park down the road. At no point did he take his eyes off the apartment block. Eventually, Byrn wondered if the woman had bedded down for the rest of the day, and he wouldn't see her again. He already felt that he'd pushed his presence in the area to the limit.

Fifteen more minutes.

Eight minutes later, a small white Toyota sedan pulled to a halt directly in front of the apartment block. A young woman dressed in a neat pale blue uniform climbed out of the driver's seat, locked the door, and walked up the path to the main door. In the shadows of the entrance, she appeared to press a buzzer, but from where he sat, Byrn couldn't tell which one. The assassin returned his scrutiny to the vehicle. Byrn could make out a logo. He got up and walked towards the building, staying on the opposite side of the street.

Tallinna Koduhooldus

Byrn reached into his pocket as he walked. After turning on his phone, he checked his translator.

Tallinn Homecare

Byrn strode back to his motorcycle around the corner, put on his helmet and waited. Five minutes later, the front door swung open, and the younger woman stepped onto the porch. Beside her, she supported Kristiina Volk.

He watched the young woman support the elder as they made their way to the car. After opening the passenger door and helping her charge climb inside, the younger woman stepped around the rear of the vehicle and seated herself back in the driver's seat.

Byrn started his engine.

A moment later, the Toyota pulled away from the curb.

Byrn followed.

The assassin hung back, but never let the Toyota out of his sight. After numerous turns down residential streets and ten minutes heading along Sopruse pst, the cityscape opened up to reveal a wide-open space. At the center of the block, an enormous cream-colored building towered over the neighboring structures. Its surrounding areas were a mixture of treed areas and car parks.

The Toyota turned left into one of the car parks. Byrn kept going before turning in at the next opportunity. He quickly parked the bike before hastily making his way toward the building's entrance. To his left, he saw Kristiina Volk being led up the main steps by her chaperone.

Byrn paused.

The moment the pair passed through the doors, he scurried forward. As he did so, he glanced at the large sign above the door.

POHJA-EESTI REGIONAALHAIGLA

The assassin didn't need to be Sherlock Holmes to realize he was entering a massive hospital complex.

Ahead of him, the two women had almost made it to the elevator. For Byrn, this was the trickiest part. He needed to know where they were going but wouldn't entertain the concept of riding the elevator with them. He ambled past just as the doors were closing. Glancing to his right, he saw only one other person inside. That narrowed the odds. Byrn stopped walking once the door had closed before returning to stand facing the elevator, as though he were awaiting the next available.

He scanned the array of numbers above the doors. First, the elevator paused at level two. After a few seconds, it proceeded to level five. That was all Byrn needed. He strolled back to the main foyer and studied the facility's directory, using his online translator to guide him.

Level 2 Administration
Level 5 Oncology and Hematology Clinic

Kristiina Volk had cancer.

Byrn waited in the car park for over an hour. Eventually, the two women reappeared through the hospital doors. They walked slowly toward the Toyota. The assassin decided to resume following, his mind gradually painting a bigger picture of the older lady's life.

As they finally turned back into the apartment's street, the Toyota abruptly pulled over to the curb. Byrn drove past before pulling up around the corner. Although the car had pulled over next to the park where Byrn had spent the morning and early afternoon, the two women headed elsewhere. The young woman assisted the older woman out of the car and walked her across the road.

A church.

St Michael's of the Estonian Evangelical Lutheran Church

Once more, standing well into the parkland, Byrn waited for the women to reappear. To his surprise, barely ten minutes after entering, only the younger woman emerged. She walked briskly down to her car, opened the door, climbed in, and drove away.

Another forty-five minutes passed before Kristiina Volk reappeared. Using her cane as support, she slowly made her way down the footpath leading from the church. Byrn was surprised once more when she didn't turn right toward her apartment. Instead, after checking the road carefully, she crossed it and strolled into the park.

Byrn backed off behind some trees and continued his surveillance. The woman sat down at the first park bench she came to, propped the cane up next to her and gazed ahead. To the assassin's eye, she wasn't looking at anything in particular, just staring into thin air.

Interesting.

After thirty minutes, the old lady stood up, crossed the road carefully, and made her way back to her apartment building.

Lachlan Byrn was consistently amazed by what he could learn about a person through simple observation. It was a skill he'd honed to an art. As he sat on a bench in the park, Byrn considered what he'd seen today. The controlling winds of Kristiina Volk's life.

Age.

Sickness.

Death.

God.

Reflection.

Possibly even regret.

The assassin had a lot to think about.

Chapter 19

Lachlan Byrn lay on his bed once more. His eyes may have been tracing the edges of the ceiling, but his mind examined every possible outcome and obstacle to the plan that was gradually hatching before him.

Byrn worked alone. He'd always worked alone. The last time he'd attempted a mission with a partner was years earlier in Colombia. Disaster.

No. He'd do this on his own, as always.

But now he was tasked with taking out a head of state. A world leader in the true sense of the term. Nearly two weeks into his commission, he'd constructed no plan that would allow him a totally independent operation. The clock was ticking. Experience taught him to make the most of the situations that presented themselves. While flexibility wasn't his strongest suit, strategy was.

And only one strategy currently presented itself.

Although there remained one alternative.

Walk away.

Lachlan Byrn had never walked away from a fight in his life.

An hour of reflection later, the assassin decided he would advance a single step forward. Byrn needed to make contact with the woman. It was the only way he could judge whether the plan had legs. It was a dangerous thing to do. He'd be exposing himself on the local stage while in the midst of an operation. He's never done that before.

How would he cover himself if it didn't work out with the woman? He hadn't shaved since before the Monaco job. Going into a mission with a beard gave him an instant change of appearance if required. He could dispose of all his phones, shift addresses and still move ahead.

Or there was a more permanent way to ensure the woman never spoke about him to anyone.

Byrn mused on all the arguments.

He had one chance of cutting ties with his Chinese masters.

He had one chance of taking out the Russian president.

Tomorrow, he would take one chance with Kristiina Volk.

God help them both.

Chapter 20

Byrn sat in the park across the road from the building and watched the postman make his deliveries, just like the day before. The sky was clear, the temperature could be described as brisk with an edgy breeze. The cold didn't worry the assassin; it kept him alert.

It took over two hours before Kristiina Volk ventured out to check her mail. As she had the previous morning, she moved slowly and carefully down the path, relying on her trusted cane for support.

Today there was less mail. Byrn watched the old lady shuffle through it before shoving the bundle deep into her coat pocket. Unlike the day before, she didn't turn and retreat toward the building's front door. Instead, she glanced up and down the street before stepping out onto the footpath and heading east toward the church.

Byrn watched her pause at the property's grand timber arched doorway before continuing inside. He waited for over an hour until she came out.

Clearly, God had more time allocated to him today.

As she had previously, the woman crossed the road carefully and slowly hobbled into the park. She chose a bench near the small pond deeper into the space. Perhaps she had more energy than on her previous visit.

Lachlan Byrn was nothing if not patient. He waited some distance away, allowing ten minutes to pass before he made his approach.

"Good afternoon," said Byrn as he sat down on the bench beside her.

The woman turned, scrutinizing Byrn from head to toe.

"I wondered when you'd make contact with me," she responded.

Unexpected.

"I beg your pardon," said Byrn.

"Well, yesterday you seemed to put a lot of work into observing my daily routine. When you failed to make an approach by the end of the afternoon, I assumed you waited for a reason, or perhaps just the right time."

Byrn was genuinely surprised. Although he hadn't been over the top with precautions, he'd been careful and professional in his movements the day before. Being caught out by an old lady was unacceptable. His trepidation must have shown on his face.

"Oh, don't look so concerned, young man. Decades ago, I was well trained by experts in what today's spy books call 'tradecraft'. Apparently, old habits die hard."

Byrn smiled. He was now almost certain he'd located the right 'Kristiina'.

"Would one of your trainers have been a young Vadim Aleyev?"

Byrn studied the woman's face as she decided how to react. Up close, it was clear her skin had lost much of its color, and Byrn noted that her breathing seemed labored.

"You seem to assume some knowledge of my past," she said.

"Who are you?"

"It's best you don't know my name."

"Best for you or best for me?"

"Probably both."

Kristiina Volk nodded.

"Well then, let's go a different route. Who do you work for?"

"I'm afraid I can't say."

It was clear to the assassin that although her physical health may be failing, the woman's mind remained sharp.

"Are those you work for good people?" she asked.

"Perhaps some of them," he replied.

As she turned to him, Byrn found the penetrating stare of her sky-blue eyes slightly unnerving. That was unusual.

"So, you work for a government."

Amazing.

She continued. "Which government? From your accent, I would have said British. Or are you what we used to call an independent?"

"I can't say."

Byrn had intended to control the conversation from the beginning. But the interchange so far had amused him, so he let it roll out.

Kristiina Volk turned her gaze away from Byrn and back to the pond on the other side of the path. They sat in silence for a minute or so. Byrn decided that the next few words may well dictate the success of his operation. He would choose them carefully.

Finally, the old lady spoke.

"You want to know about me, yet you bring nothing of yourself to this conversation, young man. What on God's earth can you possibly offer an old woman in my situation?"

Byrn paused, as much for effect as to give him a moment to think.

"Redemption."

The woman laughed. It began as a deep laugh and ended in a small coughing fit.

"Unless you are God, or perhaps work for him. I don't see how you could be in a position to provide me with redemption."

"Some would say I've allowed them to take a step closer to God."

She nodded.

"I see. And would any of those people be available as a character reference for you?"

"Sadly, no."

"I thought not." Kristiina turned back to face him, again confronting Byrn with her eyes. "Am I in danger?"

"From me? Probably not."

"How reassuring."

Byrn decided to gain some control over the direction of their conversation.

"How long do you have?"

"To live?"

"Yes."

She sighed deeply, contemplating her response.

"All right, I'll share. A few weeks at most."

"What type of cancer?"

"Lymphoma."

"I'm sorry." Byrn surprised himself with his reply. The assassin was rarely sorry.

The old lady nodded.

Byrn pushed further.

"The disease, death approaching, seeking refuge in the church and probably spending a fair amount of time sitting in this park reflecting. I suspect you have regrets."

"Don't we all?" replied the woman.

"But some of us seek a deeper level of atonement than others."

The woman raised a palm, as though attempting to silence Byrn, but then lowered it.

"What degree of absolution do you believe I am searching for?" she asked.

Byrn looked directly into her eyes, fighting their beguiling quality.

"I refer you to my original question. Was Vadim Aleyev the one who taught you your skills in tradecraft?" This was the point of no return.

Again, the woman turned her gaze to the pond, following the progress of a couple of ducks across the water.

"Yes," she answered.

"Then your burden is heavy. The path to redemption will be difficult if not..."

"Impossible," she interrupted.

"Yes," agreed Byrn. "Impossible. But maybe I can help you begin the journey. In the end, only you can determine if the turmoil in your soul is worth any potential outcome."

"You sound more like a philosopher than an assassin or spy."

"In my line of work, the two go hand in hand. I believe it's important that people understand the lives they've lived, and that they appreciate how their mistakes have impacted others."

"And I suspect you bring them news of the price they'll need to pay for those mistakes."

The assassin nodded.

"Have you been sent to bring me news?" she asked.

"No, I'm here to ask you to help me deliver it."

"I see. I suppose I should be relieved. You offer a job to an old lady in the final throes of her life. Perhaps a mission that invokes redemption for her sins. That is a lot to ponder."

Again, Kristiina Volk eyed Byrn, searching his face for an indication of intent.

"Do you enjoy your work?

"I love it, maybe too much."

"I see."

The moment had arrived.

"Ms. Volk, Kristiina. How do you feel about Vadim Aleyev?"

The woman inhaled sharply, as if caught by surprise.

"I hope you have time to spare my new young friend. Because the answer to that question holds more complexity than you can imagine."

Lachlan Byrn sat back on the bench and smiled.

"I have time."

Chapter 21

"You take an old lady for a stroll down memory lane. You should expect some detours."

"I understand," said Byrn.

"You ask me how I feel about Vadim Aleyev. I will answer with honesty. I've never despised a human being more in my whole life. And there, of course, is the problem. My time with Vadim affected my whole life. His influence has been catastrophically destructive."

Kristiina searched Byrn's face for a reaction before continuing.

"So, it may come as some surprise to you that we were once deeply in love."

"I suspected as much."

"I'll spare you the romantic details, suffice to say he was a dashing man, five years my senior and extremely self-assured. To a young, barely twenty-year-old Estonian girl, he appeared the epitome of style and sophistication."

Byrn nodded.

"We met, we dated, we fell in love."

"Are you certain those feelings were genuinely reciprocated?"

"Without doubt, and that's not just a young girl's wish. I

have evidence to support my belief. But I'll get to that later."

She looked at Byrn.

"If you've done the research, and I suspect you have, you'll already know that Vadim's expertise lay in his power to recruit people from all walks of life. In his time in Estonia, his focus was on members of the resistance. You probably know he used several young women to lure individuals in, until, through blackmail, those victims had no choice but to follow his directions."

"I'm aware of that," Byrn.

"At first Vadim kept me separated from his work. Our relationship was personal. But as time wore on, he became more driven. Eventually he requested some simple tasks of me. Gradually they became increasingly complicated until they became too complicated, if you understand what I mean."

Again, Byrn nodded.

Kristiina paused, perhaps deciding how far to go.

"Tell me about the politics," he asked.

She looked up.

"I didn't care one iota about politics. Of course, I was aware the Soviets had taken over our lives and that Soviet law was now our law. But you need to remember, I'd grown up in that environment. My parents had done all right for themselves under the regime. I was more interested in boys and parties. I was a fool."

"What changed?"

"There's the question I've asked myself my whole life. How could I not have realized the ramifications of my actions? I suppose it's easier to judge yourself in retrospect. At the time, everything was in increments. I partook in the gradual demise of my own morality."

The old lady sighed. The weight of the world.

"It took a couple of years before I truly appreciated that Vadim sought more than just information. The intelligence we passed on to him had ramifications. At first, the consequences seemed mild. People I vaguely knew being brought in for questioning. Bit by bit the questioning became re-education and then…"

Kristiina paused. Byrn saw the first trace of a tear in her eye.

"Then people started disappearing. That's the moment I realized Vadim Aleyev was not the man I believed him to be. It was also the moment I fully understood that I was willingly contributing to a regime dedicated to the darkest side of human nature. You ask about politics. None of this was about politics. It was about power, manipulation, greed, and, in the end, murder. And I was part of it."

She continued.

"Do you appreciate how many Estonians were sent to Gulag camps or murdered because they wanted their country and their culture returned to them?" she asked. "No need to answer. I suppose no one ever counted. But one fact I do understand to the depths of my soul, is that I personally carry the responsibility for the disappearance and or death of a great number of my countrymen."

Kristiina paused and began to tremble, as though recalling the past had taken her right back in time.

Byrn waited patiently as she decided which road to walk next. She didn't need his prompting.

"I'm sorry. This is not easy for me, but perhaps it is cathartic in my final days."

Another moment slipped by.

"I expect you'd like to hear how I got out of it. Well, the truth is I didn't. If I'd told Vadim that I'd had some sort of epiphany, I would have been shipped off to a Gulag or worse. Despite my belief that his love for me was genuine, his love for himself was far greater. In the end, I started feeding him false information whenever I could. I protected as many people as I could. But of course, for a great number of people, my epiphany came too late."

"So, what happened next? I understand his masters lost some of their faith in him."

"At least I can take some credit for that. He probably still doesn't know to this day that I was the resistance's late blooming mole, feeding the false intelligence that cost him Moscow's trust. In fact, when the summons came to return to Russia, he begged me to go with him. Of course, I refused."

"And what of your life since then?" asked Byrn.

Kristiina Volk shook her head.

"What life? I wouldn't call my existence a life. I've spent my time dedicated to supporting my country, my community, and my culture. I couldn't bring myself to love, to start a family. It was impossible for me to see I deserved that level of happiness. I don't know if you can comprehend this, but guilt is like a cancer. It ravaged me well before the physical disease that now knocks on my door."

Although it was a lot to take in, Byrn deemed the woman to be sincere.

"What about Aleyev, the man? Is he a true believer? Is he as devoted to the Russian cause as his publicity suggests?"

"Even back then, Vadim's quest for power and money had become obvious. There were times when individuals who clearly stood against the Soviets accidentally slipped through

Vadim's clutches. By coincidence, they were always people of substance, if you see what I mean. When I read later about the rumors of Vadim's lust for opulence and his tendency toward corruption, I was not surprised. He displayed a wealth far beyond his earnings as KGB officer."

Byrn leaned forward as he asked his next question. The whole operation depended on the answer.

"You mentioned earlier you had evidence that Aleyev's feelings for you were genuine. I don't want to pry, but this is important. What proof do you have?"

"These," she said, reaching into her purse.

Kristiina produced a small bunch of letters held together by an elastic band. She thrust them forward. Byrn took them, removed the band, unfolded the papers, and began reading. Their content astounded him.

"He's still in love with you?"

"At least in his mind, he believes that. You'll see there are three letters in your hand. The first one is dated a short time after his wife, Tatiana, died, five years ago."

"Incredible."

For Byrn, this couldn't have been better.

"At one point, after his wife died, he sent two of his people to speak to me, to inquire if I wished to meet with him. Before you ask, I threw them out and told them never to contact me again. I keep the letters with me as a memento of the shame I carry."

The two strangers sat in silence, both feigning amusement from the ducks swimming in circles around the pond.

Byrn considered Kristiina Volk and her story. The two of them clearly shared a common disappointment in the circumstances life had presented to them.

"How do you feel about Vadim Aleyev now?" he asked.

"Do you really need to ask? That man destroyed my country. He ruined the lives of hundreds of Estonians and probably even more Russians. He is currently spreading his plague of death around the globe like it's his personal destiny."

Kristiina gasped a little, losing breath. Then she continued.

"And for me personally, Vadim Aleyev is the man who stained my soul with blood. He may as well have killed me because he stole my life. I have a deeper affection for the devil himself."

The woman virtually spat out her final words, her agitation obvious. Byrn allowed her a few moments to reflect.

She broke the silence.

"I trust that I've provided you with the information you sought, young man. I've also, perhaps foolishly, trusted a complete stranger by sharing these intimate thoughts. I hope my faith is not misplaced."

"It is not."

Kristiina looked once more into Byrn's eyes, as though she were aware of the power her own gaze carried. The assassin noted that her tears now flowed more freely. Then she spoke.

"For all I've given you today, I can't help but believe there is something more you require of me. This is the time to speak up. If you have some redemption to offer my tortured soul, offer it now. My time is running out."

Byrn held her stare. There was no longer any need to hide his purpose in their meeting.

"I want you to meet with Vadim Aleyev. And I want you to help me kill him."

Chapter 22

The Whitehouse, Washington DC

PRESIDENT JEFFERSON BLAKE

Jefferson Blake swiveled his chair and gazed out the large south-facing window. He found the view of the tranquil green lawn, the rows of fastidiously maintained hedges and, of course, the roses, meditative.

His was a demanding job. People frequently perceived the role of President of the United States to be a calm, big decisions only kind of thing. If you truly cared about your country, it was anything but that. Certainly, he had the world's largest bureaucracy and most powerful military machine at his disposal, but Blake thought the old analogy of the circus clown balancing a bunch of simultaneously spinning plates appropriate.

For sure, he had a large staff to spin the plates for him, but only he could decide where they landed. And right now, there were a lot of plates spinning.

He'd only been in the job for a couple of years. It wasn't a position he'd sought. Blake's background was military through and through. He'd been seconded into the role of vice president when the incumbent VP had been embroiled in a major scandal that threatened the previous administration. President Carlton had needed a candidate with a squeaky-clean past. Blake had agreed reluctantly, assenting to stay only until the end of the administration's first term.

The scenario had changed dramatically when the president had died in office, and Blake ascended into the role. He'd never asked to be here, but by God, he'd do his best while he sat in this chair.

Jefferson Blake believed in service to his country. He was also proud to be the second person of African descent to hold the position.

There was a brief knock on the door before Sandra, his secretary, stepped into the room.

Blake turned back to his desk.

"Mr. President, sorry to disturb you, but Abe Peterson would like a quick word with you if he could," she said.

"Send him through, Sandra. I'm sure he's keen to take another shot at talking me out of the summit."

"Yes, sir." She disappeared through the doorway.

Abe Peterson was head of the Secret Service, but to Jefferson Blake, the man had been much more than that. Peterson had been in charge of Blake's detail when he was VP and had been crucial in foiling an assassination attempt on Blake's life by a Sudanese terrorist group shortly after he took over the top job.

Abe Peterson was also Jefferson Blake's friend.

Another knock.

"Mr. President?"

Blake looked up from his desk.

"Come in Abe, take a seat." Blake waved the Secret Service

man over to the comfortable couches on either side of the fireplace.

"Mr. President, are you certain I can't talk…"

Blake raised his palm.

"No, Abe, you can't talk me out of attending the summit. You and I both know what's at stake."

"Yes, Mr. President."

The big man sighed. Blake was aware he valued his leader's life as much as his own.

Blake continued. "I understand that it's going to be difficult for your team to protect me in Estonia, Abe, but the situation is deteriorating rapidly. I've just had a briefing from Cynthia Ford, who tells me that idiot Aleyev is now rattling his saber on the borders of Estonia, Latvia, and Finland. Cynthia is convinced that Finland is only a distraction, at least for now, but the man's actions are incomprehensible. Does he really believe he can time travel back to the era of Soviet domination?"

Peterson respected Cynthia Ford's perspective. She was as dedicated to her role as National Security Advisor as Peterson was to his own position.

"I understand, Mr. President, but does it need to be Estonia? We'll be virtually visiting in President Aleyev's backyard."

"Yes, I'm afraid we are Abe. And we're doing it for two reasons. First is that Estonia is the only place our team could convince his team to meet, and I don't want to wait another six months, and hundreds or thousands more deaths, until we can persuade them of an alternative location."

Peterson nodded.

"And the second reason, Mr. President?"

"It's precisely because Estonia used to be part of the Soviet

111

Union and used to be his backyard that it's appropriate to meet him there. I want Vadim Aleyev to understand that Estonia is now part of NATO and, if not in our own backyard, is at least in our neighborhood."

"Point taken, sir. You have your own saber to rattle. You'll get no further argument from me."

Blake smiled. He knew Abe would come around.

"I'm aware it's relatively short notice for a trip of this magnitude, Abe, but I have every confidence in your team. For what it's worth, we've tried other avenues of approach. We've had extensive discussions with the Chinese government, but despite not outwardly supporting Vadim Aleyev, President Xiong Lei is not willing to publicly condemn him, either."

"Thank you, Mr. President. Now, I've got some additional information that has just come across my desk. I know they'll cover it later, in today's security briefing, but I thought you'd want to hear it now."

Jefferson leaned forward.

"Your expression speaks volumes, Abe. Please tell me now."

"Mr. President. The CIA analysts have picked up some communication chatter, and I should point out that chatter is all it is at this stage."

Blake nodded.

Peterson continued. "It appears that there is some talk of a small hit team crossing the Estonian border."

"Who is their target?"

"At this stage, we don't know, sir. But coincidentally we've picked up another report that there was a house fire not far from Kiiu, in the country's northeast. The building affected was a remote farmhouse. The local authorities have found seven bodies in the burned-out wreckage."

"And you suspect this is related to the insertion of this supposed hit team?"

"It's a possibility, sir."

Blake sat back on the couch and scratched his chin.

"Interesting."

"It gets more interesting, Mr. President."

"Go on."

"We're waiting for confirmation, but it appears the corpses in the farmhouse are of Asian descent."

Peterson waited while his boss considered the information. Eventually.

"I don't need to tell you, Abe, there are several possibilities that explain these circumstances. But let's take this for a walk for a moment."

"Yes, sir."

"First. We need to determine if the hit team in the country is targeting me, the Russian president, or someone else entirely. Second. Are these dead bodies the result of the hit team's work, or are they the hit team itself?"

"You can be certain our people are working twenty-four seven to find the answers to those questions, Mr. President."

"I've no doubt about that, Abe, none at all. But the most important question to me, at this point, is that if there really is or was a hit team in place, who sent them?"

"As yet, we can't be certain, sir. In the meantime, we'll interpret this situation as a direct threat and boost the security arrangements for the summit accordingly."

The two men sat in silence, Peterson waiting to be dismissed by his boss.

The President said nothing.

"Is there anything else, sir?"

"Yes, think with me for a second here. I know this is out of your direct area, but I'd appreciate your view. Suppose that was a hit team, and it was they who died in the fire. Who instigated their deaths? I presume it wasn't us."

"No sir, it wasn't."

"Then it may have been the Russians, or someone else with a completely different agenda."

"Our people will be examining all possibilities, Mr. President."

Jefferson Blake rounded his left hand in a fist before holding it to his mouth. He then tapped it back and forth against his lips. Abe Peterson knew the signs. His boss was deep in thought. Peterson appreciated his president's adroit ability to analyze a myriad of details quickly and succinctly.

"Abe, have your team and the CIA consider this. What if Xiong Lei has decided on a new strategy? Suppose for a second that he's accepted defeat at being unable to talk Aleyev down from the ledge. Russia's expansionist stance is causing great harm around the globe, including to China. My understanding is that privately, Xiong has admitted Aleyev is an embarrassment."

"So, the hit team could be operating under Chinese direction," suggested Peterson.

"Quite possibly. That leads to the question of who the hell stopped them?"

"The Russians?"

"Have we've picked up any chatter about a Russian team in place?"

"Negative, sir."

"If the facts line up a certain way, the United States is in a tricky position here."

"How so, Mr. President?"

"If we've received intelligence regarding an assassination attempt on the president of the Russian Federation, if we don't share it with them, and that fact sees the light of day, the US becomes an international pariah."

"Do you wish me to request that the Director of the CIA formally warn the Russian government, or would you prefer the State Department to handle it?" Peterson asked.

The president resumed his tapping.

"No, neither one, Abe. You currently have a direct line into the Russian president's security team, don't you? Part of a security alliance for the summit?"

"Yes, sir, we do. I've established a personal relationship with Viktor Sidorov, my counterpart on President Aleyev's team."

"Then, Abe, I want you to use that open line to inform the Russians of our preliminary level of concern and pass on any information we possess, as long as it doesn't compromise our own security."

"Yes, Mr. President. Consider it done."

"And one more thing, Abe."

"Yes, Mr. President."

"Please pay extremely close attention to the way the Russians, and Mr. Sidorov in particular, react to the news. Your man's initial response may tell us more than we'd learn through official high-level channels."

Abe Peterson smiled.

"Yes, Mr. President."

Chapter 23

LACHLAN BYRN

It was just after midnight.

Lachlan Byrn could feel the icy gulf waters penetrate his wetsuit. The situation wasn't comfortable, but it was tolerable.

Stage two of his reconnaissance of the abandoned submarine base couldn't be achieved through a simple tourist visit during opening hours. Byrn had to immerse himself in every aspect of his evolving plan. Nothing had been set in stone in the assassin's mind yet, but this recon would be the point of no return for how he approached the job.

He entered the waters from the forest, several hundred yards west. From time to time, he risked using a flashlight. He had no scuba gear, so he came up for air every couple of minutes. If the plan panned out as he expected, he'd have to make further arrangements to acquire equipment. That was standard procedure.

The water was dark and foreboding, but for a man of Byrn's skills, it was a straightforward insertion. Eventually, his light exposed the foundations of the old pier rising from the depths below.

This is where things would get interesting.

The assassin's first task was to climb back onto the structure to gauge his bearings. Byrn was aware of a ladder down by the beach, but it was too close to the shore for his needs. As he climbed, the moss-covered stone caused his hands and feet to slip. Each crevice in the stone was a victory, each slip a setback. Once above the waterline, the relative dryness of the wall made his job considerably easier.

When he reached the uneven surface of the top of the pier, he lay flat, raising his head to scan the area for any possible impediment to his task.

Nothing.

His breathing still heavy from the swim, the assassin rose to a crouching position before making his way along to the building he'd identified during his first visit as having the most potential for what he had in mind. The torpedo room. He entered through the northern doorway at the end of the structure. There were no doors and no locks because there was nothing to steal. The whole facility had been ransacked of anything of worth decades before.

Once inside the building, Byrn used his flashlight to orientate himself. A concrete pit ran the entire length of the room along the western side. A metal grate covering the pit appeared to be the only recent addition to the space. Byrn assumed it had been put in place for the safety of tourists.

His initial task was to find an access point and climb down under the grate. Five minutes later, the assassin crawled on his hands and knees along the full length of the pit. Satisfied the pit would give him further access to any section of the structure he required, Byrn then began examining its walls. There appeared to be several points where the bricks had crumbled, not completely, but enough to allow egress to the neighboring underfloor.

This was the interesting part. Byrn's plan would be made or broken with this next exploration.

Byrn noted the weak spots in the pit wall, then climbed out at the far end onto the main floor. Running down the eastern side of the floor, parallel to the pit, was a series of smaller, separated concrete foxholes. Most had heavy covers made of either metal or wood solidly bolted to the concrete floor. Byrn was unaware of the original purpose of the foxholes, but it was irrelevant to him.

The assassin's next task was to associate each weakness in the long pit wall with a neighboring foxhole. This was the crux of his investigation.

Ten minutes later, Byrn found what he'd sought. One of the deeper foxholes correlated with one of the weaker spots in the pit wall. Byrn pulled at the hatch covering the foxhole. It wouldn't budge. The assassin cast his flashlight around the trapdoor's outer edges. Four large bolts held it down. They were rusty, but secure. Byrn assumed the trapdoor hadn't been opened since the Soviet occupation.

Perfect.

With one more vital task to perform, Byrn headed to the southern end of the building. The long pit ran under the outside wall, providing an exit point to the pier. He scurried back to the northern end to find a similar layout.

Options.

Byrn loved options.

The assassin glanced back toward the beach before he ventured out of the building.

No one was in sight.

After walking the length of the pier on either side, to check points of egress, Byrn moved quickly back to the torpedo room and flashed his torch around its edges one last time. He was now satisfied he had his bearings locked in.

Byrn was going to earn every dollar that Zhen Su and his people paid him, but for the first time, Byrn considered the job doable. Several factors had to align for that to occur. A lot of ducks need to form a long row.

Lachlan Byrn allowed himself a small wry grin before easing himself back into the water.

Chapter 24

The Kremlin, Moscow

PRESIDENT VADIM ALEYEV

The morning had been busy. Aleyev preferred it that way. He'd received a briefing from the military regarding the overnight progress of their current 'special operations'. An hour after that, he received another briefing on exactly the same subject. Both teams that briefed him were unaware of the other. Accordingly, the president could ensure the accuracy of his information.

Trust no one. It was an adage that had served him well through the years.

Vadim Aleyev allowed himself a moment to reflect. As his gaze wandered around the room, he speculated that his own personal office probably didn't appear like the dark wood-paneled Kremlin headquarters portrayed in the cliched Hollywood blockbusters. The paneling had been painted over in a neutral cream. The rug on the floor matched. Behind his chair, the Russian flag stood proudly. The mammoth desk before him had enough space for screens, mounds of paperwork, and several phones. Aleyev had ensured the desk was considerably larger than his American counterpart in the Oval Office in Washington.

This was modern Russia. Yet the world would soon understand that modern Russia was reconnecting with her roots, the great Soviet Union.

Aleyev felt impregnable here at the Kremlin. No one could touch him. No one would dare try. The Americans can keep Tom Cruise, his plastic disguises, and his tendency to drop down on cables into enemy strongholds. Aleyev found amusement in the banal American rubbish, knowing how far it was from the truth.

No, he couldn't be touched here, and his security team was the most thorough and brutal in the world.

In fact, Aleyev couldn't be threatened anywhere.

A knock on the door. The president glanced at the wall clock. It would be Sidorov, his head of presidential security. Aleyev trusted the man to the extent that Sidorov was aware that if anything happened to his leader, his own life would be forfeited.

"*Vkhodit*, enter."

"President Aleyev."

"Come in Viktor. Sit down."

Aleyev neither stood up nor guided Sidorov to one of the more comfortable seats in the room. The director of security sat across from his boss in an upright chair.

"Tell me, Viktor, are you satisfied with the plans you've put in place for my security at this ridiculous summit?"

"Yes, sir. Our preliminary team is going in next week. They will cover and sweep all locations on the itinerary. In each case, we will leave armed personnel on site to ensure there are no last-minute transgressions."

"And the Estonians. Have they been accommodating?"

"Yes, Mr. President. In fact, they've provided every support we've requested. They are a little unhappy about our people remaining fully armed in the lead up to the summit, but they've acquiesced."

"The Americans would have requested no less."

"No, sir."

"And what about the Americans?" asked Aleyev. "I understand you've been coordinating your preparations with theirs."

"Yes, sir. Director Abe Peterson is my equivalent in Washington. He has been cooperative and willing to coordinate our arrangements together for the actual times you and the American president are meeting."

"Excellent, Viktor. I suppose that gives us a clear understanding of what protections they are putting in place?"

"Yes, Mr. President. It does."

Aleyev paused momentarily before resuming the discussion.

"Viktor, it may be a good idea to provide me with full details of the American security plans."

He spoke as though it was an afterthought.

"You would like that much detail, sir?"

Aleyev smiled.

"Yes, I'm certain studying how the Americans develop such intricacies will aid me in understanding how these people may approach the broader perspective."

The Russian president didn't believe there was one iota of truth in what he'd just said.

Sidorov hesitated for a fraction of a second before complying.

"Of course, Mr. President. It will be done."

"Thank you, Viktor. I believe that concludes our business for today."

"Yes, sir. Well, perhaps not Mr. President."

"You have something further."

"Yes, Mr. President."

Sidorov leaned forward in his chair, searching for the words. Nothing.

"Well, spit it out, man."

The last thing Aleyev needed was another imbecile, hesitant to speak his mind.

"I'm afraid it is a delicate subject, Mr. President. I've been uncertain whether to bring it up, but I believe you may have some interest in the matter."

"Your hesitancy is acknowledged. Speak your mind, Viktor."

Viktor Sidorov was a large man with a military history beyond question. He was also one of the most deadly men in the Kremlin, yet still he found difficulty in the task at hand.

Inhaling deeply, he began.

"Mr. President. I'm sure you are aware that part of my role is to monitor all communications and requests for personal access to you."

"Yes, Viktor, I am." Aleyev's patience was waning.

"Since your wife's passing, I'm aware you've attempted to contact an old friend in Tallinn."

"I have many old friends, Viktor. Of whom do you refer?"

"The person I speak of is one Kristiina Volk."

Aleyev sat back in his chair. Conscious that he'd failed to conceal his surprise, the president quickly reclaimed his mask of neutrality.

"Yes, I believe I recall her, Victor."

"Mr. President, we've had an inquiry. You'd be aware we receive hundreds of requests each month for a personal audience with you, and most don't make it past our team's initial scrutiny. Due to our assumption that this lady is an old acquaintance of yours, her request has made it this far."

"Her request?"

"Yes, Mr. President. Ms. Kristiina Volk has requested to meet with you while you are in Estonia."

Vadim Aleyev sensed the blood rushing to his head.

Kristiina.

Sidorov waited for a response from his leader.

"Mr. President. Shall I decline in the usual manner? Almost every moment in your brief time in the country is already accounted for."

Kristiina.

"Mr. President?"

Chapter 25

LACHLAN BYRN

The assassin had some housekeeping to take care of.

Following the midnight visit to the old submarine base, Byrn dedicated most of the next day to planning. Detailed planning. He considered every possible scenario and designed a counter-scenario to accommodate each circumstance. Of course, the one thing Byrn could not totally control was human behavior. A crucial ingredient in devising a successful kill was steering people's actions towards the intended outcome, but there was no certainty. The human factor played a greater part in this situation than Byrn would have liked, but there were no alternatives that had a chance in hell of working.

As Byrn finalized his plan, he noted down a list of required equipment. He'd brought an array of gear with him, but he always knew he'd have to access more resources on site. This is where things got sticky. Byrn had trusted suppliers in a range of locations throughout the world. The key word was trust. It had taken the assassin a long time to build up his network. A very few of his suppliers he'd met in person. He had never seen most of them, and they had never seen him.

Although most of the equipment he needed wasn't weaponry, it was still specialized gear. There lay the trouble. Specialized gear required specialized shops. Byrn could easily acquire the dive gear he needed in Tallinn, but there were less than a dozen dive shops in the city. Any astute investigator, post the event, would be able to locate where he'd acquired the equipment. Accordingly, his description at the least, or perhaps video footage of him at the worst, would be accessible.

An unacceptable risk.

Byrn would use one of his two northern European suppliers. He had one in Helsinki and one in Riga. Helsinki was accessible from Estonia only by water or air. Both means of travel were a needless complication. Riga, in Latvia, was just over a four-hour drive, but it meant crossing a border. This time, Byrn would access back roads to make the crossing. The time for taking unnecessary chances had passed.

The assassin was on the road at dawn, two days later. He'd sent his list of requirements through to his contact in Riga. He'd known Barda for years, and the old man had been in business for decades before that. Longevity begat confidentiality in Byrn's trade. The two of them had even met on a couple of occasions when Byrn had required some local expertise. Barda had given Byrn no reason to regret their relationship.

Byrn detoured through Leipste and down to Talcis in Latvia to avoid the main border crossings. The road was steep, and at times wound tightly through the hills, but the Volkswagen he'd stolen from the long-term parking lot at Lennart Meri Tallinn Airport handled it well. There was a strong chance Byrn would be done with the vehicle by the time the owner found it gone. He changed the registration plates anyway, just to be sure.

By mid-morning, the assassin was pulling into a laneway off the Kalnciema Iela just inside the Marupe Municipality a few miles from the Riga city center. The address Barda had texted him turned out to be a large industrial factory, set amongst a plethora of other similar buildings. Byrn was right on time. He texted the word 'here' to the number he'd been given and within seconds, the mammoth roller door rattled before slowly opening. As soon as the opening was high enough, Byrn drove straight in.

An almost empty cavern greeted him. There was no machinery, no equipment in sight, and no pallets of storage. The barren space appeared completely unused, except for two shipping containers in the far corner.

Byrn was not surprised. Barda had remained in business this long by being adaptable and almost invisible. With any inkling of the authorities' interest in his location, he could have his entire operation relocated within an hour.

Byrn opened the Volkswagen's door and got out, expecting to hear Barda's semi-evil chuckle along with some smart-ass comment about Byrn only coming to visit him when he wanted something.

It didn't happen. Byrn was greeted with stony silence.

The hairs on the back of his neck began to prickle.

Then.

"I have your order ready. I believe you'll be satisfied."

Byrn swung around, withdrawing the SIG from his jacket.

"There is no need for that, my friend."

Byrn leveled the pistol at the man approaching him. He'd obviously been waiting in the small factory office beside the roller door.

"You're not Barda. Where is he?" Byrn demanded.

"No, Sir, I'm not Barda. I regret to inform you that the old man passed a few weeks ago. I am his nephew, Mikelis. I have taken over my uncle's business. It was his wish."

Byrn eyed the guy off. Probably early thirties, unshaved, solid but not particularly fit. His grin exposed uneven and slightly yellowing teeth.

"I was not informed of any change of proprietorship. You had plenty of opportunity to make that clear. This changes the circumstances completely."

"I do apologize, sir. That is our mistake. Would you care to inspect your order? I'm certain you will find our service as efficient and confidential as my uncle's."

Byrn was fully alert and deeply concerned, so the SIG remained pointed at the other man's heart. This change of arrangement was totally out of line. Anyone legitimately taking over from Barda would know that face-to-face meetings were the exception, not the norm. Barda would also have ensured a smooth transition if he'd decided to pass the business on, which Byrn considered unlikely, nephew or not. The other thing that worried Byrn was this man's reference to 'our'. He'd said it twice. The confidential supply trade was based on a single supplier's integrity, not the corporate 'we'.

"Please, sir, take a moment to inspect your order. I'm sure we can work through this small issue."

Byrn sensed that he was in no immediate danger. He may as well check out the goods. No matter how this ended, he was certain he'd depart with them in his possession. He nodded.

"This way please."

The man who'd introduced himself as Mikelis strode over to

the closest container and heaved the door open. He then stood to one side, pointing to a neatly arranged row of assorted equipment. Byrn lowered his weapon and took a moment to inspect it. The issue wasn't with the gear.

"The equipment is satisfactory," Byrn began, "but this new arrangement is not."

"No sir, I don't believe the arrangement is satisfactory either."

"I beg your pardon?" said Byrn, once more raising the SIG.

"Forgive me," said Mikelis. "My uncle was an honorable person, but perhaps not such a great businessman. I have been thinking. The equipment you have requested points to a distinct intention. I think we both know what that intention is. In a typical business environment in our line of work, that would not be an issue. However, the current conditions are anything but typical, aren't they?"

Every fiber in Byrn's body tensed. He held no doubt where this conversation was heading.

"Go on."

Mikelis cleared his throat. Not nervous, but perhaps apprehensive.

"I am aware that a significant meeting is scheduled to take place soon, across the border. It seems to me that the people attending may have made many enemies through the years. Enemies that may want to, let's say, see them relinquish their roles."

"Your point?" said Byrn.

Mikelis glanced at the concrete floor before looking Byrn in the eye. A sure sign of trepidation.

"I assume you will be extremely well paid for your work, sir. Accordingly, we must double the price quoted to you for these goods."

Byrn smiled.

"Why didn't you say it was only a matter of money? I'm sure the increase in cost won't be an issue."

The other man seemed relieved.

Byrn lowered his gun.

The assassin began walking towards his vehicle. "Perhaps your associate could help me load the gear into my car," he said.

"My associate?"

"Of course. Mikelis, you are clearly a smart operator. You wouldn't have confronted an armed man so confidently without preparation. Please ask your friend to join us."

Byrn paused in his walk before reaching into his trousers to pull out his wallet.

He started pealing notes away from a large pad of cash.

Mikelis shrugged his shoulders.

"Andris, come on out. The deal is done."

To his left, Byrn noticed some movement in his peripheral vision. The office door opened, and a tall, slender man walked into the factory space. He carried a Luger in his right hand.

"Put the weapon away, Andris. We are all friends here," instructed Mikelis.

Andris appeared hesitant. He didn't stow the gun, but he lowered it.

In the same moment, Byrn dropped a couple of bills on the floor. An accident.

"Clumsy me," he said, reaching down to reclaim them.

Andris seemed to relax a little.

Lachlan Byrn decided to ensure the man would never feel tension again.

Just before the tips of his fingers touched the first hundred dollar note, he reached for his ankle, unclasped the diver's knife, and in a single movement sent it propelling through the air.

Andris would have screamed out if the blade hadn't plunged directly into his throat, severing his larynx and one of his two carotid arteries.

Byrn didn't wait for the geyser of blood to erupt. He swung around to Mikelis, who stepped backward in surprise. The man then attempted to dash for the shelter of the container. Mid-step, Byrn raised his pistol and shot him in the right foot. He went down.

Lachlan Byrn exhaled deeply. He glanced briefly at Andris' bloodied corpse before casually strolling back towards Mikelis. To his credit, the guy hadn't shrieked in pain. Byrn smiled as Mikelis struggled with his jacket, clearly trying to retrieve some sort of weapon.

Without faltering, Byrn fired again, hitting his target in the lower forearm. The man grunted in pain but ceased his movement as the blood poured down his sleeve.

"Mmm, you seem to be quite a tough one, Mikelis, if that is your real name."

Mikelis grunted again.

"So, let's chat," said Byrn.

The assassin crouched down next to the struggling man.

"Tell me about Barda. You're not really his nephew, are you?"

Mikelis appeared uncertain how to respond.

"I suggest you cling to the truth as though your life depends on it, Mikelis."

The man nodded.

"No, but Barda sold me his business. He told me negotiation with the customer was standard practice."

"Oh dear," said Byrn as he casually fired a round into the prone man's shoulder.

He cried out.

"I apologize Mikelis. I overestimated your understanding of English and I'm afraid I don't speak Latvian. I had tried to make a reference to the importance of truth. You may have missed it."

The man's skin slowly drained of color.

"Now, one more time. What has become of my dear friend Barda?"

"He is dead."

"That saddens me," replied Byrn. "Was it an accident?"

As he spoke, Byrn raised the SIG and pressed its hot barrel against the other man's temple. He automatically yanked his head away.

"No, it was not an accident," Mikelis responded.

"That news makes me even sadder, Mikelis. Tell me, did you kill him?"

Mikelis remained silent, not wanting to answer.

"Our current understanding implies that silence is the equivalent of a lie, my friend. I repeat, did you kill Barda?"

Mikelis closed his eyes. "Yes, I killed him."

"It feels better to get it off your chest, doesn't it?"

More silence.

"So, here's how this is going to play out, Mikelis."

The man opened his eyes expectantly.

"I like to do what I can for those involved in a negative situation such as this. In the case of your friend Andris, I was able to provide a swift, painless exit from this world. He probably doesn't even know he's dead yet."

Byrn sniggered.

"For you Mikelis, I have decided on a different approach."

In an instant Mikelis' skin had turned ash white, sweat oozed from his pores. Byrn knew it wasn't just from the blood loss.

"We'll begin with some business advice. I really think you can do better in the way you conduct yourself. First. If you wish to obtain a business, either start one yourself or offer the vendor a decent amount for his achievement and years of labor. Barda spent his whole life constructing a dependable enterprise based on his personal integrity and didn't merit to have it snatched away from him. Do you understand my point, Mikelis?"

The man nodded.

"Good. Now, second. When you agree to perform a commercial transaction, at least in my line of work, your word is everything. To change conditions, including the price, once negotiations have been finalized, is just tacky. It won't get you repeat business."

Mikelis groaned and nodded again.

"Okay. The final point I'd like to make today regards respect for people's privacy. I had agreed to meet Barda face to face because we knew and trusted each other. You and I have no such relationship. The moment you laid eyes on me, you disrespected my privacy. For what it's worth, no matter what you'd said during our meeting, your fate had been decided by this one act."

Mikelis slumped back, almost sinking into the concrete floor.

"Well, all right then," continued Byrn. "I think that just

about concludes our chat. Tell me, Mikelis, do you feel more confident in managing a small business now?"

Mikelis whispered, "Yes, sir. I do."

The assassin leaned in closer, his weapon remaining trained on his victim.

"Okay then," said Byrn. "So, for each of those three transgressions, you've already received considerable punishment, Mikelis. A bullet in your foot, in your arm and in your shoulder. I can tell from the look on your face that the pain is really starting to kick in now. Are your senses being overpowered by the agony of your wounds? I do believe you're close to passing out. Am I correct?"

Mikelis grunted a nod.

"I'm not so sorry to hear that. Before I depart Mikelis, would you like me to leave you with some hope, possibly a little light at the end of what must appear to be a very bleak tunnel from your point of view?"

"Yes... please."

"Well, here it is, then. As you go forward with your newly acquired business acumen, I suggest you consider cats."

"Cats... are you insane" Mikelis barely managed to get the words out.

"Yes, my sanity has been a bone of contention, but that's not the point I wish to make. I need you to ponder the relationship between humans and cats. What do we actually have in common with our feline friends?"

"I, I... I don't know."

Byrn paused as a grin spread across his face.

"Well mother fucker, you better hope like all hell you both have nine lives."

In one movement, Byrn stood up, leaned over his victim,

and double tapped him right between his struggling eyes.

Thirty minutes later, Lachlan Byrn was back on the road to Estonia, enjoying the northern European sunshine. His goods were secured safely in the car's trunk.

He would miss Barda.

That being said, the resolution of such an awkward situation was most gratifying.

Chapter 26

"How are you feeling?"

"Each day, the struggle is slightly greater than the day before. I fear I don't have long."

"I'm sorry to hear that."

"Because you're worried that I will die before I can help you?"

"No," said Byrn, quite surprised that he had experienced some genuine concern. Just a little.

The assassin was certain that Kristiina Volk looked more drawn and listless than their previous meeting.

Byrn could hear the rain belting down on the church roof. It was far too wet to meet in the park. Sufficient shadow haunted the rear corner of the building so that nobody entering the church could identify him if they were questioned later. And there would be questions.

"Don't worry, young man. This old bird has a bit of fight left in her yet. I won't let you down." The old lady sighed as she spoke, as though convincing herself that she believed her own words.

"I'm sure you won't. You're committed to easing your conscience."

"That's true." Kristiina coughed heavily. Byrn waited until

she settled.

Before he could speak, she continued.

"Yes, I'm certain I won't find complete solace with this single act, but there is one thing that has surprised me."

Byrn raised his eyebrows.

"I must say," she added, "the thought of revenge, even after all these years, excites me. And I can tell you it takes a great deal for a person of my age, in my condition, to get excited."

Byrn smiled.

"Welcome to my world."

"Your world," repeated Kristiina. "I really don't understand what your world consists of, although I do have a few suspicions. Would you care to share?"

"No."

"What about your name? You haven't even told me that."

"I've told you, it's better you don't know," Byrn replied.

"I suppose you know best, my mysterious new friend."

Byrn nodded.

Kristiina Volk paused, took a moment to scrutinize the young man next to her. She knew she'd get no more information than the sparse details he'd already given her. He clearly wasn't the sharing type. She put a hand on his knee, probably too familiar a gesture for their limited relationship, but what the heck, she had nothing too loose.

"Well, I've received some news which may please you."

Byrn stared her in the eye.

"Yes."

"I've received a reply."

"And?"

"Look at you, suddenly so interested in what I have to say."

Byrn shrugged his shoulders and waited.

"All right, I'm just playing with you. Why do I think not many people would have the courage to do that? Anyway. Yes, I have a reply and yes, Vadim wishes to meet with me."

She smiled.

"That's good news," said Byrn. "It speaks to the depth of your relationship so long ago." As he spoke Lachlan Byrn realized he had absolutely no understanding of what would cause a man like Aleyev to risk everything to catch up with an old flame. The assassin just didn't fathom the magnitude of emotion that would lead the Russian president to this point. He really couldn't understand such a euphoric connection between two human beings. It was beyond him… and he was okay with that.

"Did you receive a confirmation of when and where?" he asked.

"Time, no. The message I received said that would be conveyed to me closer to his visit. The location, however, has been confirmed. The Hara base. Vadim seemed to like the idea of revisiting his Soviet past with me. I think my mention of his father having been in the submarine service, and the fact I'd remembered that, may have gotten the venue for our meeting across the line."

As she looked at Byrn, her mouth grew tight into a wry smile.

"That was a nice touch, by the way. I had no recollection whatsoever of his father's service," she said.

"I do what I can," said Byrn.

"You're quite the poet of death, aren't you?" she said.

Byrn didn't respond.

After a few minutes of listening to the rain pattering on the roof, he said, "We need to talk about afterwards. After the

138

event."

"I don't consider that there is much to talk about," replied Kristiina.

"You understand, I won't be available. You can't count on me for support."

Once again Kristiina smiled.

"I think we both appreciate that I won't be available either," she stated candidly.

Byrn stared at the church's stone floor. He remained silent.

"Oh, don't look so glum," announced the old woman. "I understood what I was signing on for, and truth be told, so did you."

Byrn nodded. Despite the fact that his plan was gaining momentum, he felt surprisingly joyless.

"It is what it is," he said.

More rain.

Byrn continued.

"We won't be meeting again until the day. When you receive confirmation of the time, text it to me on the number I gave you."

"What if it arrives at the last minute?"

"It won't matter. I'll be ready. It just makes it a little easier to know the precise hour."

The woman nodded.

Byrn continued. "Do we need to go over everything again? Are you sure you understand exactly what is required of you? There cannot be any variation or inaccuracy."

The old lady laughed.

"You seem to forget what I used to do for a living. It may have been a long time ago, but I remember my craft. Beside you've been over it many times."

Byrn chuckled.

"If you managed to pick me out the first day I followed you, I suspect you haven't lost much."

"That's it then," said the old woman.

"Yes, that's it."

Byrn considered whether to say more.

Finally.

"I hope you find what you've sought for so many years. I hope this one act will bring some comfort."

Again, the woman sighed, considering her response.

"I would say the same thing to you, but I suspect comfort isn't something you seek, young man. I pray that one day you'll find some measure of peace, or at least acceptance."

Byrn didn't respond.

Kristiina continued.

"As regards what I am about to do, what we are about to do, we both know there will be no satisfactory measure of solace for either of us."

Byrn smiled.

"You're correct in what you say, but you are also completely right when you say redemption and solace are not the targets I seek. I couldn't really care less."

Kristiina Volk tilted her head to the side and allowed herself an internal chuckle.

"Well, I can tell you one thing. What we do will count."

Byrn sat back on the pew and reached an arm over, touching the old lady's shoulder.

"Yes," he said, "it will count."

Chapter 27

The Kremlin, Moscow

PRESIDENT VADIM ALEYEV

Vadim Aleyev studied the man across his desk. General Yuri Varkov was slight, yet muscular. Today, his brow was severely creased. In his role as director of the Federal Security Service of the Russian Federation, Varkov reported directly to the president. The FSB was widely respected and universally feared throughout the federation. Aleyev had directed Varkov to maintain the organization's formidable reputation, and his protégé had done well. Aleyev knew the function of the director's role all too well. He had held the position for over a decade before his ascension to greater heights.

"Have you had a chance to read the reports I sent you, Mr. President?"

"Yes, Yuri. As ever, you've been thorough."

Varkov dipped his head.

"*Spasibo*," thank you.

"But I've got a few questions," continued Aleyev.

"Of course, sir."

"The information I passed on from Viktor Sidorov was

useful?"

"Yes, sir. Most useful. Having an insider's view of the Americans' security strategy provides us with options we might not have otherwise considered."

"That is excellent, Yuri. But you know the Americans won't have told us everything. We are allies in terms of ensuring the summit is secure, but in nothing else."

"Yes, Mr. President. Fortunately, we also retain access to other means of intelligence. That said, the American Secret Service should never be underestimated. They are professionals."

"As are our people."

"Of course, that is so, Mr. President. Our Presidential Security personnel are unparalleled, and of course the FSB are the best in the world, just as you shaped them to be, sir."

Aleyev sat back in his chair. Varkov was extremely capable. He was also adept at kissing ass when required.

"Speaking of our people, Yuri. You are satisfied with your team?"

"Most definitely. They are the best in their field."

"You are, of course, aware that they may not return from this assignment and must never allow themselves be captured?"

"Of course, Mr. President. And I've indicated this to the squad. Precautions have been taken."

Varkov coughed, as though nervous to ask a question.

"Speak up if you've something on your mind, Yuri. We are friends."

Varkov was pleased the president regarded him as a friend, but he was all too aware of how many 'friends' of Vadim Aleyev had died an unexpected and early death.

"Thank you, Mr. President. I have two questions."

Aleyev nodded.

"First. I'd like to confirm that my colleague, Viktor Sidorov, and his team possess no knowledge of the special operations we've planned. Any leak at all would be detrimental to the outcome."

"Viktor is a good man, Yuri, but no, he is not familiar with your assignment. If he knows anything, it would only be because you told him. I presume you've said nothing in either the summit briefings or privately?"

"No, sir. Not a word."

"That is good, Yuri, because if you did, I'd need to set you upon yourself."

Aleyev laughed. Varkov hesitantly joined in.

"Your second question, Yuri?"

"Yes, Mr. President. But may I say, I ask this out of loyalty, not out of questioning your judgement, sir."

Aleyev's brow furrowed.

"Go on."

Varkov coughed nervously before continuing.

"I just want to ensure, Mr. President, that you are aware of the international and internal ramifications if our mission is successful. A great deal of pressure will be brought to bear."

Aleyev smiled reassuringly. Like an Arctic wolf.

"There is no need to concern yourself about either the external or internal implications. The west knows that Russia remains strong, despite their attempts to weaken us. They know I remain strong. I'll handle and publicly dismiss their absurd accusations. With regard to internal pressures, I'm certain that the second part of our plan will put out that fire before it even starts. You've confirmed those arrangements?"

"Of course, sir. Everything is in place and the timing has

been carefully calculated so that the location is appropriate."

"Excellent, Yuri. As always, you've done well. Just ensure that your team doesn't get carried away. They must wait for my word before enacting the second plan. I'm still hopeful it won't be necessary."

"Nothing will happen without your say so, Mr. President. I can see how carefully you've considered all aspects of our operations."

Aleyev sat forward and clasped his hands in front of him. His most presidential pose.

"Yes, Yuri. I have considered everything. You would do well to remember that."

The director of the FSB rose and nodded.

"Thank you, sir."

Varkov turned and walked briskly out of the room. The president's final words had only succeeded in raising his fears. But there was no turning back now.

Chapter 28

PRESIDENT JEFFERSON BLAKE

"You look concerned, Mr. President."

"I am concerned, Abe. Cynthia Ford will be joining us in a moment. I want her view, as NSA, of our security arrangements for the summit."

Abe Peterson looked his president directly in the eye. He didn't feel threatened by others checking his practices, and he held National Security Advisor, Cynthia Ford, in high esteem, but he wasn't used to his arrangements being questioned.

"Don't look so worried, old friend. It's not you or your work. Something has come up," said Jefferson Blake.

"May I…"

"Of course, you can ask, Abe. I've just come from the Situation Room. That idiot, Aleyev, has ordered his people to board a Turkish ship in the Black Sea. It's part of his plan to quarantine Ukraine."

"But Turkey…"

"Is a NATO country."

The buzzer sounded, interrupting their conversion. Sandra

Scully, the president's personal secretary, stuck her head around the Oval Office door.

"Sorry to interrupt, Mr. President. Cynthia Ford is here to see you."

"Show her in please, Sandra."

"Yes, sir."

The door remained open and NSA Cynthia Ford strode directly in. She was dressed in a dark business suit, white shirt, and her ever practical flat-heeled shoes.

"Well, that was quite a shit show downstairs, Mr. President... oh, hello Abe."

"Good morning, Cynthia."

Ford sat down on the same sofa as Peterson.

"Are you sticking to your guns, Mr. President, or should I say in this case, sticking to your 'not guns'?"

Blake glanced over to Abe Peterson, whose crinkled face exposed his confusion.

"I should clarify, Abe," he began. "Several of the joint chiefs would like to see us enter the situation in the Black Sea with all guns blazing, to make a point."

"Or start a war," added Ford.

"Would I be out of line to say that's a worry?" asked Peterson.

"Not in the slightest, Abe," replied the president. "While part of me would love to put Vadim Aleyev out of our misery, I can't help but feel that's just what he wants us to do."

"Forgive my ignorance. This is far out of my wheelhouse, but what about the traditional proportional response?" asked Peterson.

Blake nodded towards Cynthia Ford to field the question.

"Normally, yes, that's how the US would respond. Send a

message of equivalent force. But this situation is different. Given the Russians' special operation in Ukraine, and their threatening behaviors along other borders, even the slightest military response could trigger the war we've been trying to avoid."

"You mean world war?" asked Peterson.

"So, Abe, this is where you come in," said the president. "With the summit being so close, everyone has agreed we hold off until I can talk directly with Aleyev. In the meantime, we'll increase sanctions and tighten the stranglehold on the Russian economy. That means the pressure on the summit security has probably just doubled. I have zero trust that Vadim Aleyev won't try to even the odds at that meeting."

"You consider it likely an assassination attempt will be made on your life, Mr. President?" asked Peterson.

"Possible to probable," responded Ford.

"Over my dead body," replied Peterson.

"I'd prefer both our bodies to come out of the summit intact," said the president. "So, I've requested Cynthia go over some of the arrangements with you, Abe, keeping the current international volatilities in mind."

"Of course, sir, not a problem."

Cynthia Ford edged forward on the couch and turned towards Peterson.

"Abe, you've been in direct contact with your opposite number in the Kremlin?"

"Yes, Director Viktor Sidorov."

"What's your take on the man?" she asked.

"He's reserved, but thus far, seems like a straight shooter."

Jefferson Blake laughed. "Perhaps you could have phrased that better, my friend."

Peterson smiled.

"What have you shared with Sidorov so far?" asked Ford.

"We've exchanged the standard outline of security arrangements that we usually share with foreign services when planning a combined operation out of the US."

"I imagine there's a great deal they still won't know about how we do business," said Ford.

"We do have a few tricks up our sleeve. There is little chance they'll get to you, Mr. President," said Peterson.

"But not 'no chance'," observed the president.

"It's never 'no chance', sir."

"Point taken," said Blake. "Now, I assume you passed on the intel regarding the chatter we picked up re the possibility of a hit team in Estonia?

"Yes, sir."

"What was Sidorov's reaction to the information?" inquired Blake.

"There was almost no reaction, Mr. President. Sidorov is one cool customer, he's not likely to give anything away in an exchange with me."

"But?" asked Ford.

"My bet is he had no idea about the situation. I informed Sidorov at the beginning of what was scheduled to be a fairly lengthy online meeting. Ten minutes into the session, he begged off, saying he needed to gather some more intel on the Russian preparations before we could continue."

"You don't think that was the case?" asked Ford.

"I'm certain it wasn't the case," replied Peterson. "The information I required was on the agenda we'd established together two weeks earlier."

"You're a clever operator, Abe," said the president. "You

knew Sidorov couldn't sit on the hit team intel for long. Nice set up."

Cynthia Ford chuckled.

"Well played, Abe. But there's one additional aspect I believe we need to consider, Mr. President."

"Go on, Cynthia."

"We should think further down the line. What would happen if an assassin took you out? What would happen if an assassin took Aleyev out? What would be the repercussions? What would the political landscape look like then?"

"Thanks for lightening up my day, Cynthia." Blake chuckled.

"Sorry, sir. But we need to think this through. Our intelligence suggests that there may be some Russian generals in positions of influence who are less than happy with the direction Aleyev is taking the country."

"Are they in a position to do anything about it? Can they depose him? Can they remove him?" asked the president.

"It depends how you define 'remove,'" replied Ford. "But the bottom line is, we believe they will do nothing while Aleyev remains so powerful. His personal network, which he started building back in his KGB and FSB days, is too strong. It threads like a cancer through the Kremlin's power structure. President Aleyev has been clear about his attitude to betrayal throughout his career."

"Oppose me and die," said Peterson.

"Essentially yes," responded Ford. "And he has the track record to prove it."

"If I go down, the US will maintain its current position. What would either the Russians or the Chinese have to gain?"

"Possibly confusion, sir. There would be a domestic demand for an instant reaction. You've already said that some of the joint chiefs are biting at the bit. Will the current vice president have the strength and guile to oppose them? Many an attack has exploited the enemy's confused state. Our country would grieve for its president and fear the threat to our democracy. While only momentary in terms of history, there would be an opportunity for an enemy to take advantage."

"Well then, don't grieve too long," said Blake, a tinge of irony in his voice. "What about if Aleyev goes down?"

"For the US, Mr. President, that's probably a win. There is a possibility his successor may not be as internationally aggressive. It's not a guaranteed outcome, however. You might have a window of opportunity to weave your negotiating magic."

"Forgive me airing such a thought out loud, Mr. President," began Peterson. "But with my Secret Service hat squarely on my shoulders, I must consider all possible outcomes. As unlikely as it is, what if an assassin takes out both you and the Russian president?"

The room dissolved into a stony silence.

Eventually.

"Then we're all fucked," declared Ford.

"All right then," announced the president. "I'm going to leave you two to go over the security arrangements. I don't need to tell you that there is more riding on this summit than possibly any other high-level meeting in US history. Your diligence may well save our country and the world from stepping into a frightening abyss."

Chapter 29

LACHLAN BYRN

It was going to take two trips over a couple of days. That wasn't a problem. Byrn had time.

The first trip would be the riskiest. He'd procured a small tender from a fishing trawler moored off the coast just west of the submarine base. Byrn had monitored the trawler's lack of use for forty-eight hours before swimming out after sunset on the third day to procure it. The assassin planned on returning the boat before sunrise. Minimizing your trail was as important to a professional as enabling a successful hit.

He'd returned with the craft to the shore and loaded his supplies. These were things you just couldn't swim with. Now, with the dark of night as his shield, Byrn slowly rowed toward the abandoned base. The light wind supplemented the brushing of the waves against the wooden hull to provide a meditative backdrop to his heavy breathing. He slowly guided the boat closer to his target.

An hour into the journey, the unmistakable outline of the submarine base appeared silhouetted by the moonlight. There was more brightness than Byrn would have liked, but he couldn't afford any more time sitting around waiting until the ideal conditions presented themselves.

Pausing his rowing, he scanned the horizon and listened for anything unexpected. Nature provided the only soundscape, and the assassin noted no sign of human activity.

Perfect.

Two hundred yards west of the base, Byrn held his starboard oar still in the water while continuing to row with the port. When the boat had turned a neat ninety degrees, Byrn resumed rowing with both oars, heading directly for the beach.

As the bow nudged up on the gravelly sand, Byrn jumped out and pulled the craft further ashore. This was his most exposed moment, so haste was everything. He reached into the dinghy and grabbed the first of three bags of supplies. The heaviest. The assassin heaved the bag up into his arms and carried it like a forklift towards the trees.

After stashing the load just inside the tree line, Byrn returned for the other two loads, each one progressively lighter.

Now the boat was empty, the immediate pressure was off. Byrn retreated three hundred yards into the trees and dug a shallow hole. When he was satisfied with the result, he returned to the forest edge and retrieved his bags, one at a time. After placing them in the hole and covering it with dirt and ground cover, he buried his spade with his hands.

Lachlan Byrn then jogged down to the beach, pushed the boat out from the shore, and began rowing. Small white caps had appeared across the water. The wind had picked up while he'd been completing his tasks. A pleasantly light mist sprayed the assassin's face as he headed back toward the trawler.

Everything in Byrn's world was a balance of probabilities.

The assassin considered it improbable that anyone would locate his forest stash in the twenty-four hours it would remain there. If he'd attempted to conceal his equipment somewhere on the abandoned base's actual structure, the chances of detection would have increased significantly.

Lachlan Byrn always played the shortest odds.

Chapter 30

Byrn awoke early in the afternoon.

The assassin felt the same edginess he always experienced as a kill approached. It was tinged with slight apprehension. He knew he'd spend the next hour revisiting all his planning, just to be sure he'd covered every possibility.

After that came the expectancy.

This job was different from most. There would be a delay between his current actions and the kill itself. That said, after today there was no going back.

Lachlan Byrn never went back.

Byrn's first task was to go through the house. Every surface he may have inadvertently left a fingerprint, or an element of DNA on had to be cleaned. After ninety minutes had passed, he was satisfied his presence in the dwelling had been extinguished.

He then loaded his remaining belongings into his backpack and climbed onto the Kawasaki. He'd enjoyed the bike. It would be a shame to destroy it. Byrn jumped on, revved the engine, and then headed south.

Lehtmetsa was a small village in Järva County. The assassin turned off Perila-Janeda and passed through the tiny settlement before venturing down a series of side roads. Eventually, he found the old farmhouse he'd located in his earlier research. Next to the house was a large wooden barn. The building contained most of the farm implements used on the land. Amongst them, Byrn had noted two KTM trail bikes parked near the entrance. They currently stood leaning on their stands in front of the other farm equipment. To Byrn, they appeared dusty and accessible, like working bikes. Just what he had in mind.

After checking that the KTMs were still there, Byrn proceeded down the dirt road and into the forest about a mile and a half away. He rode another mile into the woods before the track ran out. He then ventured down an over-grown walking trail. Three hundred yards down the trail, Byrn came to a small clearing. He looked around. Tall pine and spruce trees surrounded the space formed a large green wall protecting the tiny dell from the outside world.

Perfect.

Byrn climbed off the Kawasaki and laid it on the ground. Placing his backpack a safe distance away, he used his hands and feet to rake up sounding leaves before scattering them all over the motorcycle. When he was done, he plonked down on the dirt and waited.

Nearly an hour later, the assassin was satisfied that the darkness had fully enveloped the forest. He leaned over, reached into his backpack, and retrieved a container of petrol. He got up, walked over to the bike, and doused the petrol liberally over the machine and the leaves. He then pulled a lighter out of his pocket, bent down, picked up a leaf, lit it, and flicked it onto the small pyre.

The flames soared up into the night but didn't reach above the surrounding trees. The area of cleared space around the fire would keep it from spreading into the surrounding forest. Byrn waited a few moments until the flames had peaked before grabbing his backpack and retracing his route.

It would be a long walk back to the farmhouse.

An hour later, Byrn sat crouched behind a large bush near the barn. He watched the house carefully. Two lights had been turned on in the dwelling. The highest probability was that one or two individuals were inside. Byrn waited until the occupants were settled before sneaking into the barn.

He risked a brief flicker on his flashlight to assess each KTM. Both trail bikes appeared to be in good condition. It came as no surprise to Byrn that the key remained in the ignition of each. Most farmers were more worried about losing their keys than having their machines stolen. It saved Byrn the trouble of hot wiring.

Byrn checked inside each bike's fuel tank. One nearly empty, one almost full. That made the decision for him. He grabbed the bars of the bike with the full tank, kicked its stand back into its home position, and wheeled it outside.

No one came out of the house. No dogs barked. No one was going to stop him now.

Byrn pushed the KTM several hundred yards up the road before throwing his leg over the seat. The bike started at the first kick.

The assassin rode off into the night.

The trees of the Lahemaa Rahvuspark towered above the road on either side as Byrn sped along the asphalt. Although slower than the Kawasaki, the KTM was the superior machine for Byrn's purposes. The assassin was pleased how the exchange had panned out. Reconnaissance and forward planning were everything.

The next phase of the Byrn's plan involved making a difficult decision. If Byrn left the KTM too near the submarine base, he risked it being discovered when the Russian security team scoped the area for threats. If he played safe and hid the machine further away, there was a danger the greater distance would render it ineffectual. Like everything in Lachlan Byrn's world, this was a calculated judgement.

Three miles before reaching the water's edge, the assassin did as he had done earlier, venturing off the highway onto a dirt path that eventually led to a more secluded hiking trail. Byrn hid the bike in a clump of trees, again screening it with leaves and fallen foliage. This time he didn't set a fire.

It was a while before Byrn made it down to the water. Once he got his bearings, he backtracked to the spot he'd dug the hole and buried his equipment the night before. The assassin was fortunate to have enough moonlight to navigate the forest without a flashlight. He retrieved his small shovel, uncovered his three bags, and began the process of hauling them back down to the beach.

Zhen Su's intel indicated the facility should now be temporarily closed to tourists, and the Russian security team wouldn't secure the abandoned submarine base for another forty-eight hours. Zhen's schedule had stated that the full security sweep of the area would take place twenty-four hours after the initial team had arrived. At that point, the Hara base would become an impregnable fortress.

Byrn had a limited window of opportunity. Unfazed, the assassin glanced at his watch. Plenty of time remained before sunrise to complete the tasks at hand.

Byrn grabbed the heaviest bag and traipsed along the small beach. Before rounding the point, he paused and peered cautiously around the headland toward the submarine base. He scanned the foreshore first, finally allowing his gaze to drift along the full length of the pier.

Nothing.

Ever prudent, Byrn edged his way toward the facility, remaining in the forest shadows that ran parallel to the sand. A few minutes later, he scrutinized the entire area one more time. From his point of concealment, the assassin stood less than thirty yards from the structure that housed the small harbor office. As expected, the lights were out, and no sound emanated from the building. It was highly likely the office would be manned twenty-four seven when the Russian team arrived on site.

Satisfied, Byrn jogged down to the end of the pier. Now more exposed to the weather, the sea air stabbed like darts of ice against his face, although the wet suit he wore retained body heat. He continued along the pier until he came to the building he'd scoped out weeks earlier. Once inside, he checked all the entry points.

Relieved to finally get the heavy bag off his back, he placed it down on the metal grating that ran over the length of the pit on the building's western side. He then scurried toward the far entrance on the northern seaward end. Before passing through the doorway, he paused, listening for any untoward sound. He heard only waves and wind. The breeze seemed to be picking up, but that should have no impact on the operation.

The assassin then prowled the final length of the pier. As he passed the second smaller structure, he glanced inside. He saw nothing, nor did he expect to. He went as far as he could before turning back to the shore. There was a great deal to accomplish before the sun rose.

He'd made it five yards further along the pier when he heard a scraping sound, like a boot on gravel. The assassin spun.

"*Stoy, kto ty, chert voz'mi*? Who the fuck are you?"

Dressed in combat fatigues, Byrn immediately recognized his accoster. Even in the moonlight, the red, white and gold insignia of the Russian National Guard was evident on the soldier's sleeve, as was the AS Val subsonic suppressed assault rifle in his hands.

Zhen's intel had been wrong.

"*Kas sa räägid eesti keelt*? Do you speak Estonian?" asked Byrn.

"*Net*. No."

Byrn was relieved, because he didn't either, but he was playing for additional seconds.

"English?" he asked.

"*Nekotoryy*, some," the guard responded.

Byrn took a step closer. The soldier held his weapon high, pointing it directly at Byrn's chest.

"*Net*."

The assassin raised his arms in submission.

"I've been sent by the harbor master to ensure the structure is safe before the president's..." Mid-sentence Byrn noted the increased tension in the soldier's shoulder muscles. He was going to shoot.

In a combined movement, Byrn lifted his left foot and sent it pounding into the soldier's groin while simultaneously grabbing the rifle's barrel and yanking it from the man's hands. Throughout the action, he stared fixedly into his opponent's eyes.

After he'd established control of the weapon, the assassin used his momentum to spin around and smash the rifle's butt against the side of the soldier's face. Although dazed, the man was highly trained and reached into a scabbard on his belt. Byrn noted the flash of steel in the moonlight as his opponent brought the blade to bear. Byrn head-butted his opponent, dropped the rifle, and grabbed the soldier's knife wrist with both hands. Pivoting, the assassin now presented his back to the guard. He pressed his thumbs down into the man's wrist, working the weapon free. It clanged to the ground.

Byrn's mind raced. Two things were paramount if the operation was to continue. This warrior must die quickly and quietly, and his death must appear like an accident. In the meantime, he couldn't be allowed to call for help.

Byrn used his right elbow to jab backward into the guard's solar plexus before pivoting again. With his opponent now doubled over, Byrn stepped forward. He stooped down and threw his arms around the guard's torso in a bear hug. The assassin squeezed tightly, forcing the air out of the man's lungs. The soldier fought and struggled, but Byrn held him in a vice-like grip. His proximity to the soldier's body rendered his opponent's limbs useless as weapons.

The assassin had complete control now.

Abruptly, Byrn removed his arms from around the soldier. As he did, he repeatedly pummeled the man hard in the gut, winding him badly. Before his victim knew what was happening, Byrn turned him, launched his left arm over his neck, and locked it tightly, pulling his own wrist with his right hand. He walked the soldier rearwards until they both teetered on the edge of the pier. Byrn drew a deep breath before diving backwards into the water, his arm still gripping his attacker's neck. Like a noose.

The man flailed wildly, just as Byrn expected him to. This would come down to the assassin's ability to maintain control of his prisoner while outlasting him underwater. That's why he'd winded his victim before they'd entered the water together. Part of Byrn's Special Boat Service training had been in extended freediving. Slowly, the soldier's movements became weaker. Byrn held his captive tight but craned his head around to catch a glimpse of his face. Despite the murky water, he saw the soldier's eyes bulge in fear as he realized the futility of his struggle. The soldier made one last desperate attempt for freedom, trying in vain to punch Byrn's face over his shoulders.

Byrn gave the warrior credit for his attempts, until the credit ran out.

Finally, the guardsman's movements waned into listlessness. His lungs yielded, forcing the involuntary opening of his mouth. The seawater rushed in. Byrn held on. A few spasms and then the man's limbs stopped moving altogether. Byrn waited, clasping his victim's body close to his own while lurking six feet below the surface. Once he'd ensured the man's lungs had expunged all his air, Byrn released his hold. The soldier's body hung listlessly, suspended in the icy cold water.

Now having reached his own limit, Byrn swam to the surface, inhaling the fresh air as he broke through the waves. He scanned the structure above him and down to the shore. There was no movement. Byrn hauled himself up onto the pier and caught his breath. He stared down at the water's surface. The assassin felt no remorse about the life he'd just taken. Working for bad people is a choice that entwines one's destiny with their employer. This man had met his fate. It was black and white. There was no gray.

There was never any gray.

Any autopsy or examination of the Russian National Guardsman's body would reveal saltwater in the lungs and facial bruising resulting from the jagged stones and rocks at the side of the pier. In the high wind, the man miss-stepped and fell into the water, knocking himself unconscious on the rocks as he fell. A simple accident.

The immediate threat was resolved, but the number of Russian security troops present at the facility remained uncertain. Byrn walked briskly back to the torpedo room where he'd deposited his bag, pushed it into a corner, strode up to the southern doorway, and waited.

Nothing happened.

The assassin allowed fifteen minutes to pass before continuing his preparations. He could allow no more. He had no doubt that other Russian personnel were stationed somewhere on the abandoned base. The most likely scenario was that there would be only one or two others. They were clearly an advance party sent to watch over rather than secure the facility now that the public had no access. Byrn figured they would be running their watch in shifts, but the key question was how long was each shift? That was a question Byrn couldn't answer. He also needed to find out where any remaining guards may be positioned. He'd need to find an answer to that question before even considering resuming work.

The harbor office. That was clearly the most likely base of operations for the security team.

The assassin padded carefully down the pier toward the shore and the office. He reached the building undetected. Keeping low, he stalked the wall of the structure, checking out ingress and egress points. He returned to the main door and tried the doorknob. It turned silently. Byrn eased it open. Instantly, his suspicions were confirmed.

Snoring. Loud and nasally.

Byrn stole quietly into the room. Three stretcher beds had been laid out randomly across the floor. Two of them were occupied. Byrn could kill both men in their sleep without difficulty, but there was no point. One drowned corpse may be regarded as an accident. Three dead soldiers and the Russian president's visit to the base would probably be called off.

That meant Byrn's operation would have to be abandoned. It also meant he wouldn't yet be free of his Chinese tormentors.

No. The assassin would let these men live. The pragmatic decision gave him no pleasure.

Byrn eased himself out of the room, closed the door gently, and went back to work. If there was no shift change until sunrise, he still stood a chance of success. If either Russian left the building before sunrise, his plan was destined to fail.

Chapter 31

Even in the best laid plans, moments of potential exposure couldn't be totally avoided. For Lachlan Byrn, this was the time that concerned him most. He'd have to make some noise to complete his preparations. That wouldn't really have been an issue if the submarine base had been completely abandoned as predicted, but of course, now it wasn't.

Damn Zhen Su and his inaccurate intelligence.

Byrn decided to press on as though no one was there. If he worked too slowly, concentrated too much on being quiet, or interrupted his progress to check on the sleeping Russin guardsmen, then all would be lost, anyway.

Victory favors the bold... or the mad.

Byrn had chosen the exact location within the building on his daytime reconnaissance. He'd counted down the number of small foxholes in the walkway next to the grate until he came to the one whose metal hatch appeared totally secure. The rusted bolts holding the hatch down had probably not been moved for years. Neither had the two wooden crossbars than ran across the hatch, double securing it. It seemed unlikely any presidential security team would tamper with an object that clearly hadn't been touched for decades.

Byrn was betting his life on it.

Now perched in the pit beside his chosen foxhole, Byrn calculated where the height of the foxhole floor would be in relation to where he currently crouched. Based on the few exposed foxholes, he estimated that each was approximately three feet and a half deep. That meant the foxhole floor was just a couple of inches higher than the channel pit's base, indicating that one would have to bend down to observe any irregularity in the wall.

Having retrieved his final two bags from the beach, the assassin had all his relevant equipment laid out around him. He reached down and grabbed the hand drill. Ten minutes later, he'd drilled eight holes directly into the mortar that glued the old rock wall together. He replaced the drill and withdrew a small plastic container from one of the bags. He opened it before grabbing a large syringe that lay next to the drill. Inserting the syringe into the container, he filled it with the yellowish liquid. He then inserted the syringe's needle into one of the holes, filling it almost entirely. Byrn knew the muriatic acid would instantly begin softening the aging mortar. He repeated the process seven times.

Byrn inhaled deeply. The next step was unavoidably noisy but had to be done.

The assassin wrapped his fingers around the small pick next to him and began scraping the mortar away. Much of it gave way easily, but eventually he hit a solid layer. He gave it half a dozen hard pecks before pausing for a reaction from outside.

Nothing.

The rising wind was certainly working in Byrn's favor. He glanced at his watch. With only two hours until sunrise, and no doubt the change of guard, he would not be stopping again. The assassin began fervently picking away at the mortar.

Thirty minutes later, Byrn pushed one of the loosened stones into the foxhole and reached his arm through the hole in the wall. He felt around until his fingers touched the cubicle's concrete base a few inches below his incision.

Perfect.

A short time after that, there was a breach in the stone wall just big enough for Byrn to squeeze through. He shone his flashlight through the hole. What he saw pleased him. He gathered up his tools and equipment, placed everything back in the bags, and pushed them through the gap. After shoving them to one side, Byrn looked around his work area. He retrieved all the broken and crushed mortar and swept it into a bag, which he then shoved through the opening. The assassin then used his fingers to brush away any evidence remaining. He then allowed himself a moment to fully scan the surroundings, ensuring no trace of his presence remained. Byrn clambered carefully through the opening in the wall. The fit was tight around his hips, but with a bit of wriggling, he made it.

Once inside the foxhole, the assassin inspected it with his flashlight. The space was small, not more than a yard square and just over forty inches high. There was barely room for Byrn and his equipment, but he'd get by. This tiny cubicle would either be his home for the next few days, or if he was discovered, it would become his grave.

Again, the assassin glanced at his watch. Time was pressing.

Now it was all about speed and efficiency. Byrn began by retrieving a tube of quarter inch black poly piping from his bag. He cut it into appropriate lengths, matching the width of the wall plus a few inches. He placed two at the bottom of the hole.

Byrn then retrieved a small plastic pre-measured container of water from one of his bags. He removed the lid, reached back into the bag and pulled out a soft plastic pouch, sealed at the top. He undid the seal and poured the quick dry mortar into the water. He mixed it up with a spatula and began applying it over the exposed stone edge and the poly pipe. He ladled enough mortar to fill most of the space, but not enough to bulge out into the channel pit. Small gaps in the mortar may not be noticed, but new cement flowing from the stonework could draw unwanted attention.

He then placed the previously removed rocks on top of the layer of mortar. He double checked to ensure the rocks hadn't squashed the piping closed.

All good.

Byrn repeated the process on the next row, but this time, he added three rows of tubing. The top tier of rocks was augmented by two more tubes before replacing the stones. The moment the final stone was in place, Byrn felt a foreboding sense of claustrophobia. It wasn't unexpected. He'd deal with it later.

Satisfied with his work, Byrn reached back into a different bag and retrieved another tube. This one was unlike the others. The beam of the flashlight revealed a coil of tubing with a slightly wider end. With all sounds outside the pit heavily muffled, the night vision borescope would help the assassin monitor the outside world. He shoved the semi-ridged device through one of the tubes of poly pipe. The fit was snug, but still functional. He checked the vision on the small screen. Equipped with two-way articulation to cover different angles, the picture, although not great, was adequate. It would provide Byrn with some idea of what events took place outside his hide.

The smallness of the oxygen holes was a concern, but they couldn't be any larger and remain concealed. Byrn had calculated that the difference in air pressure between inside the foxhole and outside would aid an adequate flow of air through the holes. If he ran into strife, he had two re-breathers as backup, which would help him in replacing any oxygen he used. Byrn didn't want to resort to them as they were allocated for another purpose.

Byrn's final act was to open his third bag and take out the small bucket shaped chemical toilet, his food rations, and his supply of bottled water.

One last time, the assassin shone the flashlight at his watch. The sun would be rising outside, and the missing guard would soon be noticed and presumably his body discovered.

From this point on, Byrn would allow himself no sleep. The occasional light doze would be permissible, but nothing deep enough to withdraw himself from the ability to respond quickly in changing circumstances. He reached into a pocket inside one of the bags, his fingers touching a small plastic vial. He pulled it out, opened it, and popped two tablets. His old friend, modafinil, the Night Eagle would see him through. He yanked a thermal blanket out of the same bag, wrapped it around himself and waited.

For most people, surviving for several days in the conditions in which Byrn now existed would be intolerable. The claustrophobia, the darkness, the lack of amenity and above all the uncertainty, would overwhelm them.

But Lachlan Byrn had been trained to withstand and survive these exact conditions. Several years of captivity and torture at the hands of the enemy will do that to you. Byrn realized that those dark memories would probably haunt him over the next few days. He'd prepared himself for the ride. If they couldn't kill him then, this wouldn't kill him now.

He knew they were there, yet he couldn't see them, nor touch them.

The walls.

They hid like malevolent sentries behind a veil of darkness. There was no escape, no relief. The damp bricks entombed him like a rat in a stone cage. Or was it the darkness that entombed him? Perhaps the darkness coiled inside him like a snake awaiting its moment, anticipating its prey.

The rat.

It didn't matter. He was beyond caring. The blackness now wrapped him in its cold merciless arms. There would be no light... ever. There would be no freedom... ever.

When there is no light, seek solace in the darkness.

The black cloud enveloped him, rising through his body, penetrating every pore, every muscle, every artery, every thought, until his mind became a dusky shadow. Somber. Devoid of activity. Moment by moment the glacial numbness slithered through his flesh and bones.

You become the darkness. You are the darkness.

Byrn jolted himself awake.

Fuck Zhen Su and his miserable miscreants.

The irony wasn't lost on Byrn. The assassin had chosen to imprison himself in pursuit of the holy grail of freedom.

Chapter 32

The Whitehouse, Washington DC

PRESIDENT JEFFERSON BLAKE

President Jefferson Blake studied the man sitting on the other side of his oval office desk. He trusted no one more, both in terms of loyalty and competence.

"Are you satisfied with the security arrangements, Abe?"

Abe Peterson frowned as he considered his boss' question.

"As much as I can be, Mr. President, and probably as much as I'll ever be."

"What do you mean, my old friend?"

"Well, sir, there is an outline of the plans in that folder. Everything is as it should be. The Estonian government is providing over three thousand police and soldiers to ensure the security of the event. As per our usual protocol when traveling overseas, the Secret Service personnel accompanying you have been documented and their firearms registered with the Estonian authorities. Our people will be with you at all times, Mr. President."

"So, your problem is?"

"The Russians have exactly the same arrangement with the

Estonians. Their security team and their weapons are also documented."

"That makes sense," Blake responded.

"Yes, sir, it does. But it does mean that when you and President Aleyev are sitting down together, in the same room, armed Russian agents will also be present. I can't really get my head around Russian personnel carrying weapons being in such proximity to our president."

Blake sat back in his chair and chuckled.

"You're a very hard man to make happy, Abe. I wonder if Aleyev's security guy, what was his name?"

"Sidorov, Viktor Sidorov."

"Yes, Sidorov. I wonder if he's having the same conversation with his boss."

"More than likely, sir."

"It seems to me we only have two choices, Abe. Everyone is armed, or no one is armed. And I'm willing to bet you'd also be unhappy if I entered that room with no armed security."

"That would be unacceptable, Mr. President."

"Of course it would, Abe. So, it's going to come down to who is the quickest."

"Mr. President?"

"If one of their men pulls out a gun to shoot me, one of ours will need to be quicker on the draw to take the Russian down."

The president laughed at his gallows humor.

"I'm glad you think that's funny, Mr. President." Although he was trying to scowl, Abe Peterson couldn't avoid a slight smirk.

"Just to confirm, Abe, there's been no more talk of an assassination attempt on either president?"

"No, sir, that trail has gone cold. The CIA believe it was

171

a red herring. They hold the view that with such elaborate security, no one man could make much of a difference."

The president raised his eyebrows.

"I wonder how our recently departed Secretary of Defense would feel about that statement. Anyway, let's move on. Abe. Tell me about the schedule."

"It's pretty straightforward, sir. There will be two days of summit meetings held over a three-day period. The first meeting on day one will essentially be between you and President Aleyev, with a couple of support personnel from either side. A kind of 'getting to know you' moment."

Blake nodded.

"Later that afternoon, there'll be a more formal meeting that will include the two presidents and a much larger delegation from both countries. On our team will include the Secretary of State, the National Security Advisor, the Under Secretary of State for Political Affairs, the United States Ambassador to Russia and two National Security Council Russian advisors."

"And the Russians?"

"Pretty much the same or equivalent, Mr. President. Accompanying President Aleyev will be the Russian Foreign Affairs Minister, Pavel Fedorov, The Russian Ambassador to the United States and a few others."

President Blake scratched his chin.

"I'm glad Fedorov will be there. I met him once, at a function here in DC, before I was president and before he'd been appointed foreign minister. He seemed like a reasonable man, more moderate than Aleyev. Both Cynthia and I had been concerned he might have been sidelined, but his appearance at the summit may indicate otherwise."

"And appearance may be what it's all about," commented

Cynthia Ford as she entered the room. Both men had been expecting her.

"You think Fedorov is just there for show, Cynthia?" Blake waved at her to pull up another chair.

"I fear so, Mr. President," she responded. "Our intelligence suggests the foreign minister doesn't hold a strong voice in government policy, either domestic or foreign. Aleyev prefers to control the strings himself."

"We'll have to see how that one pans out on the day. The meetings were originally planned to be over two days, it's now three. What's the team's latest thinking about that, Cynthia?"

"Has Abe filled you in on the schedule, sir?"

"We'd just completed day one," said Peterson.

"Please, don't let me interrupt," Ford responded.

Peterson leaned forward.

"Day two is outwardly more about ceremony. Mr. President, you'll have an opportunity to meet with the Estonian President and Prime Minister. The meeting will provide you with a chance to thank them for hosting the summit. There is an official dinner that night for all delegates, and then day three consists of a third meeting with the larger groups and, if all goes well, a combined press conference."

"Let's backtrack to the term 'outwardly' Abe. I suspect there's going to be a little more at play here, isn't there?" said the president.

"If you don't mind, Abe, I'll take that one," said Ford.

Peterson nodded.

"The Estonians are extremely concerned about Russia's recent behavior," she began. "They don't want to go back to the good old Soviet days in any form. Amongst their security forces, they'll put people on the ground gleaning whatever information they can that may aid the US in our negotiations."

"Spies," suggested Blake. "Not very neutral of them, is it?"

"They're more worried than neutral, Mr. President," said Ford.

"Okay, I can live with that, but something tells me you've got a little more up your sleeve, Cynthia," said President Blake.

"It may be something, it may be nothing, sir."

"Go on."

"There's some talk that the reluctant generals we spoke about last time may be growing more restless. Probably not enough to ignite any action yet, but there is definitely trouble brewing in the ranks."

Ford took a breath.

"So, the real reason for the extra day during the summit is for us to gather intel on Russia and receive feedback from the Estonian security team's observations of the generals' visit to the abandoned Hara submarine base. We understand the generals are making a special trip to Estonia so Aleyev can show them the base, bring the Soviet memories to life, and perhaps inspire their commitment. The Russian president requested that day personally."

"Then we resume the meeting on day three fully informed, and possibly even pull a rabbit out of the hat. You people really know your shit," said Blake.

"An official presidential commendation," replied Ford.

Peterson smiled. But he still wasn't happy.

There was too much that could go wrong.

Chapter 33

The Kremlin, Moscow

PRESIDENT VADIM ALEYEV

"Everything is in place, Viktor?"

"Yes, Mr. President," replied Sidorov. "You have the meeting schedule in front of you and the special agenda for the second day has been arranged as you requested."

"Very good, Viktor. Let's go over that."

"Yes, Mr. President." Despite his day-to-day contact with Vadim Aleyev, Sidorov was always slightly in awe, perhaps even fear, when sitting across the desk from his president.

"The generals are flying into Lennart Meri Tallinn Airport by private plane early in the morning and will join you at the Hara submarine station at 12 noon. Once your meeting and tour are concluded, they'll head straight back to the airport and return to Moscow."

"Excellent, Viktor. You've made arrangements for me to lead the tour?"

"As you requested, Mr. President. There will be Russian and Estonian security personnel accompanying you."

"That is fine, but please ensure the Estonians keep their

distance."

"Of course, sir."

"And what have you arranged after the generals leave?"

"Again, as per your request, Mr. President, we've scheduled a two-hour break where you may wander about the facility at your leisure and take a hot meal undisturbed at the harbor office."

"I can always count on you to deliver, Viktor. You do your job well. We're both aware there are many dissidents out there," Aleyev waved his hand dismissively, "who would like to see the end of me."

"Not on my watch, Mr. President."

"Let's talk about the late afternoon."

Sidorov nodded.

"At exactly 3 p.m. Ms. Kristiina Volk has been requested to make herself known to our people at the harbor office. She will then be escorted down to meet you at the first building on the pier, the torpedo room, as you asked."

"When Ms. Volk arrives, she is to be treated with the utmost courtesy and respect, Viktor."

"I shall see to it myself, Mr. President."

"Again, excellent. Now I have one more request."

Sidorov sensed his shoulders sag. What now?

"Yes, sir."

"Once you've brought Ms. Volk to me, you are to take the guardsmen and leave."

"I beg your pardon, sir. You wish us to leave you unattended in a foreign location. This is most unusual."

"Relax, Viktor, and I will forgive your impertinence. This is a personal request from me, I think I need say no more. You may, however, station guards at the end of the pier, out of earshot."

Every instinct in Sidorov's body snapped to alert. Despite his concerns, he was aware that to hesitate would mean he would be replaced in his position by the end of the day.

"Of course, sir. It will be arranged just as you've requested."

"Is there anything else, Sidorov?"

Sidorov, not Viktor. His hesitancy had been noted.

"There is one more small matter. I even hesitate to bring it up."

"Continue."

"There was an incident at the submarine base yesterday. You are aware we've taken possession of the facility in anticipation of your visit."

The president nodded.

Sidorov continued. "We sent in a light advance team, just to keep accidental interlopers away. There was only three men. They each took eight-hour shifts. It would appear the man on the night shift met with an accident."

"What sort of accident?"

"He drowned."

"The circumstances?"

"The winds rose overnight; we suspect the guardsman slipped and fell into the water. He was discovered the next morning floating near the beach. A complete field autopsy was performed immediately. Seawater was found in his lungs and his face was bruised, indicating a fall."

"Was the man sober?"

"A small trace of alcohol was detected in his system and a hip flask was found in his coat. All three men had hip flasks to help ward off the cold."

"And your reaction, Viktor?"

Viktor.

"The two remaining men have been returned to their Moscow barracks for disciplinary action. The full advance security team has since arrived at the base. They've been over the facility and surrounding area with a fine toothcomb, including an electronic sweep. No irregularities were uncovered."

"Then there is nothing for me to worry about?"

"No, Mr. President. The facility is secure."

"So, *you* say Viktor. Double up the security arrangements anyway. Please ensure that the remaining two guardsmen are shipped off to an appropriate penal colony, well clear of Moscow. The families of all three men should have all pensions or financial benefits canceled. See that the guardsmen's colleagues are clearly informed of their fate."

"It will be done, Mr. President.

Vadim Aleyev smiled, again the Arctic wolf. He was not a man who tolerated incompetence.

"That will be all, Sidorov. Our plans do not change. We leave for Estonia tomorrow."

Chapter 34

LACHLAN BYRN

The water wept in droplets, like blood from the sky. Slowly, excruciatingly slowly.

He didn't know how much time had passed. Time had become a meaningless value. The minutes, hours, days, not even the months and years meant anything anymore. His future, past and present, now merged into one ongoing cesspit of pain and despondency. Although, if he was honest with himself, true despair abandoned him long ago. To plummet into the depths of despondence required grief. He could no longer imagine what he might be grieving for. It certainly wasn't hope. Hope had also deserted him a lifetime earlier, taking flight with every other emotion or trace of optimism his soul discarded.

No, there was no point in grieving.

He was a semi-corpse. A zombie. Lifeless, but still breathing.

The dankness of the cell had become the only environment his dying mind could entertain. Water dripped from the ceiling. Relentless in its monotony, ruthless in its erratic rhythm. There was nothing to get hold of. Nothing to relate to.

There was nothing.

He almost looked forward to the interrogator's sessions when the tedium was replaced by pain. The pain gave him his only sense of being alive. Surely, he couldn't be dead if he felt pain.

But did he feel it? Did he really? Or did he just witness the sensation crawl through his body like a venom or a cancer? He no longer genuinely partook in the experience. He just observed.

How long had it been since their last attempt to break him? The fools, they didn't even know he'd been broken long ago.

How long...

Thump.

Lachlan Byrn awoke with a jolt. The Night Eagle had kept his door to consciousness ajar, allowing him a dazed and torturous reminiscence but nothing more.

Thump.

They were testing the foxhole's hatch. If the metal or wood gave way, his world would cease. Byrn eased his SIG Sauer out of his bag. If they came for him, he'd go down like a rattlesnake, stinging all within reach.

Thump.

A few seconds later, he heard another thump. Did this one appear further away? Had they moved on to the next foxhole?

Thump.

Byrn waited... for nothing. Eventually, the thumping disappeared into the distance.

There was no benefit to using his scope to check the channel pit. To do so would only provoke discovery. Instead, the assassin just waited.

He reached down beside him. The borescope sat secured in the small lead-lined box. No sweeping device Byrn was aware of would detect it. His watch wasn't digital, a good old fashion Swiss timepiece. He glanced at it with a flick of the flashlight. It was important that he kept track of time for both his mission and his sanity.

If the sounds above him were the Russian team securing the venue, then everything was on track. Byrn had heard nothing in relation to the drowned guardsman. Not that he could hear much, anyway. So, he'd remained uncertain if the Russian president's visit would proceed.

The thud promised hope.

According to the information received from Zhen and the old lady, there was eighteen hours until the president met with his generals, and twenty-one hours until his rendezvous with Kristiina Volk.

A lot of moving parts needed to merge for this kill to succeed. The remainder of Zhen's information must be accurate. After the early arrival of the Russian team, Byrn now harbored doubts about Zhen Su's reliability. The critical link remained the old lady. Would she be as good as her word? Would she live long enough to perform her task?

The assassin harbored no doubts as to his own contribution to the operation. He was here to do what he did best. Kill. Every part of his being now anticipated the gratification of the final act. The only emotion that dwelled within him was the passion for his work.

Some had labeled him compulsive. He considered himself thorough.

If he were to be frank with himself, he'd admit the odd doubt about his mental stability. Sealing himself inside a dank, dark hole would not have been the therapy any PTS shrink would have recommended. Not that Byrn had ever visited one.

The assassin popped a couple more pills and cast the doubts aside. If he'd survived nearly three years in a similar state of captivity, a few days wouldn't kill him.

Lachlan Byrn understood how to dig deep, and he knew how to kill. Now was the time for both.

Chapter 35

The assassin's watch indicated two hours until the Russian president's scheduled meeting with his generals.

Byrn anticipated that there would be a final deep sweep of the facility. With the president's arrival time approaching, his security team would be taking no chances. From what Byrn understood of the Russian security services and military, failure was a punishable offence. These people would perform their task in a thorough, professional manner.

Byrn respected that. He just needed to be better than them.

Ten minutes later, another series of thumps above him confirmed his speculation as being correct. The assassin would wait until the frantic activity above him had passed before moving onto his next phase.

Byrn looked forward not only to his approaching task but also to getting the hell out of this hole. The muscles in his body were coiled tight like a spring. The dampness had seeped through him. Despite the wet suit, and the thermal blanket, he felt saturated to his soul.

Over the last hours, as he lightly dozed, the visitations had become more vivid. His past wasn't haunting him, it was strangling him. Byrn had beaten it this time, but he'd never allow himself to be trapped in such a confined space again.

And damn this fucking dampness.

A short while later, after the noise above had abated, Byrn decided to risk a look with the borescope. He grabbed it out of the box and threaded it through one of the poly pipe tubes inserted into the mortar. The channel pit appeared empty. He swiveled the camera around to get a view of the grating above. He saw no movement.

Acutely aware that the breadth of his view was limited, and he had no real idea how many, if any, guardsman occupied the building, Byrn would have to begin.

It was time for a leap of faith.

Using the hand drill from a bag, the assassin began drilling a series of holes an inch apart into the new mortar. His aim was to weaken the bond, but not yet remove it completely. When he came out of the hole, Byrn would need to move quickly and quietly. This time, there could be no smashing away with the mortar pick. Premature discovery would mean failure.

Failure, as always, was unacceptable.

The assassin chuckled to himself. Unfailingly a fan of the classic old movies that got him through his childhood, he likened this situation to 'The Great Escape'. Only in this case, Lachlan Byrn was his own prisoner. He chuckled again.

Now there was a metaphor worth considering.

Chapter 36

PRESIDENT VADIM ALEYEV

Vadim Aleyev gazed out across the bay towards the Gulf of Finland. The sky was a clear blue, but the wind was brutal. Aleyev drew his heavy jacket tighter. Beyond the white capped water, he stared into the haze that masked a view of the Finnish coast just beyond.

But that was not the view concerning the president today.

Aleyev pivoted around and peered down the pier towards the shore. The condition of the abandoned Hara base had been disappointing, but the president really expected no different. In his mind's eye he could relive the bustle and activity surrounding the lumbering Soviet submarines, orders being barked, vessels loaded, sailors and workers frantically attending to their tasks. Their aim: maintaining the most feared and respected naval fleet on the planet.

Aleyev saw it all.

He remembered it all.

What the hell had happened?

The generals would be arriving shortly. The president hoped that they could share his vision. For him to rebuild the Russian Federation to its former glory, he would need their total support. That is what today's visit was all about. Of course, history's great leaders had taught Vadim Aleyev that strength and power ruled. Sometime ruthless decisions had to be made for the good of the motherland. If the generals could not get one hundred percent behind him, then they would be replaced.

Victory to the strong.

Aleyev slowly strolled back down the pier, his security detail strutting both ahead and at his back, their eyes darting around like hawks. His mind wandered to the previous day. His first meeting with US President Jefferson Blake.

To Aleyev, Blake seemed intelligent, astute, and perhaps more assertive than he'd imagined. As impressive as the man appeared, he was hampered by one impediment to success. The chains of democracy.

Aleyev was constrained by no such impediment.

The Russian president held no doubt that Blake and his team were meeting frantically today, discussing yesterday's meetings, making judgements on his own behavior, and on Russian policy. Tomorrow they'd be seeking compromise, and an indication that Russia would back off her expansionist agenda. They may even make use of some veiled and not so veiled economic threats. Aleyev would treat them with polite courtesy, listen seemingly respectfully and proceed to ignore every proposal. He would explain to them, as he would to a child, that Russia had no 'expansionist' policy. The federation simply intended to take back what was theirs, by any means available.

Of course, there would be one special surprise for Jefferson Blake in their final negotiations.

The Americans would learn that the Russian Federation is

a force not to be angered.

"Mr. President."

Aleyev snapped out of his daydream as he heard Sidorov's voice.

"The generals have arrived. They await you in the harbor office."

"Very good, Viktor. Let's join them."

Vadim Aleyev strode down the pier towards the future. One way or another.

Chapter 37

LACHLAN BYRN

Byrn stopped working on the mortar. There was activity above. He could sense it.

He quickly shone the flashlight on his watch face. 12.15 p.m. Aleyev should be meeting with his generals.

Byrn inserted the borescope into a hole and looked carefully at the image. Nothing appeared in the channel pit, but when he swiveled it up has saw several pairs of feet on the grate above.

The generals. Confirmed.

The assassin laid his tools down and waited.

Again.

Chapter 38

PRESIDENT VADIM ALEYEV

"Well, my colleagues, my comrades. What do you think?"

Vadim Aleyev swept his arms around as if beholding all before him.

"Before you say anything, I understand. It's not much now, but I implore you, recall how it once was."

The four men standing in the torpedo room murmured some non-committal platitudes before Aleyev interrupted.

"Admiral Kovalenko, Igor. You are old enough to remember when our brave submariners sailed out of this base to intimidate the western navy forces. Do you recall the trepidation the US Navy expressed as they encountered our deadly fish? Would it not be wonderful? Do we not deserve to take our righteous place as the most fearsome force in the ocean once again? Would your pride not swell at the thought of commanding such a powerful fleet?"

Igor Kovalenko knew there would be no evading a direct response. The admiral stood upright, raising his chin.

"*Da, Gospodin Prezident*, yes, Mr. President. It would be a great honor."

Aleyev smiled.

"And General Levitsky, Matvey."

A tall man at the rear of the group rose to attention.

"Da, Gospodin Prezident."

"Do you recall when the Americans made their Hollywood movies in such fear of our long-range bombers? The fools in the west cowered at the threat of our massive payloads. Now they fear nothing. At least not from us. Do you believe that is where Russia should be placed in the world order?"

"Net, Gospodin Prezident. I am of the opinion that our motherland should stand tall amongst the lesser countries. Our right to rule the skies should not be in question."

Aleyev nodded.

"And Dimitriy, General Stepanov, perhaps my oldest and wisest friend. How do you feel when we are challenged even when taking back our rightful territories, such as Crimea and Ukraine? Should we not have the capability and the will to stomp our challengers into submission?"

Stepanov stood in front of his colleagues, where his President expected him to be. He pushed his chest forward as he spoke.

"Konechno, Gospodin Prezident, of course. The only question is whether this is effected through military or political means."

A collective intake of breath spread through the group. Stepanov walked a fine line.

"If I might respond, Mr. President?"

"Of course, Yuri." Aleyev turned to the others. "As Director of the FSB, I'm certain General Varkov will offer a unique perspective on these issues." He nodded towards Varkov.

"For many years, Mr. President, comrades, we've tried to flex our muscle and show our willingness to lead the world through political means. Each time we do, our power grows weaker and our influence wanes. I would argue that if we don't move now, aggressively, we will not have the strength or ability in ten years to even make any attempt to restore our nation to its natural elevation. It's time that we all support our President and go forward."

Aleyev nodded. A murmur of consent echoed amongst the group like a small wave.

"Dimitriy?" asked the president.

The room froze in silence.

Stepanov coughed before he straightened his torso.

"Of course, General Varkov speaks the truth. Perhaps my hesitation was foolish."

"Yes, I believe that to be the case, Dimitriy. Now gentlemen. I wish you to take these thoughts and others we have discussed today and consider them. As the motherland's leadership group, we must decide and collectively move forward. We will discuss this further in Moscow."

More positive whispers.

Aleyev continued.

"Now I bid you all a safe flight home. I have summit related matters to attend to." Aleyev turned to Varkov. "As you know, Yuri, I require you to stay here with our team in Estonia. There is much for the FSB director to deal with. A word if you please."

"As is your wish, Mr. President," Varkov replied.

The generals filed out of the room.

"I fear I've lost them, Yuri. These men do not have the stomach for war. I suspect they have grown into fat peacetime pigs."

"Yes, Mr. President."

"Yuri, it gives me no pleasure, but you know what to do."

191

"Yes, Mr. President."

"Oh, and Yuri, one more thing. If you ever hear me use the term 'leadership group' again, please shoot me dead on the spot."

General Yuri Varkov smiled at his leader, nodded, and left.

"It's a shame," said Aleyev, to nobody at all.

Chapter 39

GENERAL DIMITRIY STEPANOV

General Dimitriy Stepanov stared out the small window of the Embraer Legacy 600. He knew that he'd probably just negated nearly thirty years of hard work with one single careless comment. Nobody he was aware of had ever contradicted Vadim Aleyev in the way he had and remained in their position. Perhaps his best strategy would be to resign as soon as they arrived in Moscow. That may at least give him a chance to escape the situation with his life.

"We'll shortly be passing over Saint Petersburg," announced the pilot. "We are currently flying over the Tver region."

Stepanov retained his gaze. Somewhere, twenty-eight thousand feet below, normal Russians were going about their usual business. These people weren't asking for war. They weren't even asking to return to the old Soviet ways. All they wanted to do was live their lives, love their families, their friends, their country, and be happy. Was that so much to ask?

"Would you care for a drink, General?" asked the young flight attendant.

"I suppose I could," he replied, smiling at the pretty girl.

"Vodka, *pozhaluysta*." He'd abstained from drinking at first so he could think things through with a clear head. Maybe there could be another way. Did he owe it to the Russian people to try? It would be risky, the outcome uncertain. Act now or don't act at all.

Stepanov stood up, turning to face the other men, who were seated around two coffee tables.

"Well, my comrades. How do you judge that went?"

"The meeting?" asked Kovalenko.

"It is not really appropriate to talk," added Levitsky.

"Seeing how I'm the one who transgressed, I will speak. I'm certain our great country is heading for an implosion of the level of Nazi Germany. We owe it to our people to change course before it's too late," announced Stepanov.

Silence.

It was too much to hope for. These people were gutless and cared only for themselves. Either way, now he'd started, he may as well continue. Stepanov's fate had been sealed by his opening words.

"I believe we must act. Together."

More silence.

Dimitriy Stepanov knew with certainty that this would now be his last free day on earth. Someone aboard this plane would speak of his treason.

The stony silence continued underscored by the jet's engines soaring through the Russian skies.

"I agree with Dimitriy. Aleyev is a madman, unfit to lead." Kovalenko.

That made two for the penal colony, at best, thought Stepanov. But it was a start. He looked at Levitsky. This was all or nothing.

General Matvey Levitsky stared at the plush carpet, not uttering a word.

Finally.

"Stepanov, Vadim Aleyev is one of your oldest friends, he said so himself today. And you are prepared to betray him?"

"I'm not prepared to betray my country and see thousands more die for one man's lustful insanity," replied Stepanov.

More silence.

Levitsky looked at the two other men.

"I agree. I totally agree. But what can we do?"

Stepanov felt a hint of relief. There was at this moment a chance. A hope.

"Between us, we control the navy, the army, and the air force. We must take back our country," he said.

"What about that snake Varkov and his FSB?" asked Kovalenko.

"My snipers will deal with him," replied Stepanov. "Now gentlemen, we must make plans, urgent plans."

They were the final words of general Dimitriy Stepanov, commander of the once mighty Russian army.

The C4 attached to the petrol tanks in each of the wings exploded simultaneously, sending the aircraft skyrocketing towards Russian soil.

There would be no hope. No plans.

Chapter 40

Kadriorg Palace, Estonia

PRESIDENT JEFFERSON BLAKE

"Now that day one and two are over, what are your impressions, everyone? I want to look at this from all sides," President Jefferson Blake had summoned some of his key players to a meeting room within the vast Kadriorg Palace.

The clock had just struck 3 p.m. on the second day of the summit. Cynthia Ford, National Security Advisor, Nate Edwards, Secretary of State, Rowena Fisk, US Ambassador to Russia, Fred Durrows, Director of the CIA and Abe Peterson, Head of the Secret Service, sat around the warm fire. The room was ornate and impressive, as it was designed to be. Several advisors perched in a second circle, ready to provide facts and information as required.

"Vadim Aleyev has presented himself as polite, intelligent and cooperative," began Nate Edwards, "But in all honesty I wouldn't trust him to take out my garbage without snooping through it."

Cynthia Ford spoke. "I'm worried that he's listening, but not really presenting any alternative paths forward. He's used the same arguments that we've heard a thousand times. The embargos insult the Russian people. They are not aggressors but are protecting regions from corrupt governments and they regard the west as interfering in their business."

"Not to mention that he regards NATO as the aggressive body in the current scenario," added Edwards.

"Then why did he agree to this summit?" asked the president. "Why come along if you have nothing to give?"

Everyone took a moment to ponder the boss' question.

"Maybe he came because he wants to take something, not give?" said Ford.

"What are your thoughts, Cynthia?" asked Blake.

"Absolutely nothing specific, I'm afraid. It's more of a gut feeling that he has a card up his sleeve. He should be more argumentative, but he's not, and I have no idea why."

"I've come to appreciate the value of your gut feelings, Cynthia. We'll keep what you are saying in mind," the president responded.

"Let's not forget this man learned his statecraft and his morality in the KGB," said Fred Durrows. "I know I haven't been present at either of the meetings, nor should I be, but from what you've all shared, the real Aleyev is elusive, bordering on deceptive. I believe it's the nature of the beast."

"To be honest Fred, I don't doubt a word you're saying, although I'd rather it wasn't repeated outside this room." The president looked around. Everyone nodded in affirmation. This was a closed session. Blake continued, "But talking to Vadim Aleyev is not like talking to any other world leader I know. He's difficult to read and seems to be proud of it."

The president paused to give everyone a chance to consider his words.

"Okay, so let's move on. Fred, Abe, do you have any scuttlebutt from our Estonian friends? Have they observed anything that would be of interest to us?"

"Not much yet, I'm afraid, Mr. President," replied Durrows. "Aleyev's security people are keeping the Estonians at bay, as distant as possible from their leader. Although that in itself may speak to some level of paranoia."

Blake nodded.

"Abe?"

Peterson sat forward in his chair. "I might have something, Mr. President, but it's only small."

"Spit it out."

"This morning President Aleyev hosted a group of his key generals at the Hara Submarine Base in north-east Estonia. Present were…" Peterson looked down at his notes, "… General Matvey Levitsky commander of the Russian Federation's Aerospace Forces, Admiral Igor Kovalenko, in charge of their navy, General Dimitriy Stepanov, in charge of the Russian Ground Forces and General Yuri Varkov, Director of the Federal Security Service."

"Go on," said Blake.

"Well, our Estonian friends who were present on the former base weren't privy to the meeting, but one of the Russian team who'd been in earshot suggested privately to a colleague that the discussion appeared to be a pep talk of some sort. Something along the lines of 'the good old Soviet days.' One of the Estonians picked up that conversation."

"Concerning," said Ford.

"Very much so", agreed the president.

"There's more, Sir," said Peterson.

Blake nodded for him to continue.

"What some of the Estonian security people did observe directly was the glum faces of the generals as they left the meeting. Perhaps it didn't turn out to be the gee up Aleyev intended."

"Interesting point," responded Blake. "Possibly some trouble at home for our elusive friend."

The president paused for a moment. Everyone in the room knew the presidential chin scratch meant another point was about to be made.

"Abe, can you confirm if Pavel Fedorov, the Foreign Minister, was present at that meeting?" asked the president.

"He was not, sir. We've been told that Fedorov has had little presence with the entourage outside our summit meetings."

"I suppose none of this information impacts directly on our responses tomorrow, but it will be interesting to observe Aleyev at this evening's dinner," said Blake. "Good work, Abe."

Thank you, Mr. President.

President Blake stood up, intending to end the meeting. As he did so, one of the CIA advisors leaned forward to speak with his boss. Blake paused.

"Mr. President. I believe you'll want to hear this," announced Durrows.

The president sat.

"We've just received preliminary intelligence suggesting the Embraer Legacy jet transporting Generals Levitsky and Stepanov, along with Admiral Kovalenko on their return trip to Moscow, has crashed just west of Saint Petersburg. According to our intel, there are no survivors."

A collective gasp filled the room.

Blake broke the silence.

"Fred, was General Varkov of the FSB on board?"

"No, sir. Our reports indicate he remained here in Estonia at president Aleyev's direction."

All eyes in the room were glued to Jefferson Blake for a response.

"Fred, find out what you can about the accident and please report back to me within the hour. Abe, please check all our security arrangements and double up where you can. I want all of our team well protected."

The president then turned his gaze to the rest of the room.

"Ladies and gentlemen, the summit continues. We are not going home. We are not running away. Do I make myself clear?"

Chapter 41

PRESIDENT VADIM ALEYEV

It was a fine meal. One of the advantages of being the president of a great nation was that you could access the best food and wine that the world had to offer. Even in this remote outpost, Aleyev had been served an excellent Solyanka with the lightest and freshest of breads.

As he sat alone at the well-laid table in the harbor office, the president sipped his glass of Kuban-Vino. It, like the food, had been tasted separately by two tasters. There were many who yearned to see Aleyev take his final meal. But not today.

Aleyev let his thoughts stray to the afternoon ahead. Kristiina. He hadn't seen her in more years than he could remember, but she had been with him every day. A woman like that leaves a hole in one's soul reserved exclusively for her use. He'd never told Tatiana about her. There was little point. He and his wife had partnered in a good marriage. He and Kristiina had shared a great love. At least, that's how Aleyev remembered it.

She would be delighted to see him; he had no doubt.

There was a knock, and the spell was broken.

"Mr. President. I'm so sorry to intrude, sir."

Viktor Sidorov poked his head around the door.

"It's all right Viktor, I was just finishing up."

Aleyev had expected to be interrupted. In fact, it would have been a disappointment if he wasn't.

"Are you well, man? You look as white as a ghost."

"I apologize, sir, but I bring devastating news."

"Speak up."

"Mr. President, the plane carrying generals Stepanov and Levitsky, along with Admiral Kovalenko, has gone down. It is believed to have crashed just out of Saint Petersburg."

Aleyev frowned. "Are there any survivors?"

"Our reports are telling us no, sir. They say the aircraft disintegrated in mid-air before plummeting down."

"A mechanical malfunction? A bomb? Do we know? Our country has many enemies, Viktor."

"As yet, we can't confirm the cause, but if the aircraft exploded in mid-air, an explosive device or a missile is the most likely explanation. Either way, we will find out."

"This is a national tragedy, Viktor. Please arrange phone calls this evening when we are back at our accommodation. I wish to offer my condolences to the three widows. Of course, I know them all personally."

"It will be arranged, Mr. President. Would you like me to instruct our team to prepare for your immediate departure?"

Aleyev feigned consideration.

"No, Victor, this is what leadership is all about. I'll stay. This summit was difficult enough to arrange. I won't be seen to be backing out now. However, do what you need to increase my security. It appears these westerners cannot be trusted."

"You suspect the Americans, Mr. President?"

"Your words Viktor, not mine. But we must examine all

possibilities in this time of tragedy. Now, please do as I have requested, but first, please send General Varkov to see me."

"Of course, Mr. President."

Five minutes later, there was another knock on the door.

"Come in, Yuri."

Yuri Varkov appeared around the door.

"Can we be overheard, Yuri?"

"No, Mr. President. I asked Sidorov to post his men in a larger circle around this building, for security purposes."

The president smiled.

"You have done well, Yuri, in every respect."

"*Spasibo, Gospodin Prezident.* Thank you."

"There are no witnesses, I presume?"

"None who can speak, sir."

"And the components of the explosive devices, they are all American made?"

"As you requested, Mr. President."

"The investigation, Yuri. I believe the FSB should keep their distance and allow Rosaviatsiya, our agency for air transport, to handle it. They have the expertise and are extremely transparent in their approach."

"That would make sense, Mr. President. I shall make the arrangements."

"Good. Now, this is a tragic day for the motherland. I'll need some time for reflection. You may leave."

"Yes, Mr. President.

The door closed quietly as the FSB director left.

Vadim Aleyev reached across the table and poured himself some more of the fine Kuban-Vino.

He considered the air crash; he considered the wine, and he considered the woman he would be spending at least the

afternoon with.
Perfect.

Chapter 42

KRISTIINA VOLK

Kristiina Volk sat in her car with her fingers gripped tightly on the steering wheel. She's stopped the white Skoda a couple of hundred yards up the road from the submarine base. She'd be in view of the sentries when she rounded the next and final bend, which was why she paused here.

The final bend.

Kristiina was ready, at every level. She'd lived a productive life, but as she aged, the haunting voice of guilt had become overwhelming. She'd never been able to forgive herself for the grief she's caused so many. It hadn't been enough to blame it on youthful ignorance. She couldn't even hold Vadim Aleyev solely accountable.

Theirs had been a joint venture of evil.

Kristiina had spent most of her life attempting to make up for what she'd done. She knew she'd been able to achieve good things and had helped many in her community lead better lives though her work as a nurse and her volunteering. But it had never been enough. Kristiina remained certain that guilt was now the silent and dominant partner in her life.

Today, that would change.

The old woman inhaled deeply, coughed a little, and then pressed her foot down on the accelerator. It was time.

Despite not using her car much lately, she'd chosen to drive here alone. The old lady didn't want anyone else implicated in her actions. As the vehicle rounded the bend the sentries came into view. She recognized the dark color of the Estonian Police and Border Guard uniform. Behind the Estonians stood a line of soldiers in combat fatigues. As the car drew close, she noticed the red, white and gold insignia of the Russian National Guard on their sleeves.

Vadim Aleyev was really here.

One of the Estonians approached the driver's window as the Skoda came to a halt.

"*See asutus on täna suletud,* this facility is closed today."

"I have an appointment with President Aleyev. I am Kristiina Volk."

The sentry nodded silently before striding off to consult one of the soldiers. After a brief conversation, he returned.

"Please, park over there, near the harbor office. Someone will escort you to the president."

The guard waved his arm in the direction he intended her to go. The old lady noticed that his tone now held a certain reverence.

A tall man in a dark blue suit was waiting for her as she pulled up. He opened her car door. She got out.

"Ms. Volk. I am Viktor Sidorov, the Director of Presidential Security. President Aleyev is expecting you. I shall escort you to him, but first I'm afraid we'll have to perform a discreet search of your person and authenticate your identification. I hope you understand."

As he spoke, a woman, also in fatigues, stepped out of the

office. She smiled at Kristiina.

"I'm sorry for the intrusion, but it is procedure for all who visit the president."

"I understand," the old lady responded.

The woman produced a wand and ran it over Kristiina's body, back and front. She then gently padded her down from head to foot. The director turned away and checked her driver's license.

"That is fine," said the woman. "Enjoy your visit."

Kristiina nodded.

"If you would care to come with me, Ms. Volk, the president awaits you in the first building on the pier."

The director led the way, Kristiina followed. Halfway there, she stopped and coughed. For a few seconds, she had trouble catching her breath. After the brief pause, she resumed her journey.

"Are you all right, Ms. Volk? Can I get you anything?" he asked.

"No, thank you. I'll be fine." They walked on in silence.

As they approached the building, Kristiina found herself shaking. This was it. The moment. 'Get a grip', she thought. She needed to be strong for this moment. Within seconds, she would be face to face with the man who ruined her life.

Face to face with the devil.

Chapter 43

PRESIDENT VADIM ALEYEV

Aleyev found himself faintly agitated. It was an odd sensation. The president had grown used to those around him being on edge. He expected it, even reveled in it. When he'd met the President of the United States the day before, his heart rate hadn't risen one iota.

But this was different.

He'd received word Kristiina Volk had arrived at the base. Now he paced up and down, along the metal grating that covered the pit below.

Trepidation?

The president laughed at himself.

He was an impressive man with nothing to fear in this world.

"Vadim."

Suddenly, she was there.

"Kristiina. It had been such a long, long time."

Then Aleyev noticed Viktor Sidorov standing behind the woman.

"Viktor, as we discussed. Please take your men and move to the shore end of the pier. Unless the US Navy Seals attack us unexpectedly from the sea, I shall be fine." He knew how to put on a good show.

"Yes, Mr. President." Sidorov turned and left.

"You look wonderful, Kristiina. We are both older, but you've lost none of your beauty."

The old lady straightened her posture, as though rising to a challenge.

"I fear age has wearied your eyesight, Vadim."

Aleyev laughed. He stepped forward until he stood just a couple of feet from her. He leaned in to hug her. She presented her cheek for a kiss. Aleyev wondered if there was an unexpected rigidity in her movement.

The president took a step back and looked Kristiina Volk up and down. For the first time, he noticed the pallor of her skin.

"Are you all right, Kristiina? Are you well?"

"As well as can be expected, Vadim. And you?"

"I am fine. More than fine. Life has been good for me. I've been fortunate to achieve much through the years."

"Yes, you certainly have," she responded.

Aleyev briefly wondered if he'd detected an undercurrent of malice in his former lover's voice. He dismissed the thought as ridiculous.

"You are now one of the most powerful men on the planet, Vadim. Armies march at your command. Countries fear you. You must have worked hard to get to this point in life."

As she spoke, the old woman moved to the center of the metal grate. It was a crucial move.

"And what of your life, Kristiina? Have the winds of fate been kind to you? At our age, we are both still standing. That must be a good sign."

The woman sighed.

"I've made the most of the opportunities as they've arisen. I hope I've left a positive mark."

"You know, I thought about contacting you many times. I even sent men to see you. In the end, I suppose the time was not right."

The old lady nodded.

"I hope it is right now?" the president continued.

"The timing is exactly right now, Vadim. It could not be better."

Aleyev smiled. This meeting was proceeding precisely as he planned.

Until it wasn't.

"Tell me Vadim, tell me what you've *really* achieved with your life?"

Aleyev raised his arms in astonishment.

"That is a surprising question, my dear. The media is full of my achievements."

"I've read the news; I've watched television. I understand the power you wield. I just want to know how you've used it to help others?"

Aleyev was perplexed by Kristiina's question, and the tone that accompanied it.

"I've dedicated my life to my motherland and the citizens of Russia."

"Have you Vadim? Have you really? Have you done this in the same way you dedicated yourself to the wellbeing of Estonians when your country's forces occupied our lands? Do you help people now as you helped us then?"

Aleyev grew concerned. The conversation had taken an irretrievable turn for the worse. He would call Sidorov and have this woman removed. The old lady standing before him was not the Kristiina Volk he remembered.

"Kristiina, why do you speak like this?"

Aleyev began reaching into his pocket for his phone.

The old lady stared him straight in the eyes. Her own pupils wide and clear.

"Because I've come to stop you."

Chapter 44

LACHLAN BYRN

The borescope showed two pairs of shoes on the grate, about twenty feet distant from his position. He checked his watch. According to the schedule, Kristiina had been told this was it. If everything had proceeded as expected, the operation now stood a good chance.

If something had gone wrong, Lachlan Byrn would be dead within minutes.

Byrn gently pushed out the first stone. A few inches of fall shouldn't create a loud sound to distract from the conversation above.

He checked the borescope again.

No reaction.

By reaching his hand through the hole, he could catch the other stones as they came loose. After two minutes, he'd struggled through the gap in the stone wall. In the first instant, he stretched his body to full length while lying on the concrete floor of the pit. He then flexed his arms. The relief was total.

Byrn felt the familiar coolness flow through his veins. His heart rate slowed to the level it always did during an operation. It was time to go to work.

As soon as his head protruded into the pit, he heard human voices. A man and a woman. He immediately recognized the old lady's tone. It sounded like she was beginning to show some agitation already. Although sooner than they'd planned, Byrn supposed she'd waited a long time for this moment. He just needed to move quickly.

The assassin raised himself to a crouching position and half ran to the end of the pit, furthest from the voices. Kristiina had been instructed to ensure Aleyev was facing the southern end of the building. When Byrn reached his destination, he craned his head up to the level of the floor.

Two people. The man stood with his back turned towards Byrn's position.

He pulled himself out of the pit, landing quietly on the concrete floor. He padded along the floor towards the figures, the soles of his wetsuit masking his footsteps.

Then he froze.

The man, Aleyev, raised his arms. His body language suggested he was about to pivot around. There was nowhere for the assassin to hide. The assassin froze.

A few seconds later, the arms were lowered, and the conversation resumed.

He knew that Kristiina would have seen him already. They'd been over this moment. The importance of not showing any flash of recognition or relief had been impressed upon her.

The old lady didn't falter.

Byrn could now hear every word.

"Kristiina, why do you speak like this?"

"Because I have come to stop you."

Byrn heard the president laugh loudly.

"Oh Kristiina. You are a disillusioned and frail old woman.

213

I have hundreds of armed guards at my disposal, just a phone call away."

Byrn saw the president produce a cell phone from his jacket pocket. He began to press the keypad.

"Tell me, who is going to help you impede the most powerful man in Europe?"

Byrn smashed the phone out of Vadim Aleyev's hand.

"That would be me."

Chapter 45

KRISTIINA VOLK

Kristiina flinched as the young man chopped the phone out of the Aleyev's hand. She was also slightly relieved.

She watched in silence as he threw his arm around the president's neck, forcing him into a chokehold. The man's speed was astonishing.

Aleyev struggled, but age and strength were not on his side. In the end, he gave up.

"I can give you two minutes to say what you need. Then we must move," announced the man.

Kristiina nodded. Although her torrent of pain was a lifetime in the making, she would make her point quickly.

She stared the Russian president directly in the eye. Her face trembling in a restrained rage.

"Vadim, your world is about to change, just as you changed my world. I hope you are ready."

Aleyev gazed back at her, stunned.

She continued.

"You stole my life and my self-worth. You left me feeling stained and dirty. There are no words to describe the drenching guilt that has been my constant shadow for so long."

"You did what you did, Kristiina. Why search for absolution?" Aleyev struggled to speak, the grip around his throat so tight.

The old lady sighed.

"I understand what I did all those years ago, and I recognize my actions were heinous. But we both know how you manipulated a young girl and used her, me, and so many others to destroy the lives of good people. I acknowledge my part and have been repentant to God every single day since. My life has not been a search for redemption, but a constant flight from the talons of regret."

"You are deluded, old lady. What can you hope to gain from this?" Aleyev's voice was strained.

"In this one act today, I'll regain the control you stole from me. I may now be able to seek the peace in the next world that has eluded me in this."

Kristiina Volk stared into the president's eyes.

Penetrating.

"Goodbye Vadim."

Kristiina coughed and gasped for some air. Without realizing, she'd held her breath for the duration of her speech.

She nodded at the young man.

With his free arm, he reached into his pocket and produced a syringe. Flicking the cap off, he plowed the needle into Aleyev's neck. Almost instantaneously, the president's body slumped.

"Gamma Hydroxy-Butyrate, GHB," he announced.

"A date rape drug. Appropriate," Kristiina responded.

"We need to leave. You, though the front door as we discussed. If you can tell the guards that the president wants ten minutes alone, they may believe you. The time would help."

"No."

The young man appeared confused.

"We had an arrangement," he stated bluntly.

"Yes, we did, but I have changed that arrangement and I will not back down, nor be told what to do."

It was the first time since she'd told him she'd noticed him following her in Tallinn that Kristiina had seen her deadly new friend surprised.

"You will leave. I'll remain here," she began. "I'll stay as long as I can. That will give you time to escape. When Vadim's phone rings, it will mean his men are concerned. I'll leave then. At that point, I'll tell them their president wants a few extra minutes."

"They won't believe you."

"Probably not."

"You understand that you will almost certainly be walking to your death?"

"I'm already walking to my death. The only question is the length of the path."

The young man smiled.

Kristiina continued. "My doctors have told me I'll be lucky to see the month out. In fact, they're surprised I'm still active and not confined to my deathbed. It's amazing what a little motivation does. Now go on, get out of here."

"There is no chance of talking you down from this ledge?"

"No chance and no point."

The young man shrugged his shoulders before laying the president on the ground. He disappeared to the other end of the building and back down to the channel pit. He returned with waterproof equipment and two small tanks with attached masks.

"Dive re-breathers," he said.

Kristiina was surprised.

"You have two of them. I told you; I'm not going with you."

"I accept that. The second is for him," the young man nodded toward Aleyev spread out on the floor.

"I assumed you'd take his life here. Wasn't that the plan?"

"It was your assumption, not my plan."

"Why complicate your escape? it makes no sense."

The young man took a moment to respond. Then he shrugged.

"Death can be complicated. Trust me, it's what I do. A simple, relatively painless death is too good for this man. We both know what he has done. There is now a price that he must pay. I will personally extract the charge."

The man cast his gaze to the prone body on the floor in front of him, before raising his head to match Kristiina's own stare.

"To be truthful with you, I will enjoy the process."

The darkness in his eyes was unsettling.

"You're scaring me."

"That is not my intent. But I will ensure Vadim Aleyev suffers the death his life has earned him."

Suddenly Kristiina felt cold. Who was this stranger? What universe of morality did he exist in?

"You're obviously aware taking him with you will impede your escape?"

"I have means, and the risk has been fully calculated. Don't worry, if it appears I'm caught in a net, he'll die instantaneously. That is guaranteed."

"Then thank you, young man. I appreciate what has happened today guarantees me no ongoing peace, but it does provide some hope. You'd better leave while you can."

Kristiina watched the man gather what he needed. When he reached down to throw Aleyev over his shoulder in a 'fireman's hold', she was surprised that the president wasn't totally unconscious.

"Just the right amount of GHB slows the heart and breathing. It inhibits the victim's ability to think or physically react. The president is now pliable to my whim."

"I'm surprised it worked," Kristiina responded. "Because that man has no heart."

Her accomplice nodded.

"Goodbye and good luck, old lady. Thank you for your help. I hope you find what you seek."

"And to you as well."

With Aleyev drooped over his shoulder, the young man strode confidently to the northern entrance to the building, away from the guards and towards the water.

Chapter 46

LACHLAN BYRN

Byrn had almost made it to the exit when he swung around. The old lady stood silhouetted in the afternoon sun, infiltrating through the windows.

Momentarily, they gazed at each other.

"Kristiina," the assassin began, "you should know. My name is Lachlan."

Chapter 47

KRTISTIINA VOLK

The cell phone laying on the concrete vibrated. Kristiina Volk looked at her watch. It had been thirty minutes. Clearly, no one wanted to disturb the president unless they had to.

The old lady gazed at the phone. It was time. The bell tolls for thee.

She took a deep breath, straightened her posture, and walked through the southern entrance of the building. Kristiina noted the armed Russian Guardsmen standing at the end of the pier. Next to them stood their boss, the director, Viktor Sidorov. He held a phone to his ear. When Sidorov looked up and saw her, his body language relaxed.

Relief.

He began striding down the pier to meet her. Two men accompanied him. They moved quicker than she could manage, so they met about a third of the way between the building and the shore.

"Ms. Volk. I assume your meeting with the president has finished?" asked the director.

"Yes, it was wonderful to see Vadim again after all these years," she replied.

Vadim. Familiarity.

Sidorov looked her up and down.

"Are you all right, Ms. Volk? You seem very pale and perhaps a little unsteady on your feet. Can I get you some help?"

"No, no. Thank you. I'll be fine. I have some medication in my car. Now the president has asked me to tell you to give him ten minutes. He wants some reflective time. I fear I may have broken his heart."

Sidorov smiled compassionately.

"Of course. But I'm afraid we do have a duty of care." He turned to the guardsman on his left. "Obolensky, you and Baklanov, please go down to the president and confirm his wishes. Ms. Volk, if you could just wait here."

The reaction was as Kristiina had expected.

"But my medication."

"Please give me your keys. I will fetch your medicine for you. I'm afraid we have protocols to follow. I must insist."

"Very well, please be quick."

Sidorov nodded, took the keys from Kristiina's hand, and headed towards the Skoda. The two guardsmen disappeared behind her on their way to check on their leader.

They were going to be disappointed.

Kristiina raised her head and arched her back. She felt the wind brushing at her cheek. It was a refreshing sensation. She inhaled deeply. The sea air felt cold in her lungs, but also invigorating. She looked up. The sun was beginning to sink, dimming the earlier bright blue sky.

How appropriate.

The old lady thought briefly of her life. Apart from the early Soviet years, she'd had a good run. At least as good as it was going to get, all things considered.

She glanced behind her. The guards had almost reached the building.

Kristiina Volk turned back towards the shore and started walking. She was in no hurry. She understood her destination.

A few seconds later.

"He's gone. The president is not here," the guard's panicked voice screamed through the wind.

Ahead of her, Sidorov had made it to the car, but now looked up, his frowning face betraying his alarm. He reached into his pocket and withdrew his phone. As he spoke, the fear in his eyes intensified.

Kristiina kept walking. One step and then the next.

Suddenly, guardsmen rushed everywhere. Six began the journey along the pier toward Kristiina. She walked on.

"*Ostanovka!* Halt! You must stop!" the guards behind her yelled.

The wind felt good, soothing. Kristiina strode forward, her eyes cast ahead.

Viktor Sidorov now advanced with his men.

"Ms. Volk. You must stop. Please raise your hands."

They all held guns aimed at Kristiina. She assumed it would be the same behind her. But there was hesitation. No one wanted to shoot the president's girlfriend. On the other hand, no one could afford to let his assassin escape.

Kristiina smiled to herself. It was a bit too late for that.

Each step was a gratifying moment of defiance.

"We will shoot."

Again, Kristiina smiled. She figured they would. In fact, she was counting on it.

The old lady walked on.

She heard the first crack in the same instant her shoulder flicked back at the impact.

Another step.

Defiant.

Another crack.

She felt a searing heat tear through her chest, burning at her heart. The sensation of warm moisture soaked her top.

Another step. That surprised her. This was a moment of victory. She'd beaten Aleyev, and she'd beaten the cancer, cheating the disease of its chance to ravage her further. Kristiina would remember this moment for the rest of her...

Crack.

Suddenly, the old lady lay on the ragged stones, staring at the sky. She sensed a thick liquid oozing down her cheeks. Above her, the blue hue was growing dimmer. More quickly than the sunset.

Forgive me, oh Lord.

Chapter 48

LACHLAN BYRN

Byrn had been trained in attack diving, and he'd been trained in how to rescue a semi-conscious diver from the ocean floor. His actions now were a combination of the two skill sets.

The assassin swam on his back, just below the surface, every muscle in his body straining. He had an arm around Aleyev's chest as he powered forward, doing the kicking for both of them. The re-breather's mask was securely fitted to the president's face, but Byrn kept a close eye on it anyway. Above them, the waves would disguise any trail of bubbles, although the choice of using a re-breather as their source of oxygen meant there would be few bubbles.

Byrn's original plan had allowed for an extremely tight timeline to make his escape. The old lady's insistence on buying him more time had helped considerably.

Byrn understood why she had made that choice. She wanted to be in control. Given the same situation, he would have done the same.

After twenty minutes, Byrn risked a quick glance above the surface. He craned his neck to see they were only yards away from rounding the point. He kicked back down until they were at least six feet under the waves.

Ten minutes later, the assassin was dragging Aleyev's slumped body across the rocks. The man was aware enough to contribute to his movement, yet not sufficiently awake to have any say in where he was going. Byrn chose this as the extraction point because they could reach the forest edge on foot by stepping only on rocks and stones.

A trail in the sand was too big a gift for those who would follow.

Once in the shadows of the trees, Byrn hoisted the president back over his shoulder and carefully made his way along the forest path. After several minutes, he deviated off the track, quickly reaching the spot where he'd left the KTM trail bike. He dropped Aleyev to the ground and righted the bike. The next part was tricky.

Byrn grabbed four tie-down straps out of his bag and strapped the president's chest to his back, and each of Aleyev's legs to one of his own. He guided the president onto the KTM by lifting his left leg over the bike with his own.

An instant yet semiconscious pillion passenger.

The assassin glanced at his watch. Forty minutes since they'd left the pier at the abandoned base. Any minute now, all hell would…

The gunshots cracked through the late afternoon air. Byrn felt himself inhale involuntarily.

Rest in peace, old lady.

The KTM started on the second kick. The assassin figured he had around ten minutes until the area was flooded with both Russian Guardsmen and the *Estonian Police and Border Guards.*

Byrn guided the bike along the rough track before hitting

a wider dirt road. The route had been carefully planned out well in advance. The assassin made good time along the road covering several miles. Without leaving the Lahemaa Rahvuspark he then veered off the road back onto a smaller track. With every mile into the forest, he became less visible to any possible satellite surveillance. Gradually the paths grew more difficult to negotiate until to go any further would create a new track in itself.

Byrn stopped the bike, put it up on its stand, and guided the president off the machine. After unstrapping Aleyev, he laid him on the ground and checked his pulse. Weak but steady, as expected. He then walked the bike further into the forest, disturbing as little undergrowth as possible.

Five hundred yards in, Byrn laid the KTM down in a thicket of bushes and did his best to cover it. He only needed twenty-four hours. Byrn was confident his location was far enough from the Hara facility to buy the time required. And he hadn't exposed himself or his prisoner to anyone on his trek here.

Perfect.

Chapter 49

The irony of the situation wasn't lost on Byrn.

He had just spent several days secured in a confined stone and concrete box in order to perform a mission intended to escape forever the clutches of an intelligence service who held him captive for years in an equally confined space, only to bring his quarry here.

A cave.

Byrn accepted that the irony brought a certain poetry to the kill.

That was fine by him.

President Vadim Aleyev lay on the hard earth and stone floor of the cave. Byrn had left him in his wet clothes but removed his shoes. The president drifted in and out of consciousness, but according to Bryn's calculations, the man would be ready for a conversation within the next ninety minutes. The assassin bound his prisoner's hands and feet for added security.

Byrn's own state of mind was verging on the precarious. Even with the modafinil, he caught himself dozing off at times. Now, having changed out of his wet suit into the dry clothes that were waiting for him, he reached into his jacket to retrieve his vial of pills. He popped some into his mouth, upping the dose by fifty percent. Additional security.

The cave was a gem of a find and had taken some work to locate. The assassin had read stories about the famed Forest Brothers, the partisans who'd hidden in the forests of Lithuania, Latvia and Estonia and rebelled against the Soviet occupation. They were brave people who risked and often lost everything to fight for their country's freedom. Byrn held them in silent admiration.

Logic dictated that the partisans would have maintained hideouts in the forest, in locations unknown to their occupiers. In the time since the occupation, the positions of many hideouts became public knowledge. The assassin figured that there would be some that remained a mystery. This cave was one of them.

Byrn hadn't scoured the forest for such a location; he didn't have the time for that. Instead, he hit the bars around Muuga Harbor, Tallinn's biggest container port. Eventually he'd found what he needed, a drinking place frequented by several old seafarers. Experience taught Byrn that the older people grow, the greater their inclination to tell stories. Sailors liked to tell yarns and talk about boats. Byrn could talk boats. That was his way in.

Over a couple of nights, he'd befriended and bought drinks for an old Estonian salt named Toomas. Over several rums, Byrn expressed his disgust for the Soviet empire. Toomas shared the view passionately. Byrn guided the conversation to the partisans, the Forest Brothers, and Toomas had been unstoppable. When the assassin finally confessed that he sought a place to store some contraband goods he was bringing into the country, Toomas had suggested this cave. He knew of it because his father had been one of the partisans.

Toomas was certain that very few people were aware of its existence.

Toomas' directions were thorough, but it still took Byrn half a day to locate the cave. When he explored it, he realized the hidden entrance and its depth into the stony mountain side made it ideal for his purposes. The time with Toomas was well spent.

Byrn gazed at the prone man before him. The old lady's speech had clearly stunned him and dented his pride. After Byrn finished with him, her words would seem like a walk in the park. The assassin had seen his face on television and in the media many times. The Russian president portrayed himself as a serious and respected leader, a force to be feared. Byrn snickered to himself. We'll see how this alpha male reacts when he's facing his own fear rather than dishing it out on others.

Somewhere at the back of the cave, a tiny underground stream dripped water across the rocks. As ever, the tempo was inconsistent. Byrn grew accustomed to the irritation. There was zero natural light, so he'd placed a couple of small LED lanterns around the cavern. It was enough to see Aleyev clearly. It was also enough for Aleyev to see him. The assassin wondered how long it would take the president to comprehend the significance of that.

They must have been at least fifty feet underground. No one outside could possibly hear them, although Byrn fitted a MODX-9 segmented, titanium printed, 9mm suppressor to his SIG Sauer to be certain. The cave had been fairly low and narrow on the way in. Byrn worked hard to get the semiconscious man through. He was sure the cuts and bruises the president suffered along the journey would be painful when he became fully conscious. He hoped so.

The area where he sat now, perched against a natural rock wall, was at least six feet high and around sixty square feet in size. There was only one way in and out. The Forest brothers had done well to find this place. Byrn was sure it would have served their needs.

The assassin maintained his vigil. Slowly, Aleyev's mumblings turned into slurred words.

Byrn waited.

After a while, the single words turned into incomprehensible sentences.

Byrn waited.

Eventually.

"*Kto ty?* Who are you?"

Byrn remained silent.

"*Chto ty khochesh?* What do you want?"

Byrn leaned forward and tilted his head. As though speaking to a child.

"Speak English please."

"*Ya ne govoryu po-angliyski.* I don't speak English."

"Well, you did just fine back at the sub-base talking to Kristiina Volk." Byrn realized Aleyev would not have seen his face at that point.

"*Net.*"

Byrn shrugged his shoulders, reached a hand into his jacket, and pulled out the Sig. He raised it, pointed it at Aleyev's right foot and shot off his big toe.

The president screamed.

"Okay. Now we understand the rules, Mr. President. Let's begin."

Chapter 50

"Today's session will be split into two parts. The first will deal with reflection. After that, you'll get an opportunity to present your case."

Byrn's words were emphasized by a slight echo within the cavern.

Aleyev looked his accoster dead in the eye.

"You're insane."

"Raised. Discussed. No verdict reached."

"What do you want from me?" pleaded the president.

Byrn paused to study the man. He'd wrapped a bandage around his foot. It was far too early for him to be allowed to pass out through loss of blood. The assassin was slightly surprised that his prisoner remained somewhat defiant, even after being shot. He supposed you didn't reach the zenith of power in a formidable federation such as Russia without having the '*cajones*' to see it through.

"It's not so much what I want from you, Mr. President, as what I can do for you. I fear that at this point you are still in the stage of denial, but I assure you what is happening to you is very real."

"You won't get away with this," said Aleyev. "My people will come for me."

Bargaining. Threatening. It was all the same to Byrn.

"Please don't rush the proceedings, Mr. President. You will be given the opportunity to make a plea, a bargain if you like, at a later time. And if you can't follow the rules, there will be further consequences."

Byrn glanced at Aleyev's foot. The president inhaled as though about to speak before changing his mind.

Byrn continued talking.

"My first task here today is to hold up a kind of prognostic mirror, if you will. I urge you to participate fully. Others before you have found it a sobering experience."

"Others?"

"Let's not dwell on *my* past, sir. This is all about you."

Silence.

"Okay. For a moment, I want you to imagine I'm holding this large mirror in front of you. Think of it as a real mirror. Take a look and tell me what you see?"

More silence.

Byrn had placed the gun on the stony cave floor. He reached down and picked it up, grasping it loosely in his hand.

"I urge you, sir. It's best to avoid disciplinary consequences."

Aleyev surveyed the weapon and then fixed his gaze on the assassin's face. His brow creased, and he held his bound hands tight to his stomach.

Not broken, not defiant.

Eventually.

"I would see a man who is strong, purposeful. A leader of other men. A professional who works at a level pissants like you couldn't comprehend."

"Okay, well, that's a start, but please refrain from personal insults. They serve you no purpose but may risk my irritation."

Byrn lowered his eyes to the SIG as he spoke.

"All right," the assassin continued. "A dialog begins. It's been my experience that when a person looks into a mirror, they see either what they want to see, or what their life circumstances lead them to assume is there. In your case, your observations appear to be a mixture of the two."

Aleyev didn't respond.

"Let me explain. I believe it comes down to a matter of ego. It's a funny thing, ego. Everyone needs some, but if you have too much, it can turn dangerous. I'll give you an example. I need to possess a certain confidence, ego, if you like, to sit here threatening one of the most powerful men in the world. With no ego, I'd collapse, degenerate into a quivering mess, and you'd walk, or should I say limp, right out of here."

Aleyev nodded, a slight sneer forming on his lips.

Byrn smiled before continuing.

"On the other hand, if I possess too much ego, I could become overconfident. I might make a mistake, given my belief that I can do no wrong. It may be a small error, such as accidentally placing my weapon within your reach. Once again, you would walk right over me, and it would have been my ego that let me down."

"What is your point?" asked the president.

"Good. Questions that are relevant. My point, sir, is that ego is what you are currently seeing in our mirror. You are seeing who you think you are, not really who you are. My role is to help you make a deeper connection with yourself. A kind of therapy if you like."

"You have no idea…"

Byrn sprung up in a flash. In two paces he stood over the president. He flipped his SIG over in his hand and pistol

234

whipped the man hard across his face. Aleyev's neck cracked as the side of his head smashed against the rock wall behind him.

"You would do well not to make accusations or insult me, Mr. President. I thought I'd made that clear," he spat.

Byrn resumed his seat against the opposite wall and tilted his head to one side. Softening.

"I suppose if I was to reflect a little, I would confess to you that I may have accidentally induced your indiscretion."

"How?" asked Aleyev.

"In my analogy, I called you one of the most powerful men in the world. But I lied. Sorry about that. At this moment, you are probably the least powerful human being on this planet. Your every whim, your every move, your every opportunity to survive are in my hands. Do you understand, Mr. former President? For the first time in your pathetic life, you have no power at all."

Byrn waited, gazing at the man, as his words sunk in. Byrn wondered if the initial gray clouds of acceptance had crossed his prisoner's eyes. No, it was too soon. There was more work to do.

"Let's talk about your life and the way you view it. As you speak, I urge you to cast your ego aside and see the real Vadim Aleyev. Perhaps we should begin with a subject simple to define. Achievement. What have you really achieved, Mr. President?"

Byrn watched as the man before him pushed his shoulders back, straightening as much as he could, given his restrained position. Clearly, he'd heard nothing Byrn had said.

"I've been ambitious for my country. I've led my people towards a stronger, more secure existence, where Russia holds her rightful place in the world order."

"Bullshit."

"Who are you to judge?"

"Stupid question, Mr. President. To you, right now, in this moment, I am the most powerful judge you will ever face in this world."

Aleyev straightened himself even further before spitting across the cavern, his saliva landing on Byrn's shoe.

"You have no…"

Byrn picked up the gun and shot the president in his right ankle. The man screamed.

Byrn paused while his victim came to grips with his pain.

"Well, we've established at least one thing, Mr. President. You're a slow learner."

Byrn withdrew a bandage from his bag and wrapped it tightly around Aleyev's latest wound. His prisoner grimaced as he tied it tight.

"I'm beginning to think I need to speak more simply and perhaps make things a little clearer," said the assassin.

"You talk to me as though I'm a child."

"You may have hit the nail on the head there, sir. A child is born believing the whole world revolves around him or her. And it does. That's the job of being a good parent. People like you, Mr. President, people who have created a power vacuum around themselves by associating only with those who either agree with you, pretend they agree with you or serve your every whim because they are scared of you, create the same effect."

"How can you possibly…"

Byrn raised his palm.

"Please don't interrupt, Mr. President. It's rude." Byrn

glanced at his SIG. Aleyev leaned back against the wall, a slight gasp audible. The training was beginning to work. "As I was saying, it comes back to ego. Parents create that sense of entitlement in their youngsters because they pamper them. A false ego. You've done the same in your world. I congratulate you. It's a very hard thing to do. This is a feat that can only be accomplished by men of great power."

Byrn watched as Aleyev allowed himself a small grin. He knew he would.

"Or bullies," added the assassin. "You know the type. The abusive and controlling husband and father who intimidates his family to bend to his every whim. Your kind of person."

"I object..."

"Don't."

Aleyev thought better and didn't finish his sentence.

Byrn continued. "We could go on all night about what you consider you've achieved, but to be honest, I don't have the time. So, let's get to the point. I have a few simple questions. I want only simple answers. A yes, no, or numeric response would be preferable."

Aleyev nodded.

"How many innocent people have you had killed?" asked Byrn.

"Less than you, I suspect," Aleyev replied.

"Nice try at deflection, but an incorrect answer."

Aleyev flinched, pressing hard back against the rock.

"Don't worry, Mr. President. You don't receive a punishment for every incorrect answer. In this case, I can supplement your response with some additional information. I Googled it. Speculation is that you've had at least fourteen direct opponents assassinated. I imagine the real number is triple that amount. Now if we go back to your early days here, in Estonia, Kristiina Volk bore witness to the many countrymen of hers you caused to either be shipped off to a Gulag or killed. Assuming your pattern of behavior continued between your beginnings and your current practices, well, surely the number of innocent deaths at your hands must be in the thousands."

Aleyev didn't speak.

"So as for your comparison to my own humble endeavors, you are well wide of the mark."

"Sometimes people need to be sacrificed for the greater good," said Aleyev.

"You know, I'm so glad you brought that up. Once again, sir, you are looking in our mirror and seeing two things that you want to see but aren't really there. That old ego is getting in the way again, isn't it? First. You've assumed these people had to be 'sacrificed' as you say because they disagreed with your views. Are you aware that democracies are designed to withstand disagreement and still move forward?"

"They are weak…"

"No, you are weak President Aleyev. Didn't we just cover that? Have a look around. Remind yourself who holds the power here. It certainly isn't you."

Silence.

"Second point. The greater good. Let's gaze into that mirror and give it another try. Is your country better off than when you took over its reins?"

"Of course, we are respected, feared. The world trembles at our actions. Our people are proud of what we've achieved. They respect my leadership."

Byrn looked at the man. The assassin was a little disappointed, but not surprised.

"You're really trying to bust my bullshit meter here. Let's do a quick fact check. The Russian Federation's economy is tanking. You've been in a negative growth phase for some years and the western sanctions are killing you. So, it can't be the current financial situation that's making your people so proud of you."

No reaction.

"All right, let's look at your military might. Your forces are generally being trounced in Ukraine. They are in disarray, and their families back home know it. You thought you'd bring the opposition to heel in a few days. It's been over a year and now your own hold on the Crimean Peninsula is also threatened. It's the old thing, you know. Drive too far on an empty tank and you're going to run out of petrol eventually. Your tank, sir, is bone dry and the whole world knows it. Plus, your people are growing more pissed by the day."

Byrn offered a condescending smile. It gave him some pleasure.

"Okay. Tell me about your world influence. Surely you can tick that one off as a win?"

"The west now understands that Russia is not a country to be toyed with. We have been provoked and they fear our reprisals."

Byrn smiled again.

"Actually, I don't think they give a shit. From what I understand, more countries have joined NATO since you started your little campaign. The only thing the west is wrestling with is whether to stomp Russia out in one strike of their superior weapons or not. Of course, they won't, because they have nothing against the Russian people. They are not their enemy. You, Vadim Aleyev, are their enemy. How does it feel as a brave leader to be hiding behind women and children?"

For a couple of minutes, Byrn didn't speak. In the confined space, only Aleyev's labored breathing could be heard. Along with the dripping water.

Like a clock.

A ticking clock.

Finally.

"To be truthful, I didn't really expect you to answer that, so I'll give you one more chance, Mr. President. A bonus question. Who will miss you? When you're gone, who genuinely will miss you?"

Aleyev paused, as though weighing up his words carefully.

"If she were alive, my wife Tatiana..."

"Maybe, maybe not. From what I understand, that was somewhat a marriage of convenience. She may have missed her position, but probably not you. Until earlier today, you might have assumed that Kristiina Volk, the flame from your past, would mourn your passing. I think she pretty much confirmed that not to be the case. It didn't go well, did it?"

Aleyev cast his eyes downwards.

"I'll give you a helping hand, shall I? What about your closest colleagues? What about the famed Generals, the leaders of your armed forces? Will they miss Vadim Aleyev, the man?"

Aleyev didn't respond.

"I asked you a question."

Silence.

"A zero response will be met with a consequence," said the assassin.

Aleyev looked up.

"No, they will not miss me."

"They won't? Why not?"

Byrn was genuinely surprised.

Aleyev didn't speak.

"I asked you why not."

More silence.

Byrn stood up, the SIG hanging menacingly in his fingers.

"Speak." The assassin allowed the harsh edge of an angry teacher to envelop his tone.

He took a step forward.

"Because they are dead," yelled Aleyev, his voice almost shrill.

Byrn stopped mid-step. He sank down on his knees in front of the president and began to chuckle. Within two seconds, the chuckle had turned into a full bellied laugh. Byrn felt his eyes watering.

"I'm sorry, that was rude," he said eventually. "It just struck me that as we slip away the layers, as any good therapist should, we're not finding too much underneath."

Byrn paused.

"How many of your trusted leaders did you murder?"

Aleyev shook his head.

"How many?"

"Three."

"Who?"

"Kovalenko, Levitsky and Stepanov."

"They didn't buy in to your plan?"

"*Net.*"

"How?"

"Plane crash."

"Really, how?"

"Bomb."

"You are one evil motherfucker. A tantrum throwing toddler clutching a hand grenade."

"I am a visionary."

"I bet you didn't see this coming."

Lachlan Byrn Dropped his gun to the ground, reached forward and grabbed the president's right hand. As he did so, he reached into the scabbard on his ankle, withdrawing his diver's knife. Aleyev's face seemed transfixed by the weapon's metallic glint as he swept it across between them.

"No," yelled the president, unsuccessfully trying to pull his arm away.

With mechanical precision Byrn bunched Aleyev's middle three fingers together, holding them by their tips, tight in his fist. He then sliced the razor-sharp blade through them just below the knuckles, leaving three bloody stumps.

Not for the first time, President Vadim Aleyev cried out in pain.

"A finger for each man, motherfucker. We're done here. Unsurprisingly, you've failed in your reflection. I can't wait to see how you go in your appeal."

"*Ty zloy chertov ablyudok*. You evil fucking bastard!" yelled the president.

"Wonderful," Byrn responded.

"Anger, right on cue."

Chapter 51

Byrn decided to take a break.

The Russian president wasn't going anywhere, and the assassin didn't want to rush the process. Experience had taught him that the projection of misery was often more distressing than the misery itself. And he intended that Aleyev's misery be maximized.

Byrn knew that Aleyev would be running through every available avenue in his mind. It was important he complete the process and realize that negotiating with Byrn remained his only option. What the president wouldn't know was that Byrn rarely negotiated at all. He wondered what the old lady would make of his progress so far. She'd probably have found it disdainful, yet the assassin figured that some small part of her would find Vadim Aleyev's desperation satisfying.

Byrn stood just outside the cave's entrance, staring into the darkness. There was no sound apart from the natural movements of the forest. He expected the scene back at the submarine base would be a different story. This wouldn't be the first time Lachlan Byrn had been on a country's most wanted list. Truth be told, it would probably be the last.

Byrn sensed a yawn emerging. Once more, he reached into his pocket, flipped open the lid of the vial and popped a few pills. He needed all his senses alert for the next part of the journey.

Anticipation flooded through the assassin's veins like a drug. He turned to retrace his steps into the cave. It was time to go back to work.

Chapter 52

PRESIDENT JEFFERSON BLAKE

Jefferson Blake gazed into the mirror as he tugged down at the edges of his suit jacket. Having your own personal tailor had its advantages, although Blake insisted on paying for the man's services out of his own pocket. He figured the American taxpayers had been slugged enough for the vanity of their presidents. A quick glance around the opulent luxury of his penthouse suite confirmed the view.

His thoughts were interrupted by a sharp knock at the door.

A member of his security team poked her head in the room.

"Mr. President. Director Peterson and Director Durrows would like to have a brief word with you before you leave for the dinner."

"Show them in Jillian."

"Mr. President," said both men almost simultaneously as they entered.

"Fred, Abe, what can I do for you? Time is tight and we don't want to keep President Aleyev waiting."

"About that," said Fred Durrows.

Blake raised an eyebrow.

"We've just received a communication from the Russian

delegation. They've told us that due to the sad deaths of Generals Stepanov and Levitsky, in addition to that of Admiral Kovalenko in an aircraft accident this afternoon, President Aleyev won't be present at the dinner tonight. They say he's returned to Moscow to lead the Russian nation in its time of grief. They have also said that the president is expected back tomorrow morning to resume our summit talks as scheduled. The Russians said they are hopeful that we will accept foreign secretary Pavel Fedorov substituting for the president this evening. They send their profound apologies."

"Well, that confirms what we suspected," said the president. He then eyed the two men.

"You're not telling me everything, are you, gentlemen?"

Durrows glanced at Abe Peterson. Peterson nodded.

"Mr. President. For the first time since we arrived, the Estonians have begun tightening their lips. Our flow of information has gone quiet, if not totally dead," he said.

"What am I missing here?" inquired Blake.

Durrows continued. "There have been some unsubstantiated rumors, sir. Nothing is confirmed, but we've heard that President Aleyev may not actually be back in Moscow as we've been told."

"So where is he?" asked Blake.

"That's the thing, Mr. President. Nobody seems to know. There is every chance that President Aleyev has gone missing... or worse."

"Holy shit," said Blake. "I think you better take a seat and call Secretary Edwards, Cynthia Ford and Ambassador Fisk up here." He waved Durrows and Peterson to a large lounge area of the suite.

"They're already on their way, sir," said Abe Peterson.

Five minutes later, the six of them gathered around the small coffee table. The president sat in a wingback chair by the fire. Secretary Edwards sat opposite him. Fisk sat on the lounge with Durrows while Peterson and Ford remained standing.

"So, what do we do?" asked the president.

"Option one is to stay and continue as though we believe the Russians, and hope Aleyev turns up. That would minimize any possible disruption to the summit process," suggested Nate Edwards.

"Alternatively, we can put everything on pause while my people gather more intelligence before making a final decision. They're running overtime back at Langley now," offered Durrows.

"Abe?" queried the president.

"Sir, we have no choice. The summit has been compromised. For your safety, we must return to Washington immediately."

The group entered a familiar silence while their boss considered the situation. Jefferson Blake was known for his sharp, analytical brain. Everyone in the room knew better than to interrupt him.

Then Blake broke the silence.

"All right. Let's take this one step at a time. We'll attend the dinner tonight. Maybe Fedorov will let something slip and give us a better handle on the situation. After the dinner, we'll make the call on staying or leaving."

Blake turned to the secretary of state on the chair opposite.

"Nate?"

Agreed.

"Rowena?"

"Your call Mr. President."

"Fred?"

"With you all the way, sir."

"Cynthia?"

"I'm not that keen, but I see your point."

"Abe?"

Abe Peterson probably knew his boss better than anyone else present. An outsider would perceive the president's action of calling on each person as inclusive leadership. But Peterson understood that by working the room in that particular order, the president had stacked the odds against him.

"I respectively reiterate my previous statement, Mr. President. My position is that I believe we should go. I do, however, acquiesce to the consensus of my colleagues."

The president looked at his old friend and smiled. He knew that Abe knew what he'd done.

"Matter settled. Now let's go and get a bite to eat."

Chapter 53

LACHLAN BYRN

"Please present your case."

Byrn gazed into the Russian president's eyes. They'd dulled a little. The man was obviously in intense pain. That pleased the assassin.

"What?"

"I said present your case. You're a reasonably intelligent man. I assume you have a grip on the most likely outcome of our meeting today. I shall probably kill you. So here is your opportunity. Persuade me. Give me a reason to let you live."

"Who made you the judge and jury?"

"I thought we'd been through that. The gun in my hand and the ties on your arms and legs offer me that privilege. And of course, you left out part of my role description. The full title is judge, jury, and executioner. I'm sure the exclusion was just a Freudian slip on your behalf."

Byrn laughed.

"I'm waiting."

"You know my people will find you. When they succeed, they'll kill you without asking questions," said Aleyev. "If you release me now, you may have a chance."

"I'm really not that sure your people are trying all that hard to find me or you. We've already established that there aren't too many people who are going to mourn your loss. I expect there are some diehard fans, but I suspect most will only be going through the motions. Certainly, the Estonians won't bust their gut trying to locate you. Next argument."

Aleyev sighed deeply. Each breath seemed to herald more pain.

"I am a wealthy man. You've no idea how much money I can provide you with."

"Two points here," Byrn responded. "I'm already as financially secure as I need to be. Also, I don't receive stolen goods. Well, not on that scale anyway."

"I beg your pardon?"

"Come on, get with the game. Your wealth comes from the money you stole from your people. I'm not interested."

The president's shoulders appeared to sag. His gray eyes seemed to be searching. Byrn appreciated that no matter which door he opened, Aleyev would find the room empty.

A quiet silence flooded the room. Byrn got the impression that Aleyev was at odds with himself. Eventually, he found some resolution.

"I am in a position to offer you information."

The assassin leaned forward and spoke in a whisper.

"Do I look like James fucking Bond? I'm not some half-witted spy trying to pump you for intelligence. I don't work for any country. Well, at least not usually. By the way, President Xiong Lei says hi."

Aleyev recoiled at the revelation.

"You're working for China?"

"A temporary relationship. I'm about to break it off."

"Would you be interested in employment with the Russian Federation?"

Desperation.

"In my line of work, it's dangerous to break contracts in the middle of a job. Thanks, but no thanks."

Aleyev paused. Byrn knew he was searching, despairingly.

"The information, do you want it?" asked the president.

Maybe Byrn was wrong. Perhaps one room had a small box within its walls. Despite what he'd just said, his curiosity was slightly piqued. Curiosity could be a killer.

"Okay, let's take that thought for a walk for a moment. What information do you possibly possess that may be of interest to me?"

"If I tell you, will you release me?"

"I'll consider it."

Negotiation stalled.

Despite his agony, Byrn could see the Russian president attempting to read him. Good luck with that.

Finally, Aleyev shrugged his shoulders. "It would appear I have little to lose."

"You have nothing to lose."

The Russian president drew a deep breath. From his involuntary flinch, Byrn could tell the pain was beginning to dominate the man's thinking.

"Very well," Aleyev began. "Tomorrow, Jefferson Blake, the American president, is going to die."

"And you know this how?"

"My people are going to kill him."

"Your people?"

"I have three operatives, including the finest marksman in the federation, already in position. No matter what you do to

251

me, the man will be dead by the day's end."

Byrn was honestly surprised. This guy never gave up.

Aleyev crouched forward, as much as he was able, anticipating Byrn's reply. The assassin mulled the information over in his head.

The water kept dripping.

Eventually.

"Ahh, nah. On reflection, I really don't give a shit if Blake lives or dies. No deal."

Byrn scrutinized the Russian's response. He'd been wrong. The man did give up. Byrn watched it happen. The president's eyes glazed over, and his body slumped back against the wall.

Depression and acceptance. This time it came as a package deal.

Byrn could live with that.

Of course, the Russian president wouldn't.

Chapter 54

JEFFERSON BLAKE

"Minister Fedorov, I'm glad to have this opportunity to have a quiet chat."

"No, it is I, Mr. President, who should be grateful. Thank you for allowing me to step in on President Aleyev's behalf while he is indisposed."

Jefferson Blake and Pavel Fedorov stood facing the majestic French doors, which lead out onto a patio overlooking the sculptured and manicured gardens of Kadriorg Palace. Blake thought it an impressive sight. The president was also aware that the Secret Service snipers that would be secreted around the grounds would be nervous at best, watching their president stand in front of such a large window in a foreign landscape.

"Kadriorg is a majestic environment, isn't it, minister? We have been quite fortunate that the Estonians were prepared to host our meetings here."

"Indeed, the architectural beauty almost matches that of my homeland."

Blake smiled.

The formalities now over, the president was pleased to have

some one-on-one time with the Russian foreign minister.

"I recall our first meeting. It was at your embassy in Washington. We both held significantly different roles back then," said Blake.

"It is kind of you to remember, Mr. President. I recall we spoke at the time of our hopes for a developing relationship between our two countries."

"Indeed, we did minister. It would seem history has relegated that to be a missed opportunity."

Pavel Fedorov turned from the window and looked up at the American president. Blake had a good six inches on him.

"Opportunity is a word that can mean many things, Mr. President. Don't you believe so?"

Blake scanned the vast room. No one was within listening distance.

"In what sense, minister?"

"Opportunity has brought you and I here together."

"Yes, that's true. Although I will certainly be passing my condolences on the loss of his colleagues directly to President Aleyev tomorrow. It was a terrible accident. It must have come as quite a shock?"

Fedorov smiled, just a little.

"Yes, to me it was a great shock. But sometimes a shock is different from a surprise."

Blake sensed the Russian foreign minister was trying to make a point.

The minister continued.

"You know there are many who would take advantage of such a tragedy, and our beloved leader's absence to score some political points. Fortunately, I am loyal to the president. I am here to do his bidding even if my own personal viewpoint may differ slightly to his."

Message received, thought Blake.

"Yes, I appreciate your point. It's a fine line between making the most of an opportunity and being an opportunist," he replied.

"I see that you fully understand, Mr. President. I fear that in our game, politics, there are opportunists on both sides of the fence. Good men always need to be wary of them. Don't you agree?"

"I couldn't agree more, Minister Fedorov. We should always remain alert."

Warning received, but a warning regarding exactly what?

"We should probably rejoin the group, lest my colleagues perceive that I'm manipulating your valuable time, Mr. President," said Fedorov.

Blake nodded, gesturing towards the center of the room.

"After you, minister."

Blake was now more certain than ever that all was not well in the halls of the Kremlin. Perhaps Abe Peterson was right, and they should hightail it out of there.

Perhaps.

Chapter 55

LACHLAN BYRN

"It's time, Mr. President. Vadim."

"Time for what?"

"The inevitable."

Aleyev appeared to shrink back into a mental cocoon. Byrn noted a small tremor in his leg. The uninjured leg. Good.

"Don't beat yourself up, Vadim. You had almost no chance of dissuading me, anyway."

Even in the shadowy light, Byrn saw the color drain from Vadim Aleyev's face.

"Is there nothing…"

"There is nothing at all. Now is the time for acceptance."

The slow drip of the water permeated their silence.

Byrn allowed the man to prepare himself. The tremor had become a quiver that slowly racked his victim's body.

Then Aleyev whispered, "I don't want to die."

Byrn smiled.

"And yet here we are, Vadim. The moment. Think carefully of the thousands whose death you have caused. Consider the sensations you are experiencing, the trepidation, the paralyzing fear. You are sharing that now with all your victims. You are feeling what they were feeling. You have become one."

Aleyev uttered a guttural moan.

"Please?"

"How many of your dead pleaded with their executioners, Vadim? And how few were shown mercy?"

Silence.

Finally.

"How?"

Byrn leaned forward, his lips close to Aleyev's ear.

"This is my thing, Vadim. My specialty," he whispered.

"I have been unsuccessful in helping you repent. But taking your life, the way you stole so many others will be a pleasure."

"How?" Aleyev repeated, his voice barely audible.

"You offered me numerous options, Vadim, but I have chosen your favorite. It is my gift to you."

Byrn leaned over to his bag and extracted a pair of latex surgical gloves. He showed them to Aleyev before slipping them on.

"In my game, you can't be too careful."

He then lay down beside Aleyev, his lips once more whispering into his victim's ear.

"Have a look Vadim, there's enough light."

Byrn reached into his pocket and produced a small vial. It wasn't his modafinil. He held it in front of Aleyev's face.

"Can you read the label, Vadim?"

Aleyev squinted before making an audible gasp. He began struggling.

"No... no."

"It's too late for that, Vadim. Your body will fight enough as the poison enters your system. It's your favorite. Novichok."

Aleyev continued to struggle.

"It's best you just take it easy. Your future has already been defined. Relax now."

The Russian groaned again before finally slumping into despair.

"Now open wide, we don't want any accidents."

Aleyev clenched his mouth closed.

"It will be easier if you open up, believe me."

Aleyev continued to bite down on his lips.

"Very well then."

In a single movement, Byrn reached behind him, grabbed a builder's hammer out of his bag, and brought it slamming down on Aleyev's fortressed jaw. The crunch of smashing teeth and bone preceded the man's scream.

"That's better. Drink it all up now."

The assassin poured the thick liquid into the Russian's mouth. His prisoner was beyond struggling.

Byrn lay there, watching in the dim light, searching his victim's face. The first symptom, he noted, was the shrinking of the president's pupils into tiny dots.

"It's working Vadim. Can you feel it?"

The dose had been pure and strong. The assassin expected the onset of the symptoms to be quite rapid. He wasn't disappointed.

Aleyev began sweating. Every pore became a torrent.

Slowly, the wheezing turned into desperate gasps. Erratic at first, then building in intensity.

"You know the routine, Vadim. You virtually invented it," he whispered.

Aleyev's body started writhing in involuntary convulsions. The man who controlled everything and everyone now had no control at all.

Byrn wrinkled his nose.

"Oh, Vadim, you've soiled yourself."

The convulsions continued, growing increasingly violent.

"It won't be long now. Of course, you can never be certain whether it's the cardiac arrest or suffocation in your own fluids that will get you. I'm guessing in your case, Kristiina would assume the latter."

Byrn giggled.

A desperate gargling sound suddenly filled the cavern as the president struggled for air. It peaked like a rasping wave before gradually lessening.

"Do you see them, Vadim? Can you see their faces? Have they come to welcome you? They'll stay with you forever now. The people you've killed. The innocents you've tortured. This is their moment."

Suddenly, all movement stopped. The Russian's body lay almost motionless as the final breaths of air were expelled from his flooded lungs.

Lachlan Byrn stood up and stretched before gazing down at the corpse.

President Vadim Aleyev, once the most feared man on earth, was now a memory.

And Lachlan Byrn was free.

Chapter 56

JEFFERSON BLAKE

"That's not good news. What the hell is going on?"

Nate Edwards had just informed President Blake that the Russian president would be unable to join them for the final summit meeting later that day.

"It would suggest that last night's reports that President Aleyev has gone missing may be correct after all," replied Edwards.

"Your thoughts, Fred?"

"I concur, Mr. President. We're only getting information in small pieces, but everything we've received points to the fact the Russians can't locate their own leader."

Blake surveyed the space. It was a small meeting room on the second floor of the palace. His team from the night before were all present and sitting in a circle of chairs.

"Do you all agree?"

Fisk, Ford and Peterson all nodded.

"With respect, Mr. President, I would suggest that the news indicates the game is over and we should inform the Estonian authorities of our intention to leave the country," said Abe Peterson.

"You're probably right, Abe. Maybe I should have listened to you last night. The trouble is that something in the back of my mind was telling me it may be worth seeing this through."

"What is there to see through now, Mr. President? Aleyev is gone, the summit is over," Peterson added.

"Fred?" The president looked directly at the CIA director.

"I'm inclined to agree with Abe. We've got nothing to gain by remaining here, and we risk your exposure in an unstable environment if we do."

Blake nodded. "It's not only my exposure. It's the whole team."

"Shall I instruct my people to prepare for your departure, Mr. President?" asked Peterson.

Blake was on the verge of agreement when there was a knock on the door and one of Nate Edwards' aides stepped into the room.

"Excuse me Mr. President, everyone. I have an urgent dispatch for Secretary Edwards." The man clutched a slim folder.

Blake nodded. Edwards held out a hand and took the folder. The aide departed and everyone waited.

Eventually Edwards looked up.

"It's a communication from the Russian delegation. They say that they are hopeful the summit will continue and are offering Foreign Minister Pavel Fedorov as a surrogate in place of President Aleyev. It states that Minister Fedorov has indicated that he'd hate to see such a fine opportunity to continue our two countries' negotiations to slip by. They await our response."

Opportunity.

"Your thoughts, everyone?" asked the president.

261

"What negotiations?" asked Cynthia Ford. "So far, Aleyev and the Russians have yielded nothing."

There was a general murmur of agreement around the room.

"I believe that to be the point, Ladies and Gentlemen," the president began. "As you know, in our conversation last night, Fedorov indicated he may hold a different perspective to President Aleyev. He also emphasized that real opportunities for our relationship to move forward should not be missed. He virtually confirms that in this message."

Fred Durrows chimed in.

"Of course, I completely understand and respect your viewpoint, Mr. President, but as CIA Director, I feel obligated to present a different perspective."

"Go on, Fred," said Blake.

"The bottom line here is that we simply cannot confirm the facts required to make an informed decision," Durrows continued. "First the plane crash killing the upper Russian military hierarchy, then the Russian president returns to Moscow or, equally possible, goes missing. We also have to consider the real possibility Vadim Aleyev has been assassinated. This is a moving landscape, sir. Nothing, including your safety, is guaranteed."

"Abe, I assume you share this view?" asked Blake.

Peterson nodded.

The president sat back in his chair. There were a multitude of factors to assess. As per their normal protocol, nobody interrupted.

Until there was another knock on the door. A different aide entered, with the same apologies. This time, he strode over to Fred Durrows to deliver a folder like the earlier one.

Blake looked up.

"Mr. President, with your permission?"

"Go ahead, Fred."

"I have a note from Yuri Varkov, my opposite number in the FSB. He has expressed his endorsement for the summit to continue and will support our security measures in any way we see fit."

"Is that a bit odd?" asked Peterson. "Do the FSB usually contribute to political and diplomatic level decisions such as this?"

"No. But everything in this situation is a bit odd, Abe," Durrows responded.

"All right," began President Blake. "I'm hearing every word that Nate and Abe are saying, and in all honesty, their recommendation to leave makes the most sense. However, Minister Fedorov's words are still playing on my mind. We may never be here again. We may never have an opportunity to move forward without an Aleyev or someone like him muddying the waters."

Blake scanned the room, searching people's faces for their reactions. He continued.

"I therefore believe it's in the best interest of the United States that we stay and conclude our meetings with Pavel Fedorov leading the Russian delegation. That said, the security risk has obviously amped up considerably. Accordingly, I'll arrange for anyone who would rather leave to do so. Such a decision will not affect your career, nor my perception of your strong commitment to our country. Many of you have families. If your gut is telling you to go, please listen to it. You will not be judged."

"Dammit, Mr. President," said Cynthia Ford. "It's speeches

like that, that haul me in against my own better judgement. I'm staying with you, sir."

Blake scanned the room. Heads nodded in agreement.

"Mr. President, it appears we're all in," announced Secretary Edwards.

Blake smiled.

"I thank you. And your country thanks you. So, let's get to work."

Chapter 57

PAVEL FEDOROV

"I thank you for your support, Yuri. To be honest, I thought the FSB would be distracted by President Aleyev's disappearance and would insist we halt the summit."

FSB Director Yuri Varkov smiled across the large desk that sat between the two men. They were seated in a conference room at the prestigious hotel that accommodated the Russian delegation.

"It is not a problem, minister. Like you, I desperately hope that our president will be located safe and well. Despite Estonian protests, I'm flying more of my people over as we speak to pursue the search and the investigation."

"Excellent, Yuri."

"I'm certain that President Aleyev would wish the summit to continue. So much work has gone into the preparations." Varkov smiled again.

This time, Fedorov felt a slight chill as he watched the man opposite. It was the smile. Perhaps a little too familiar. Traces of the Arctic wolf.

"Are you sure you're telling me everything, Yuri?"

"Of course, minister. What would I have to gain by

deceiving you?"

What indeed? thought Fedorov.

Chapter 58

LACHLAN BYRN

Byrn had work to do.

He needed to tidy up around the cave and then commit to the extraction.

The assassin checked his watch. Three hours until sunrise. That should give him all the time he required. He pulled one of the burner phones out of his bag, walked to the cave entrance, and inserted a new SIM card. He'd committed Zhen Su's number to memory. Two minutes later, he'd sent the text.

Job completed. Extraction location as arranged. 0700.

Next, Byrn needed to dispose of Aleyev's body. He didn't want to hide the corpse, but rather have it discovered somewhere else. It took the assassin around an hour to wrap the messy corpse up in plastic, fling him over his shoulder and walk him a mile further into the forest.

He then jogged back to the cave.

After cleaning and wiping everything, Byrn deposited all the evidence into one of his bags. He'd dump the bag as soon as possible but wanted to do so a good distance away. It was his intention that the authorities would think Aleyev's body was dumped in the forest rather than killed there. It was all smoke and mirrors, but experience had taught him that smoke and mirrors bought time. The assassin was aware that this wasn't completely clean in terms of leaving no trace of his presence. He'd been forced to leave some gear behind. Regardless of how well he cleaned it before taking out Aleyev, Byrn suspected the foxhole at the submarine base would contain some traces of his DNA. That simply couldn't be helped.

It was now imperative he reached the extraction point before sunrise. Once the sun rose, Byrn held no doubt that the sky would be filled with choppers and light planes, searching for any sign of the missing president. In fact, he wanted it that way. One additional chopper in the Estonian airspace coming to pick him up would hardly be noticed.

After reclaiming the KTM, Byrn set off through the forest, with only the moonlight to guide him. Cautiously navigating through the undergrowth, the bike bucked under his hands. It was hard going, but when he hit the wider dirt road, he'd turn on the headlights and make a dash for it. The assassin had memorized the entire route before securing himself at the Hara base.

Everything in Lachlan Byrn's world was planned to within an inch of its life.

Byrn left the Lahemaa Rahvuspark near the village of Uuri. As the bike sped along the back roads, the assassin made his way east. As the asphalt disappeared under his front wheel, Byrn sensed his tiredness start to overwhelm him. He'd reached his limit of days awake, even flying on the Night Eagle's wings. The assassin knew the crash was coming, and he needed to be in a safe place before it did. Each oncoming headlight caused him to squint in fatigue. The white line in the middle of the road appeared to come and go, although Byrn knew it hadn't changed at all. It was his perception that was changing.

The sign indicated he'd just passed through the village of Hingu. On the outskirts, Byrn pulled over, grabbed his vial, and popped some more pills. He was now on a double dose but still fading fast.

Not long to go.

A little before sunrise, Byrn veered right at the village of Rehemäe in Lääne County. He tracked down a series of side roads, each one a little more remote to the last until he came upon the small forest he sought. The bike bumped and pulled as he rode through the bush toward the clearing that was the extraction site. Remaining in the shadows of the trees, he stopped, kicked the motorcycle up on its stand, and glanced at his watch.

0645. He'd just made it.

The assassin got off the bike and scampered to the edge of the clearing. He'd have liked more time to scope out the site, but that wasn't to be. Ten minutes later, Byrn was satisfied that no one else was present.

Byrn had two tasks left to perform before the chopper arrived. He reinserted his SIM card back into his phone and sent a brief text to the Estonian Police and Border Guard headquarters. It gave them the exact coordinates of President Vadim Aleyev's body. The assassin had a couple of reasons for the call. He knew his Chinese masters would want evidence of the kill, and he wanted the authorities to send all available resources to a location far away from his extraction point.

Two birds, one stone.

Byrn had wrestled with the second task on his long ride through the night. He was exhausted, and perhaps not even thinking straight. He couldn't give a shit about politicians of any country or persuasion. To Byrn, they were all the same. Self-centered liars and power mongers. He didn't care whether they lived or died, unless he was tasked with killing one. But something gnawed at him throughout the journey.

Jefferson bloody Blake.

From what Byrn had read, Blake seemed the best of a bad bunch. The assassin had recent experience of the worst. If it was within his gamut to make one call to warn Blake's people, should he? He didn't really care one way or another. In his fatigued state, he wondered what Kristiina Volk would have done. It took Byrn around two seconds to realize she would have made the call.

Shit.

Byrn redialed the number before leaving another brief text.

Assassination attempt planned for President Jefferson Blake at summit. Three shooters, informant reliable.

Byrn pulled out the SIM card and destroyed it with his knife. If they were smart, the authorities would twig that both his messages came from the same number. However, knowing how these butt coverers worked, Byrn reckoned they wouldn't react to the second message until they'd verified the first.

So be it. He'd done his good turn... for Kristiina.

Byrn was well aware that the planned extraction could create an opportune moment for his Chinese minders to eliminate him, wipe him from their game plan if that's what they chose. Perhaps he'd become like Pavlov's dogs, conditioned to obey, a belief in his masters, embedded into his subconscious.

A few seconds later, Byrn noted the drone of a distant aircraft. A minute after that, he recognized the distinctive whir of helicopter blades. Well, what do you know? Zhen Su was as good as his word. Life was full of surprises.

The assassin squatted at the edge of the wood as he watched the unmarked helo land, its wash flattening the surrounding grass. The engines remained active just as Byrn would have expected, but still, he paused for certainty. A man in black military fatigues climbed out of the rear door before scrutinizing the area.

Again, Byrn waited.

Perhaps Zhen really had done the right thing this time.

Byrn took two steps into the clearing. The figure in black noticed him and waved him over. He then retreated into the helo's cabin.

Relieved that his mission was almost complete, Byrn threw his backpack over his shoulder and ran towards the helicopter, keeping his head down.

The assassin had made it to within fifteen yards of the bird when the sharp morning sun exposed a slight metallic glint from within the chopper cabin. It could have been anything, but it wasn't.

Byrn plunged face down onto the grass as the first rounds flew above his head. He rolled to the right as the next burst peppered the ground where he'd just been laying. The assassin lay totally exposed and seconds away from certain death. He couldn't reach the woods or the helicopter.

As the gunfire pulverized the surrounding dirt, Byrn rolled right and then left. He may as well have been rolling dice.

Surprised he was still alive, Byrn realized he'd ended up at a forty-five-degree angle forward of the helo's rear cabin door. The shooter now had to lean out slightly to make his shot.

That was all Byrn needed.

He retrieved his SIG Sauer from his coat, straightened his arms, and aimed. Even in his exhausted state, Byrn didn't know how to panic. As his attacker swung the barrel of his automatic around, Byrn fired.

Three taps.

Three rounds found their mark, and the shooter tumbled out of the helicopter's cabin.

Immediately, the chopper rose in the air. Byrn grabbed his backpack and sprinted back to the protection of the trees.

The bird circled, its crew obviously searching for another opportunity to complete their mission. Byrn poked his head out of the forest and fired two more rounds into the aircraft's windows. The bird rose higher and headed west towards the coast.

Byrn waited for a couple of minutes before sprinting into the clearing to confirm his kill. From the look of the bloodied corpse laying splayed on the ground, each one of Byrn's shots would have been fatal.

Satisfying. Like shooting metal ducks at a fair.

Byrn dragged the body off the clearing and ten yards into the forest before dumping it. He then picked up his backpack and returned to the KTM.

A wave of tiredness punched through his body like an anesthetic. Byrn was running on empty now. Against his better judgment, he reached into his pocket and grabbed out some more pills. As he threw them down his throat, he knew he was so far over the recommended dose it was ridiculous. Soon his body would become wracked with the nervous energy that too much modafinil induced. Shortly, he'd begin sweating and shaking. More to the point, his ability to think clearly would be affected.

The clock was ticking.

Chapter 59

The morning sun lit the paddock as Byrn perched in the forest shadows. There was no sign of the deadly firefight that had just occurred. The assassin leaned against his backpack and kicked at the dirt. Part of him wondered why he was taking any time at all to decide his next move. He always had a contingency plan, and he had one now. All he needed to do was enact it.

Byrn wasn't at all surprised by Zhen Su's betrayal. He'd half expected it. It made sense to take their man on the ground out. It was the policy of the Chinese Ministry of State Security. No trails lead back to Beijing.

Lachlan Byrn was a trail.

The assassin also knew that at some point, if he made it out of his current predicament, he would be heading to Beijing. There was a conversation to be had with Zhen and a resolution to reach.

Byrn smiled at the thought.

In the meantime, the assassin's Plan B lay tied to a jetty just under an hour away. It wasn't his own sloop, but rather a thirty-foot fishing boat Byrn had bought online. It remained in its home port of Virtsu Kalasadam. Byrn had the craft checked out and serviced, all under a false name, and it stood ready to go. Now that all Estonian land borders, airports and main seaports would be either shut down or under immense scrutiny, a leisurely motor down the Baltic Sea toward Copenhagen seemed the most inconspicuous escape route.

Yet Byrn sat here kicking at dirt.

Perplexing.

In his previous calculations, the assassin gave himself a 60/40 chance of making it out of the country by boat if the Chinese let him down. Now, every moment he hesitated, stacked the odds further against him.

He kicked some more dirt.

Shit.

The assassin stood up and walked in tight circles, thinking.

Shit, shit, shit.

Damn that old woman.

Could he be having some sort of moral conundrum? Absurd. Why would he? Why the fuck was he hesitating?

More circles. More dirt.

Surely it was the fatigue catching up with him. Those damn drugs.

Another circle.

Shit.

Five minutes later, Byrn had climbed back on the KTM and rode east along the back roads. When he came to Ääsmae-Haapsalü-Rohukula road, he stopped the bike, planted his foot on the dirt and revved the engine. Without thinking further, he released the clutch, accelerated and swung sharply left.

North towards Tallinn.

As his front wheel hit the asphalt, Byrn twisted the throttle fully open.

What the fuck was he doing?

Damn Kristiina Volk and her innate moral decency.

Damn President Jefferson fucking Blake and his self-righteous campaign against the tyranny of bully nations.

Damn his own contorted principles.

Damn everyone.

As the port of Virtsu disappeared further behind him, Lachlan Byrn asked himself a simple question.

Why?

As the wind screamed past his helmet, the assassin reached one conclusion.

He simply didn't like bullies.

He knew the authorities, the Secret Service, and all the other henchmen in Blake's sphere would do nothing. At least, not until they received further information. Typical ass coverers.

Lachlan Byrn could do something.

He would do something.

He just had no idea what.

Shit.

Chapter 60

Byrn rode his motorcycle along the Lagna Tee, the main thoroughfare bordering Kadriorg Park. The vast woods and parklands housed the Kadriorg Palace, where the American-Russian summit was taking place. Every road leading into the park was blocked off, some with check points, others totally inaccessible. The dark uniforms of the Estonian Police and Border guards swarmed like ants, infiltrating the facility. Out of sight, but just as active, would be members of the US Secret Service alongside operatives from the Russian Federal Protective Service.

The place seemed as impregnable as Fort Knox.

But Lachlan Byrn knew somebody didn't think so.

Byrn motored past. He saw no point in attracting unwarranted attention. He'd dumped the KTM and stolen a BMW K1200S. He preferred the Kawasaki he'd had earlier, but beggars, or in this case thieves, can't be choosers. The bike would serve his purposes.

Once he completed his perimeter surveillance, Byrn found a quiet spot and parked. He slipped a new SIM card into one of his phones and googled Kadriorg. Within a couple of minutes, a plan and visual images of the park and the palace appeared.

The most important question that needed answering was whether the summit would continue or be canceled. The greatest likelihood was cancellation. No Russian president, no talks. At that point, Byrn would flee to the coast.

A few minutes later, a breaking news headline flashed up on his screen.

In a joint announcement, the US and Russian Federation delegations have announced that the summit talks scheduled for today will proceed. Foreign Minister Pavel Fedorov will stand in for Russian Federation President Vadim Aleyev while the Russian leader is unavailable.

No trip to the seaside yet.

Next, Byrn had to work against every ingrained instinct of his professional life. He was a researcher and a planner. He was also a master of detail. In this instance, he had only a brief window to determine Aleyev's hit squad's plan and schedule.

Dismounting the bike, the assassin found a park bench and sat to study the images. Byrn had one advantage that no security force could ever truly master. He knew what it was like to be the aggressor rather than the defender. He'd figure out a way to take Blake down and hopefully see a way to stop it.

In the time available, it was an impossible ask.

Almost.

Chapter 61

JEFFERSON BLAKE

"Thank you so much, Mr. President, for agreeing to continue the talks."

Pavel Fedorov sat opposite Blake at the large table in the center of possibly the most ornate room the president had ever seen. On Blake's left sat Secretary of State Nate Edwards, to his right National Security Advisor Cynthia Ford, perched forward on her chair. To Ford's right was the US Ambassador to Russia, Rowena Fisk and to Edward's left sat CIA Director Fred Durrows. The CIA would normally not have a chair at the summit table, but given the unusual circumstances, Blake had insisted.

Assorted assistants and advisors either filled the remaining seats at the table or perched behind their bosses, primed to offer information and advice.

The equivalent team from Russia sat opposite with Fedorov, currently making his opening remarks.

Around the edges of the room, Secret Service agents and Russian Federal Protection officers stood poised and ready. Among them, stationed by the door, was Abe Peterson. His opposite number, Viktor Sidorov, studied the proceedings from across the space.

"Thank you, Minister Fedorov. The United States is happy to continue our conversation with the Russian people. We hope and pray that President Aleyev will soon be in a position to return to his duties."

Jefferson Blake lied well. It worried him how easily the words flowed.

"Shall we make the most of our time and get straight down to business? I believe the first item on the agenda is a review of the latest sanctions the US has instigated regarding Russian trade," announced Fedorov.

"I agree, sir. Let's start there. May I suggest we couple that discussion in tandem with the US's current stance pertaining to some of your federation's border issues as the two appear related?" said Blake.

A collective intake of sharp breaths echoed around the table. No one would have begun a conversation with Vadim Aleyev in such a manner.

Fedorov paused before a small smile creased his lips.

"Of course, Mr. President, I don't see why not."

Blake grinned. Perhaps it was worth continuing the talks after all.

Chapter 62

LACHLAN BYRN

Byrn remained convinced that the park borders stood impenetrable to any single assassin, or, in fact, any small group of operators. But that wasn't really the issue here. Aleyev already had people inside, armed people. That gave his team a considerable head start.

It was common knowledge in this line of work that the one thing national leaders of all persuasions feared the most was a traitor in their midst. A single Secret Service agent, or their Russian equivalent, with an undetected grudge against their leader, could change the whole ball game. Byrn knew these people were trained to watch each other almost as much as the VIP they protected.

Assuming the US president and the Russian foreign minister now sat in a room surrounded by armed security personnel, an attack from a single renegade operator was surely doomed to failure.

They must have another plan.

Byrn kept studying the images in front of him.

What would he do?

Chapter 63

JEFFERSON BLAKE

"So, Minister Fedorov, if your side would agree to lowering your troop numbers on your shared borders with Finland, we might be able to at least begin examining the possibility of Russian banks rejoining the international banking system."

Fedorov scratched his chin.

"Sadly, I cannot make any firm decision without consulting my president, however what you are proposing, Mr. President, may have some merit."

President Blake was astonished. On one hand, he expected no clear resolution from this meeting, yet the forthrightness with which Fedorov expressed opinions that didn't align with Aleyev's known views was surprising.

Chapter 64

LACHLAN BYRN

If Aleyev's plans hadn't been to rely on the swiftness of the Russian security personnel in the room, there must be some other opportunity for his hit team to initiate an attack.

Fortunately, Byrn had been privy to much of the planned security and presidential itineraries thanks to Zhen Su. Yet for the life of him, he just couldn't see a way in.

He decided to risk a patrol of the perimeter on foot. The downside was that he may expose himself to some video surveillance. On the upside, he needed to smell what the hell was going on.

The assassin got up from his seat, pulled his jacket hood over his head and crossed the road.

Chapter 65

PAVEL FEDOROV

Fedorov was giving Blake as much as he could. While he had no idea of his president's current status, the foreign minister needed to tread a fine line. One foot wrong and half the people around the table would inform Aleyev as soon as he returned. On the other hand, for the sake of his country, it was vital he presented a morsel of hope to the Americans.

"Mr. President. If you would care to lay out some sort of pathway forward, regarding the reduction of sanctions, I would be happy to submit it to President Aleyev for his consideration."

Blake nodded.

"Minister Fedorov, we have a draft schedule prepared if you'd like to peruse it."

Fedorov smiled.

"Of course, sir."

Chapter 66

YURI VARKOV

Sitting in the back of his limousine at the abandoned submarine base, Yuri Varkov couldn't believe the reluctance of the Estonian authorities. It seemed every decision and move required the approval of at least five people. Didn't they understand it was their president that the Russians searched for?

For God's sake. The future of the federation was at stake.

Almost.

When Aleyev disappeared, the FSB director had immediately decided to proceed with the plans that he and his president had initiated. There was too much to gain to turn back now.

If Aleyev returned, he'd be pleased.

If he didn't. Well, the bridge from FSB Director to president had been crossed before.

Varkov had no obligation to attend the summit. In fact, it would be politically advantageous if he was away, overseeing the search for the country's leader. He knew exactly how the meeting would be proceeding. That fool, Fedorov, would be giving away everything but the kitchen sink. The people would then see they needed a strong leader to fill the vacuum created by Aleyev's disappearance. Not the weak idiot sitting at the negotiating table right now.

The director smiled to himself. He'd better get back to work searching hard for their missing leader.

But maybe not too hard.

Chapter 67

LACHLAN BYRN

Byrn began striding purposefully around the parkland that sheltered Kadriorg Palace. With his phone clasped in his hand providing directions and a plan of the parklands, he looked like any other interested tourist. At various points along his route, small groups of sightseers and locals gathered, trying to get a glimpse of the activities inside. The summit was a big deal for Estonia.

After leaving the Laagna Tee he made his way down a series of smaller streets until hitting the Narva Road, near the water. It seemed to Byrn that Kadriorg was an appropriate location to hold the summit. It was close to Tallinn center yet shielded by extensive parkland on all sides. The only downside that the assassin could identify was perhaps the opportunity for someone to infiltrate the parkland undetected.

Byrn dismissed the idea as quickly as it had occurred to him. With Estonian, US and Russian security personnel flooding the space, no interloper would stand a chance.

Not unexpectedly, a wave of tiredness swamped his thoughts, muddling his perception. Byrn shook his head clear. He needed to stop regarding this as a mission for a lone assassin. For the Russian squad, this was a group operation. As he walked on, he decided that should be his focus.

The team of three.

Chapter 68

JEFFERSON BLAKE

"I believe we've made significant progress, Minister Fedorov," said the US president. "While I appreciate your team will need to run everything we've discussed past President Aleyev, I'm hopeful your willingness to listen to some of the US positions on these matters bodes well for our countries' future relationship."

Pavel Fedorov smiled across the table.

"I can make no promises, Mr. President, but I shall do my best to convey your views to my president."

Blake glanced around the room. There was certainly a softening of the atmosphere compared to two days earlier. The president knew better than to place the cart before the horse, but at least they had made the most of this opportunity.

"I believe we are due for a break shortly, but there is one more issue I'd like to discuss."

Behind Blake, a door opened, and footsteps clattered across the hard floor. The aide went directly to Fred Durrows, whispering urgently in his ear as he passed his boss a single sheet of paper. Durrows brow creased as he glanced towards Blake. The stern expression on his face indicated all was not well.

"Please accept my apologies for interrupting Mr. President and Minister Fedorov. We have just received some alarming news."

Durrows passed the document to Nate Edwards, who briefly scanned it before passing it to the president.

As Blake read the memo, the seriousness of the moment weighed heavily on his shoulders. He looked up and scrutinized their Russian counterparts.

"I'm sure your people will bring you this news within minutes, but I deeply regret to inform you, all of you," Blake cast his eyes across the whole Russian team, "that we have verified reports that a body has been located in the Lahemaa Rahvuspark south of the Hara submarine base. Initial identification has confirmed the body to be that of President Vadim Aleyev."

An audible collective gasp filled the air.

Within a second, Abe Peterson was relaying instructions over the radio transmitter in his sleeve. Viktor Sidorov did the same on the other side of the room. Those sitting at the table remained speechless as color drained from several of the Russian faces.

Blake looked Fedorov directly in the eye.

"I'm so sorry, minister."

Chapter 69

LACHLAN BYRN

Byrn had reached a spot on the Narva Road just opposite the Russalka Memorial for Russian shipwreck victims. The protective angel brandishing an Orthodox cross towered high into the air. The assassin smirked to himself as he briefly wondered if she would offer any protection for those scheduled to die today.

From his position, he could see up the roadway towards the palace itself. Of course, the road was barricaded, and numerous security and police personnel manned the temporarily constructed gate.

Lachlan Byrn had studied and infiltrated enough VIP events to know how the security would work here. Once past the guards, there would be teams patrolling the parkland. In addition, there would be at least two layers of marksmen, snipers. The outer rim would be focusing on threats external to the facility. The inner circle would concentrate on the VIPs and the immediate area surrounding their location. They would be stationed on rooftops of the numerous additional buildings within the grounds. They would also be positioned in the parkland, perhaps even up trees. Height is everything when it comes to a clean shot.

This was an unusual situation. Armed US and Russian snipers would be working side by side with the common aim of protecting their leaders. It was an odd mixture of international cooperation and potential volatility.

It was also a hell of a lot of firepower.

Byrn asked himself, if he was one of those snipers, where would he be best positioned to cause maximum damage? In addition, the assassin presented himself with a second, more challenging puzzle. How in God's name could he make a shot while surrounded by people just as deadly as himself whose raison d'être was that no harm should befall their charges?

Aleyev described a team of three yet mentioned only one marksman. How was that going to work? What would the other two operatives be doing?

Byrn's thoughts were interrupted by a burst of frantic activity from the guards at the gate. Some were yelling into their radios, others had raised their weapons in alertness, while a few just pointed toward the palace. The assassin gazed past them and up the driveway towards the summit venue. Traffic in and out of the building had increased significantly in the past minutes.

What the hell was going on?

Chapter 70

JEFFERSON BLAKE

Apart from Peterson and Sidorov talking into their hand pieces, everyone in the room sat in a stunned silence.

Several seconds passed.

Fedorov turned to Viktor Sidorov. The presidential security director nodded.

"*Da ser. Eto bylo podtverzhdeno.* Yes, sir. It has been confirmed."

The tension was palatable. The leaders of the world frozen in history.

Then the silence morphed into a lethal chaos.

Blake was the first to react. As he gazed at the bewildered Fedorov, a movement over the minister's shoulder caught the president's attention. The Russian security agent directly behind Fedorov was reaching into his jacket. A millisecond later, he withdrew his hand, his fingers clutching a...

"Gun," yelled the president.

Cynthia Ford, sitting next to Blake, saw the weapon at the same moment.

"No," she screamed as she dived sideways, pushing Blake out of his chair.

Abe Peterson and his team drew their weapons in an instant, while two other agents dove on top of the president to protect him. Peterson released three rounds straight into the shooter's torso.

But it was too late.

Cynthia Ford's body lay slumped over the president's chair, a pool of deep red blood forming on her chest.

Viktor Sidorov had turned in surprise as the man next to him withdrew his weapon. Suddenly, the entire Russian security team had their guns out, focused on their traitorous colleague, now lying prone on the floor.

Except one.

A single Russian guard was positioned by the window at the end of the room. He kneeled and aimed under the table where the president was pinned. Assessing that he had no clear shot, the agent began to rise, re-aiming his weapon as he moved.

"Viktor," shouted Minister Fedorov as he indicated towards the Russian gunman. Sidorov pointed his Makarov pistol at the man and fired. In the instant he was slammed in the chest by Sidorov's round, the gunman squeezed his own trigger, hitting his secondary target in the gut. Foreign Minister Fedorov tumbled forwards onto the table.

As the gunman hit the floor, he died smiling, knowing he'd fulfilled his president's orders.

Within seconds, the two Secret Service agents who'd protected the president yanked him to his feet as the remaining agents formed a huddle around their leader and whisked him out of the room.

More Secret Service personnel entered the space, pistols drawn, stepping in front of the remaining VIPs to build a human wall of protection.

Two hostile countries. Eleven weapons ready and aimed.

Volatility defined.

Chapter 71

LACHLAN BYRN

A team of three, yet only one marksman. Why?

Crack…

As soon as the shots rang out, Byrn had his answer. The plan was brilliant in its simplicity.

At the gate, the previous flurry of frantic activity erupted into chaos as agents and police attempted to get a handle on what was happening.

Lachlan Byrn knew exactly what was going down and exactly what would happen next.

The assassin pivoted on the spot, sprinted twenty-five yards up the road and leaped the fence into the parkland. If he got shot, he got shot. Although logic dictated that every security operative and sniper would now be focusing on what was taking place inside the palace.

As he ran through the trees, Byrn saw 'the Beast', the US president's traditional form of on-road transportation, come swerving around the corner at the far end of the building. A swarm of agents in dark suits flooded the steps. Almost immediately, they formed into two lines facing outward, weapons drawn, forming a corridor of safety for their president.

Only Byrn knew it wasn't safe at all.

The assassin had only seconds to deduce the best angle for the shot that was about to drive the free world into despair.

Byrn looked on as the presidential car screeched to a halt in front of the palace steps, its engine racing and the rear door wide open. The shot would need to come from the clump of trees west of the driveway and north-west of the vehicle. Even though proximity wasn't an issue, the angle was extremely challenging. Aleyev said he had their best marksman on the job. They'd have to be damn good to make the shot once, never mind the three times required.

Byrn had made it halfway through the trees on the eastern side of the driveway before he was accosted. An agent in black fatigues stepped out from behind a tree and pointed an FN 90 submachine gun directly at his chest.

"Stop now. Down on the ground."

"I don't think so."

In the heat of the moment, the agent stood six inches too close. Byrn lunged forward and grabbed the barrel of the gun. He knew full well a highly trained warrior wouldn't let go of his weapon easily, so he bent it sideways, causing the agent to lose his grip on the trigger. The assassin then used the gun to slam the operative back into the tree. He followed up with two sharp punches to his victim's temple. Byrn had acted with such speed and ferocity that the man was unconscious before he hit the ground.

He'd have one mighty headache when he woke up.

Making the most of a bad situation, Byrn quickly relieved the agent of his weapon, hat, and jacket. If spotted from a distance, the thinly veiled disguise may help. Either way, he supposed it was a miracle he'd made it this far.

Now, because of the delay, every fiber in Byrn's being told him he was going to be too late.

But it was also too late to go back.

The entire environment had instantly become an explosive panorama of tension, nerves, and volatility. A human hand grenade hanging by a thread.

There was only forward. Aggressively forward.

This was the moment to risk exposure and cross the drive. Amongst the chaos, another figure in black might not draw attention. Alternatively, he may just be shot down in his tracks.

Whatever.

If he made it to the stand of trees on the western side of the drive and his theory was incorrect, Byrn would certainly die in a bloody hail of lead. Still, there was only one way to go.

Forward.

Byrn stuck his head out of the woods, operatives of all persuasions prowled and scanned the surrounding area, barking instructions and observations into their radios. He saw no one in the trees beyond the drive.

Nor did he expect to.

The assassin squinted through his welling fatigue, took a deep breath, and bolted across the open space.

Surprisingly, nobody shot him.

When he reached the cover of the small, treed area, Byrn immediately flung himself to the ground. He would allow five seconds to scan the area. He only needed three.

Because nobody was there.

Byrn slithered forward toward the final group of trees next to the intersection of the main driveway and the smaller thoroughfare crossing it. That would be the best position for the shot. A glance back across the driveway revealed the flood of operatives focused on that area. They'd probably found the agent he took down, and were searching the immediate surrounds. Nobody appeared concerned about the treed area in which he lay. It had been covered by designated agents and posed no threat.

Only there were no agents and one huge threat.

Byrn almost collided with the first body. Judging by the similar outfit to the man he'd just knocked out and the FN 90 in his hands, Byrn figured him to be US Secret Service. Five yards on, he spotted another lifeless body slumped sideways under a bush, drenched in blood. This time, the uniform was Russian.

Brutal.

Now inching forward silently, Byrn gazed out of the trees and down the driveway. The presidential car was still there, as were the two lines of agents. A full motorcade had assembled around the vehicle. The assassin briefly questioned the lack of a Russian entourage but dismissed the thought.

Where the hell was the shooter?

At that moment, the palace doors opened. Two men in dark suits, presumably Secret Service, stepped out. They scanned the area before the man on the right spoke into his sleeve.

A second later, a huddle of dark suits appeared. Byrn held no doubt that in the center of the group walked the most powerful man on the planet, cocooned in a useless human blanket.

Byrn was too fucking late.

Chapter 72

JEFFERSON BLAKE

Blake wasn't allowed time to assess the situation, or even decide his own actions. The Secret Service had a job to do, protect the president. It had been made clear to Blake at the very beginning of his term that nothing would stand in their way.

The president's feet barely touched the ground as he was dragged out of the meeting room. No one had asked him for direction, or even permission. Once outside the immediate danger of gunfire, the president was allowed to walk, although only amid a huddle of agents. As a former member of the military, none of this sat well with Blake, but he understood these men and women were doing their job.

"What about Cynthia Ford? She was hit."

"We'll update you on her condition as soon as we have that information, Mr. President. Right now, we need to get you into the Beast and onto Airforce One, where we can fully protect you."

"Roger that," Blake responded. "I won't make your job any harder than it already is."

When they reached the top of the staircase, an agent on each side grabbed Blake's arms and guided him quickly down the stairs. Abe Peterson strode purposefully, two steps in front of his boss.

At the bottom of the stairway, they paused. Peterson spoke into the microphone on his sleeve.

He turned to face the huddled group behind him.

"We're just waiting while our unit forms up. It won't be a moment."

Blake nodded. "I don't want the plane taking off until everyone from our team is on board. Is that clear?"

"Perfectly," lied Peterson.

Two minutes later, they were ready to go.

"I know I'm stating the obvious, Mr. President, but head down and straight into the car, please."

Blake nodded as the agents ushered him forward.

Straight into a kill zone.

Chapter 73

LACHLAN BYRN

Byrn hurriedly scrutinized the grass between himself and the driveway. No more bodies, but no shooter. He glanced up toward the building. The huddle of agents had begun their descent down the steps.

If it was his kill, Byrn would wait until the group was exactly halfway between the building's front door and the vehicle. Equidistant. Same distance to advance or retreat.

The assassin calculated he had four seconds at the most to locate the sniper. Somewhere in the back of his mind, he heard footsteps approaching. It wouldn't be the shooter. There were too many. Security. Byrn figured he'd probably been spotted.

He scanned the low-lying branches above him.

Nothing.

He glanced behind. The agents were thirty yards away.

Byrn looked higher. Desperately searching for a sign.

Then.

Second tree back from the intersection. Twenty feet off the ground. Byrn spotted the sniper as the first shot echoed past the palace wall.

"Hey."

Byrn brought his weapon to bear, but not in time.

Another round exploded.

The footsteps behind him grew louder.

Byrn didn't bother looking toward the huddled group. He knew where the first two rounds were intended to land.

It was the third bullet that would count.

The shooter remained immune to any interruption. Byrn didn't exist. Only the target.

Without aiming, Byrn frantically released an array of shots at the body perched on the limb. As he squeezed his trigger, he saw the muscles on the shooter's hand tighten around the trigger. Byrn fired again, and again. A plethora of bark, wood and leaves peppered the air.

Suddenly, the shooter's fingers relaxed before dropping off the trigger guard completely. As if in slow motion, the sniper's body rolled off the branch and plummeted to the ground with a thud, landing face up.

Fuck, thought Byrn.

A woman.

Blood poured out of wounds on her shoulder, arm, and torso, but her chest heaved up and down, laboring for breath.

Lachlan Byrn didn't wait. He hoped he'd got there in time, but he didn't even bother to look back towards the palace. Blake was either alive or dead and there was nothing anyone could do to change that now.

A barrage of gunfire peppered the trees above him.

Ungrateful bastards.

Byrn leaped up, turned north, and ran for his life.

Chapter 74

JEFFERSON BLAKE

It was a shit show.

Jefferson Blake stared out of the Beast's window as the vehicle sped off. Two secret service agents lay spreadeagled on the steps, blood gushing from their heads. There would be no hope of survival.

Now that he was cloistered in the protection of the most armored car on earth, the president felt quite secure. Abe Peterson sat across from him.

"I'm sorry for the loss of your people, Abe."

"Yes, Mr. President, so am I."

"I should have listened to you and left earlier. None of this would have happened."

Peterson considered his response carefully.

"No sir. With respect, you shouldn't have listened to me. You made a decision based on what was right for our country, not what was right for our safety. Those two agents knew what they signed on for. It wasn't to protect you, sir. It was to protect the United States of America and, by association, the free world."

"Thank you, Abe. Is there any news on Cynthia Ford?"

As the motorcade sped out the gates and onto the main road, Peterson raised a palm and pressed against his earpiece. Blake waited.

"Mr. President. Medics are currently treating National Security Advisor Ford. At this stage, they believe she has a strong chance of survival. She'll be lifted by helicopter to a hospital momentarily."

"Thank God."

"Also, Mr. President, we'll be wheels up at Lennart Meri Tallinn Airport in fifteen minutes. All local air travel is suspended, and incoming flights rerouted until our departure."

"What about Nate, Rowena, and Fred? Are we waiting for them as I instructed?"

It takes a lot to stare the president of the United States down, but that's exactly what Abe Peterson did. Without uttering a single word.

"Fair enough, Abe, your call. I won't tell you how to do your job."

Peterson nodded.

Blake suddenly realized how much he was sweating. He sat back in his seat. What a clusterfuck.

Chapter 75

LACHLAN BYRN

What a clusterfuck.

Behind him, Byrn heard the voices shouting instructions, the boots clunking rapidly down pathways and the occasional overhead whirr of a drone motor. The assassin zigzagged in and out of the trees as rounds of gunfire hounded him northward. His coordination faltering, he stumbled awkwardly, almost pounding his face into the dirt before catching himself. Damn this fucking tiredness.

Any second now, he expected his route to freedom to be blocked, or a bullet to ground him.

Even in such ridiculous circumstances, Byrn had a plan. It was thin, in fact it hung by less than a thread. Its chances of success were minimal. The plan was opportunistic, Byrn realized that. It simply came down to a matter of geography and timing.

It also meant Byrn would have to face the demon that perennially tore at his gut.

When there is no light, seek solace in the darkness.

Three rounds in quick succession plowed the earth around his feet. The assassin veered right and ran faster.

As he raced forward, Byrn wondered if he was having these thoughts because his demise appeared imminent.

Probably.

Definitely.

Another burst of gunfire strewed the ground to his right.

Good.

Byrn headed left, north-west. He wanted the change of direction to appear to be a random decision.

A minute later, he disappeared into a thick clump of trees. Once certain he was out of the view of his pursuers and their pet drones, he swung harder left. The assassin was guided only by an image from Google Earth which he'd attempted to memorize earlier.

For a moment, the gunfire ceased. Those chasing him weren't exactly sure where he was. Byrn glanced up. The foliage cover was too thick for the drones to penetrate.

Perfect.

Abruptly, in front of him, a tall brick wall with black metal bars across its top appeared through the trees. To Byrn, it looked like the ideal location for a firing squad. If he didn't keep moving, that would most likely become its function.

The layout of the park and its surrounding buildings had presented an idea, perhaps an opportunity. With only seconds until the opportunity disappeared and his pursuers caught up with him, Byrn bolted forward.

The assassin sprinted hard at the wall, jumping high as his feet touched the bricks and his fingers grabbed desperately at the metal bars above. He missed. Both hands slipped, losing all grip as he felt himself slipping downwards. He sensed the coarse bricks ripping at his skin. As he hit the ground, he took a breath and rebounded with every morsel of flagging strength he could muster.

A last shot.

Suddenly his left hand held firm, gripping the metal bar above the bricks. Byrn thrust his right hand upward once more, hoisting himself over the wall and across the bars. He vaulted into the air before crashing hard onto the earth below.

It was like being transported to a different world.

Byrn leaned back against the wall, gasping for air. He was surprised no one had immediately accosted him. There must be CTV surveillance cameras everywhere. Behind him, over the wall, the ruckus continued.

Better to advance than retreat, Byrn climbed to his feet. It was time to knock on opportunity's door.

The building was solid brick and massive. Byrn strutted down the path on the south side before turning towards the expansive front door. The entrance was set amidst an extravagant oriental façade. As he climbed the steps, the assassin noticed the voices calling out behind him.

"*Tingzhi, tingzhi!*"

Byrn glanced at the brass nameplate beside the door. It was the right place.

The Embassy of the People's Republic of China.

The door opened just as the guards behind grabbed Byrn's arms.

An armed soldier with broad shoulders and a fearsome frown scowled down at the intrusion.

The assassin caught his breath.

"Hello. My name is Lachlan Byrn. I believe you are looking for me."

Epilogue

Four weeks later

JEFFERSON BLAKE

"It turned out the shooter was Russian. One of their elite FSB snipers," said Abe Peterson.

"Do we think Vadim Aleyev knew of the plan?" asked President Blake.

They sat on the sofas and chairs by the fireplace in the oval office. The president, Secretary Edwards, Ambassador Fisk, Director Durrows, and National Security Advisor Ford.

"We not only believe he was aware of the operation, our intelligence suggests that Aleyev was its architect," said Fred Durrows.

"It would also appear the FSB Director Yuri Varkov was a key player," added Peterson.

"The arrogant fools," remarked Blake. "Although, if they thought killing a sitting American President would change the US attitude to their aggressive behaviors, they were most certainly correct. The gloves would have come off quick smart."

Everyone nodded.

"Speaking of which, Cynthia," Blake continued. "We are all so pleased to see you well on the way to recovery. I am personally so grateful for what you did, and I owe you big time. Rest assured; I will take the necessary steps to ensure that you are recognized as a national hero."

Cynthia Ford edged forward, somewhat uncomfortably, on her seat.

"Thank you, Mr. President."

Blake scratched his chin in the usual manner.

"Okay. We know the sniper who killed our Secret Service agents was FSB, but what about this mystery man? The guy who took her down and then disappeared."

"As you say, Mr. President. He simply vanished. We haven't been able to identify him or establish how he got away. There have been rumors, but nothing yet substantiated," said Durrows.

Blake nodded.

"And Aleyev's killer."

"The same."

"Coincidence."

"Yes Mr. President," replied Secretary Edwards. "Quite a coincidence."

"One more thing Fred. Can we do anything about Yuri Varkov?" asked the president.

"No, sir. Although we are all relieved that Foreign Minister Fedorov survived his wounds and is being revered within his country, his nemesis, Varkov, remains politically untouchable and totally out of our reach."

"That's disappointing," said the president.

LACHLAN BYRN

Byrn stared down at Yuri Varkov's body.

The assassin had decided that if Aleyev's legacy was to be stopped dead in its tracks, Varkov had to go as well. It wasn't a difficult kill, given Varkov's recent relegation to the recesses of the Russian bureaucracy, but a possible resurgence of the man's power and influence was unacceptable.

He figured Kristiina Volk would have approved.

Byrn decided the old lady shouldn't die for nothing.

The Chinese had inadvertently provided the assassin with the free pass he'd needed to get out of Estonia. After the embassy officials had contacted Zhen Su, they'd been delighted to smuggle Byrn across the border and arrange for him to be escorted back to China.

Of course, that never happened.

There was no chance in hell that Byrn would ever be held captive in the squalid detention of the Beijing intelligence apparatus again. His two armed escorts had found out the hard way that when Byrn says 'no', he means 'no'.

Their bodies would be discovered, eventually.

Byrn's relationship with the Chinese was about to change. He'd sought freedom from their influence on their terms and they'd rescinded the offer. Now Byrn was about to make a counteroffer.

One that couldn't be declined.

Byrn reached into his pocket and retrieved a box of matches. He lit one and flicked it downward. Varkov's corpse, already dowsed in petrol, ignited like a pyre. The assassin spat into the burning flames before turning away and heading out the door.

A quick thirty-minute journey on his stolen Irbis motorcycle through the streets of Moscow, and Byrn reached his

311

destination, Domodedovo International Airport.

A short time later, his beautifully forged travel documents having passed scrutiny, Lachlan Byrn waited in line to board his Aeroflot flight.

"Good evening, Mister Jones," began the flight attendant as Byrn stepped onto the aircraft. "I do hope you have a satisfying journey to Beijing."

Byrn smiled back.

"Thank you," he replied. "I intend the visit to be most satisfying."

THE END

Afterword

Lachlan Byrn will return in

1, 2, 3 ... Die

Byrn also makes a substantial appearance in **COUNTER-POINT** (Nicholas Sharp Thriller No. 5). **COUNTERPOINT** not only tells the story of Byrn's relationship with Nicholas Sharp, but also covers his altercation with the US Secretary of Defense.

In the meantime get your FREE electronic copy of Mark Mannock's NICHOLAS SHARP origins Novella PLAY OUT, the latest news about new releases and some other exciting freebies along the way by joining Mark's mailing list at his website: https://markmannock.com

Although you can begin reading the NICHOLAS SHARP THRILLER series at any point here is Mark's suggested order of reading:

1. **KILLSONG** (NS thriller No. 1-*available on Amazon*)

2. **BLOOD NOTE** (A NS short story-*available exclusively to my mailing list members. I'll send you the link 7 days after sign-up*)
3. **LETHAL SCORE** (NS thriller No. 2-*available on Amazon*)
4. **HELL'S CHOIR** (NS thriller No. 3-*available on Amazon*)
5. **SILENT VOICE** (NS thriller No. 4-*available on Amazon*)
6. **COUNTERPOINT** (NS thriller No. 5-*available on Amazon*)
7. **ECHO BLUE** (NS thriller No. 6-*available on Amazon*)

PLAY OUT-an origins novella (*available exclusively to Mark's mailing list members on sign-up*) can be read at any point. The story takes you back to when Nicholas Sharp left the U.S. Marines.

What readers are saying about the Nicholas Sharp Series:

"I had to keep reading to the end, could not put it away until I had finished."

"I love Lee Child and now have another author who is just as good."

"Jack Reacher's attitude... John Lennon's sensibilities."

"I really enjoyed the sniper-musician-reluctant warrior character..."

"I've read hundreds of books throughout the years and the pandemic has provided me with extra time to discover more

reading treasures. Play Out (Nicholas Sharp Origins novella) is one of the best."

"Without a doubt this is a cracking novel... the story then keeps at you in leaps and bounds! Full of action all the way. Just brilliant!"

Reviews are life's blood to an author. If you've enjoyed KILL AS YOU DIE please consider leaving a review on the book's Amazon page or on GOODREADS.

Acknowledgements

My heartfelt thanks and love to Sarah, Anisha and Jack for your love, tolerance and support. Lachlan, your counsel and wisdom has always been appreciated.

Cover by Anisha Mannock

About the Author

Mark Mannock was born in Melbourne, Australia. He has had an extensive career in the music industry including supporting, recording with or writing for Tina Turner, Joni Mitchell, The Eurythmics, Irene Cara and David Hudson. His recorded work with Lia Scallon has twice been long-listed for Grammy Awards. As a composer/songwriter Mark's music has been used across the world in countless television and theatre contexts, including the 'American Survivor' TV series and 'Sleuth' playwright Anthony Shaffer's later productions.

Mark is presently writing the successful 'Nicholas Sharp' thriller series about a disillusioned former US sniper whose past plagues him as he makes his way in the contemporary music industry. Sharp is a man whose insatiable curiosity and embedded moral compass lead him to places he ought not go. The series is currently read in over 50 countries.

Mark also writes the exciting new Lachlan Byrn Thrillers. Assassin, vigilante or serial killer? Byrn has a passion for his work that transcends the rules of engagement. He gets up close and personal with his victims... very close, very personal and he's exceptionally deadly.

Mark lives in Kettering, Tasmania with his family. His travels around the globe act as inspirations for his writing.

You can connect with me on:
- https://markmannock.com
- https://www.facebook.com/markmannockbooks

Subscribe to my newsletter:
- https://markmannock.com

Also by Mark Mannock

PLAY OUT
A Nicholas Sharp Origin Novella

<u>Sign up to Mark's mailing list and receive this book for free!</u>

Set five years before **KILLSONG**

A Terrorist attack on the London Underground. Nicholas Sharp doesn't think so.

While on leave from Iraq, the U.S. Marine Sniper finds himself intervening when innocent lives are threatened. He walks away, but for Sharp it's never that easy. Something doesn't feel right. Twenty-four hours later everything is wrong.

The brief solace he finds in his beloved piano is shattered when Sharp becomes the attacker's next target. Step up or step away. Nicholas Sharp doesn't like to kill, but he sure as hell knows how to.

Somewhere between Clancy's *Jack Ryan* and Ludlum's *Jason Bourne*, Nicholas Sharp may be a flawed and reluctant hero, but you certainly want him on your side.

"I've read hundreds of books throughout the years and the pandemic has provided me with extra time to discover more reading treasures. Play Out is one of the best." **Goodreads Reviewer-5 STARS**

The Nicholas Sharp origins novella PLAY OUT is sent to you FREE when you join my mailing list at
https://markmannock.com

KILLSONG
Nicholas Sharp Thriller #1

Reluctant, determined, lethal. Nicholas Sharp is a killer musician... literally!

Nicholas Sharp knew there would be blood on his hands. It was just a question of how much.

The death of a child and her mother, or the loss of countless thousands. Sharp is ordered to choose, but the former Marine Sniper gave up following orders long ago.

Sharp's newfound refuge as a musician is suddenly blasted apart. While he is preparing to back well-known singer Robbie West on a USO tour of Iraq, a close friend and her daughter disappear.

Trapped in a deadly maze of colliding worlds and dark agendas as competing forces race to locate discarded biological weapons, Sharp is compelled to act.

One wrong decision, one misstep… and the consequences could be disastrous.

"I had to keep reading to the end, could not put it away until I had finished." **Amazon Reader- 5 STARS**

Available on Amazon:

http://www.amazon.com/dp/B08CT1FHF5
http://www.amazon.co.uk/dp/B08CT1FHF5
http://www.amazon.com.au/dp/B08CT1FHF5
https://www.amazon.ca/dp/B08CT1FHF5

LETHAL SCORE
Nicholas Sharp Thriller #2

"A great book that has more twists and turns than you can imagine. Pick up and read at all costs." **Goodreads Reviewer 5 STARS**

You can't stop someone with nothing to lose...

Nicholas Sharp is on a tour through Europe, the concerts are sold out and the former Marine sniper turned musician is living in luxury thanks to promoter Antonio Ascardi.

Suddenly it all goes wrong. People are dying along the way and Sharp is blamed. Now a hunted man, accused of terrorist crimes across the continent, Nicholas Sharp must fight for his life and freedom.

Available on Amazon:
  http://www.amazon.com/dp/B08CSYKG18
  http://www.amazon.co.uk/dp/B08CSYKG18
  http://www.amazon.com.au/dp/B08CSYKG18
  https://www.amazon.ca/dp/B08CSYKG18

HELL'S CHOIR
Nicholas Sharp Thriller #3

A goodwill visit to Sudan, what could possibly go wrong?

Nicholas Sharp is performing as part of a political and cultural group representing the US. Suddenly caught up in the middle of a political coup, the leader of the American contingent goes missing and his security staff murdered.

Communication with the outside world is cut off. It falls to Sharp and Greatrex to track their missing leader down.

But then things get really complicated...

"The story then keeps at you in leaps and bounds! Full of action all the way. Just brilliant!" **Amazon Reader-5 STARS**

"Great read and a fun ride." **Amazon Reader-5 STARS**

Available on Amazon:
  http://www.amazon.com/dp/B08LRB8CWN
  http://www.amazon.co.uk/dp/B08LRB8CWN
  http://www.amazon.com.au/dp/B08LRB8CWN
  https://www.amazon.ca/dp/B08LRB8CWN

SILENT VOICE
Nicholas Sharp Thriller #4

It's dangerous to be right when the government is wrong...

Hunted down by their government's secret service, the members of protest band Kha Cring flee to Los Angeles to begin a new life. After an unexpected attack, the musicians' safe exile in LA is jeopardized. The desire to fight for their country's freedom undiminished, the band find their soaring popularity and politically messaged music no longer enough to protect them from the evil they escaped.

A deadlier weapon is needed. Nicholas Sharp.

In an instant things go terribly wrong as Sharp finds himself the focus of a network of international conspirators intent on wiping both he and the members of Kha Cring from the face of the planet.

Available on Amazon:

http://www.amazon.com/dp/B08W1V9FWS
http://www.amazon.co.uk/dp/B08W1V9FWS
http://www.amazon.com.au/dp/B08W1V9FWS
https://www.amazon.ca/dp/B08W1V9FWS

COUNTERPOINT
Nicholas Sharp Thriller #5

Looking in the mirror, he saw only death...

Pursued by one of the world's most efficient and ruthless assassins, Nicholas Sharp almost admires the deadly operator's meticulous talents, until the assassin starts coming after Sharp through his friends. Sharp's investigations reveal that the killer also has another target in sight: the US Secretary of Defense. Is there a dark connection?

Face to face with a past he'd considered banished from his memory, Nicholas Sharp questions not only his own moral compass but also his slim chance of survival.

Available on Amazon:
  http://www.amazon.com/dp/B0BVTVWZ6N
  http://www.amazon.co.uk/dp/B0BVTVWZ6N
  http://www.amazon.com.au/dp/B0BVTVWZ6N
  https://www.amazon.ca/dp/B0BVTVWZ6N

ECHO BLUE
Nicholas Sharp Thriller #6

Are you safe?...

Nicholas Sharp receives a mysterious phone call from Jack Greatrex... then Greatrex disappears.

In a hunt that takes him through South America, Texas, the mountains of Northern Spain and eventually the Middle East, Sharp encounters world renowned environmental activist Dr Deagan Jones from the notorious Crimson Wave. As Sharp uncovers a chain of complex deceptions, Jones' teenage son is kidnapped. The stakes never higher, the ex-Marine sniper turned musician fights to prevent an environmental and humanitarian catastrophe with unimaginable consequences.

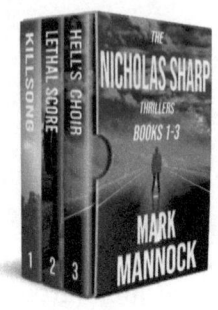

THE NICHOLAS SHARP THRILLERS BOX SET BOOKS 1-3
Nicholas Sharp is a killer musician... literally!

Nicholas Sharp is a disillusioned former US sniper fighting a troubled past and an uncertain future. Seeking solace in his work as a professional musician, Sharp is a man whose insatiable curiosity and embedded moral compass lead him into situations fraught with danger. Nicholas Sharp doesn't like to kill, but he sure as hell knows how to.

Somewhere between Tom Clancy's Jack Ryan and Robert Crais' Elvis Cole, Nicholas Sharp may be a flawed hero, but you definitely want him on your side.

Book 1: KILLSONG
  Book 2: LETHAL SCORE
  BOOK 3: HELL'S CHOIR

Available on Amazon:
  http://www.amazon.com/dp/B08NYLGW1G
  http://www.amazon.co.uk/dp/B08NYLGW1G
  http://www.amazon.com.au/dp/B08NYLGW1G
  https://www.amazon.ca/dp/B08NYLGW1G

BLOOD NOTE
A Short Story Prequel to the Thriller KILLSONG *(should be read after KILLSONG-available FREE to mailing list subscribers 7 days after sign-up)*

Just turn around and walk away. That was all Nicholas Sharp had to do when the mysterious and intoxicating Elena approached him for help.

She knew far too much about him. The warning signs were all there.

Sharp didn't listen to them.

What followed for the former Marine Sniper turned musician, was a harrowing night of violence, deceit and intrigue.

When the sunrise ushered in a new day, Sharp thought it was all over...but it was really just beginning.